PUPP ... MAKER

PM Mason

Published by Antony Rowe Publishing Services in 2005
2 Whittle Drive
Highfield Industrial Estate
Eastbourne
East Sussex
BN23 6QT
England

This is a work of fiction. Although the historical details and time frame of the book are based on actual events in the UK and Latvia, the story and characters described are products of the author's imagination. Any resemblance to actual persons - living or dead - is purely coincidental.

ISBN 1-905200-41-2

Printed and bound in England by
Antony Rowe Ltd, Chippenham, Wiltshire

DEDICATED TO MY MOTHER AND FATHER
AND TO LATVIANS EVERYWHERE

LONDON, 1999

CHAPTER 1

Arnis Rozenvalds settled himself in his swivel chair and spun round to glance through the long narrow window. The view from the back of his surgery was one of the finest in South London, but the damp autumnal mist obscured almost everything this morning save for three red lights glowing from the Crystal Palace transmitter.

Turning back to his desk, he noticed that Dawn hadn't yet changed the date on the Kabipharm calendar, so he picked it up and eased away the top sheet, consigning the seventeenth of November to the square wicker waste paper basket next to the filing cabinet.

As the low hum of conversation began to drift through his consulting room door, Arnis shifted his gaze to the model paddle steamer he had carved during woodwork classes at school in Oban. With its pair of red, white and black funnels, it was the most tangible – and the happiest – memory of Scotland, which is where he and his mother had spent fifteen years of their lives after being forced to flee from Latvia in 1945.

Making the most of the last few moments before the first patient came in, in his mind's eye, he found himself below the decks of the steamer. Down the flight of polished wood stairs to the engine room to feast his eyes and ears on his most cherished boyhood memory - the rhythmic turning of the steel paddles, one, two, three, one, two, three, one, two, three...

A sudden screech of tyres on the high street fractured his nostalgia. He listened carefully, but unable to hear anything beyond the drone of the traffic, he picked up his pen to sign the repeat prescriptions Dawn had printed out the day before. But as he reached out for the rubber-banded bundle, horns began to blare, followed by a succession of screams.

Dropping his pen, he rushed through to the waiting room. Seconds later a plump woman in a mauve mackintosh burst in through the front door. 'Doctor, quickly!' she shouted, trying to catch her breath.

Arnis hurried after her, pushing his way past the queue for the Homeless Persons' Unit. By now, the traffic was at a standstill. Horns continued to sound, red double-deckers stretched back to the traffic lights, a big delivery truck had stopped outside the Pound Shop, and a voice was bellowing in a foreign language outside the Post Office.

Then he saw the crowd in the middle of the road; twenty or so people standing in a semi-circle, their heads bowed to the ground. After squeezing past two parked cars, he edged his way through the crowd and saw immediately what had happened. A young man lay quite still on the tarmac surface with a small boy standing inches away, not uttering a single sound. Arnis squatted down at the side of the casualty and felt for the man's pulse.

Nothing.

Looking up, he spotted the woman in the mauve coat. 'Go back to the surgery,' he said in a calm, firm voice. 'Make sure my receptionist calls an ambulance.'

As she crowd moved aside to let her go, Arnis began to

attempt resuscitation. 'What happened?' he asked not aiming his question at anyone in particular.

'A motorbike hit him,' said a young woman in a dark green and yellow sari.

Arnis didn't recall seeing a bike and glanced around through the legs of the crowd.

A man with a moustache read his thoughts. 'The scum bag did a runner ... but not before I got his number.'

Suddenly the small boy began to scream. 'Daddy! Daddy!'

Those two words snapped something inside Arnis and he pressed the palm of his hand on the man's chest repeatedly. His rib cage remained sickeningly still but Arnis continued pumping, the child's shrieks driving him to attempt a miracle. Sweat pouring from his brow, he stopped only ten minutes later, when the paramedics leapt out of the ambulance. But he knew his efforts had been in vain.

When the paramedics had transferred the man on to the stretcher, he turned to look seriously at the child for the first time. A small boy, probably about four years old, with strawberry blonde hair and bright blue eyes. By now, he was in the arms of a young woman dressed in a red tracksuit.

'Are you a relative?' asked Arnis.

'No,' she replied sadly. 'There was just him and ...' Her voice caught in the back of her throat.

The little boy began to struggle in the woman's arms as the paramedics lifted the stretcher into the back of the ambulance. 'No,' he yelled. 'You can't take my daddy away.'

Arnis felt the sick empty feeling cramping his insides. He couldn't remember a time when he had ever felt so helpless. During thirty-two years as a doctor, he'd witnessed hundreds of deaths, but never one quite like this.

He stared at the boy, longing to take him in his arms and cuddle him. He knew what it felt like to be without a father. But there was a difference. Though his mother never spoke of the June night in 1941 when the Russians had forced his own father into the back of a truck, it had all happened before he was born so he'd never known his father. But this boy had. Worse, he'd actually watched him die.

The small boy's continuing screams pierced him like a knife. Like himself, this child would now have to grow up without a father. Arnis immediately recalled his first summer in Oban, fifty years earlier. Other boys going off with their dads to fly kites at Kerrera or play hide and seek at McCaig's Tower. He could never do that and it made him feel left out, alone.

Even now he still thought of his father, wondering what he'd looked like and what had happened to him after the Russians had taken him away. He'd disappeared; one of hundreds on a list in the town hall of Kuldīga, a small country town in Latvia. A list made during the Russian occupation between 1940 and 1941, then left to gather dust by the Germans after they threw the Russians out. Arnis knew little more than that. His mother never talked about his father - as if he'd never existed.

'What is your name?' Arnis asked the little boy.

'Peter,' he sobbed, rubbing a grubby hand across his cheek.

'Where's your Mummy?'

'Work,' he replied in a single word.

'Where does she work?'

'Tesco.'

'The one opposite the church?' Arnis quizzed.

Peter looked blank and started to struggle as he saw one of the paramedics moving toward the front of the ambulance.

'I'll take him,' Arnis said to the woman.

'Are you sure? My car's just round the corner. If it's the big Tesco at the roundabout ...'

But Arnis cut her short. He could not leave the little boy with someone else. 'No, I'll take him. Come on, Peter,' he said soothingly as he held out his arms. 'We'll find your Mummy.'

Peter looked momentarily uncertain then he stretched out his arms. Arnis carried him back to the surgery and spoke to his receptionist. 'I'm going to Tesco to find this little boy's mother.'

Dawn looked bewildered. 'Have you seen the waiting room? What shall I tell the patients? You're needed here. Can't I take him?'

'No,' Arnis said firmly.

'But when will you be back?'

'When I've found his mother,' he snapped. 'And you can tell the patients anything you like.'

Dawn made no effort to hide her astonishment. She had worked with him for nearly ten years and knew how he hated getting behind. 'Are you OK?' she asked.

'I'm fine,' he insisted, then his voice softened. 'I'll be back as soon as I can.'

Arnis arrived at the Tesco shop five minutes later and Peter immediately spotted his mother working at one of the tills. He wrenched his hand from Arnis's and ran towards her.

Fortunately, the manager appeared at the same time

7

and Arnis whispered in his ear, 'Cover her duties … her husband has just died.'

The manager reacted quickly and spoke sharply into the intercom unit he carried. Another assistant appeared almost immediately and unquestioningly took over the woman's duties at the till. Arnis realised from the tears streaming down the mother's face that Peter had already said enough in his stinted fashion. He approached her quickly and put his arm round her shoulder. 'I'm a doctor,' he told her. He glanced at the shop manager before continuing, 'Let's go somewhere quiet where we can talk.'

The manager led them to his office and told his secretary to make some tea. Arnis sat the young woman in the manager's chair and squatted in front of her, taking her clasped hands in his. This was one of far too many times he'd had to be the bearer of bad news but this tragedy was closer to home – almost a repeat of his own early childhood. In front of him now was a small boy and his mother; their life changed in an instant by some mindless cretin who didn't even have the guts to face the consequences of his carelessness.

*

After getting back to the surgery, Arnis spent the next couple of hours seeing his patients. But he couldn't get the little boy out of his mind. Would Peter ache for his father in the way he had ached for the father he'd never met? Would he dream about him? Would he talk to him in his sleep? How would his friends react? Would they be frightened? Would they be embarrassed?

He hoped that Peter's classmates would be kinder than his own had been. At school in Oban, they'd accused his father of being a criminal because they'd heard he'd been sent to Siberia. They had called him the 'Russian bear' because that was where they thought he was from; then yelled that he was a Nazi because of his German sounding surname. All of them except Michael Maloney, the Irish boy with whom Arnis had made firm friends.

Many years elapsed before the others understood he was neither Russian nor German - but Latvian. And though Peter had lost his father in different circumstances, Arnis could not help but worry that he would suffer at school.

After the last patient had gone, he decided to deal with his in tray, to try to dull the pain that had flowed from the boy's tears. He picked up the letter on the top of the pile and seeing it was from the local Trust, he put it down again, turning instead to gaze at the picture of the steam ship hanging in a plan black frame to the left of the bookcase.

An unexpected find in a junk shop in Hastings, the picture of the *Helena Faulbaums* was another memory of Scotland – and a link with Latvia. A distant cousin of his mother's had served as a crew member on the ship, which had been lost during a terrific storm off the island of Luing in 1936.

While they lived in Oban, his mother liked to visit the island on each anniversary of her relative's death to place a bunch of daffodils on his grave, to say a prayer in the tiny church. At the same time, Arnis developed a keen interest in the ship, researching its history, reading the report of the wreck in *The Oban Times* and he had been particularly delighted to obtain a photograph of it.

Reluctantly, he forced his mind back to his in tray and took hold of the envelope from the Trust, slitting it open with an ebony handled paper knife. He began to read.

16 November 1999

'Dear Dr Rozenvalds

As you may know several GPs in your area have retired recently. This means that patients are having difficulty finding a GP and tend to rely quite heavily on accident and emergency and ambulance services as a source of primary care. The Trust's priority is to ensure that GP services become available for all residents and remain available as existing GPs retire.

To compensate for the difficulties of attracting GPs to an inner urban environment, and to remove the pressures which single-handed general practice can place on the quality of a GP's working life, the Trust has decided to recruit salaried GPs for employment within a Community Trust. Salaried general practice will be used to attract new doctors and to guarantee them an income whilst building up new practice lists.

In addition, the Trust is offering all single-handed GPs the opportunity to transfer to salaried status on the same terms and conditions. The Trust will be responsible for organising out-of-hours cover, managing the premises and employing the necessary support staff. You will also reduce your list size to 2,000 patients.

We anticipate that this approach will help to improve primary care services in this area, and we would ask that you give serious consideration to our proposal.

Yours sincerely
Mark Quinn
Manager, Primary Care Services'

Arnis read the letter twice, anger rising in his chest. Though he knew there was no compulsion to go along with what it said, the idea of becoming a salaried GP working in a health centre filled him with horror. Having fewer patients and the luxury of not having to get up in the night was no compensation. At the age of fifty-seven, he was not going to work for someone else.

He tore up the letter and was about to throw it in the waste paper basket when Dawn came in with a cup of tea and a ham sandwich. 'You'll need this,' she said.

He frowned. She didn't usually make him a sandwich just before he went home.

She returned his frown with a smile. 'Don't say you've forgotten. You're off into London tonight. To meet Antons.'

As soon as she mentioned his youngest son's name, he remembered. It was November the eighteenth: Latvian Independence Day. Antons was due to receive a prize at the ceremony tonight for getting his degree. He looked at the clock: it was an hour before the gathering was due to begin.

He swallowed his sandwich, grabbed his coat and set off for the ten-minute walk to the railway station, glad that he didn't have to go home to fetch his mother. She was recovering from a bad bout of influenza and he'd insisted on her not coming out tonight. It was the first Independence Day celebration she'd missed in the thirty years they'd lived in London. To her it was one of the most important days of the year, an occasion to remember that her home country had gained its first independence from Russia in 1918.

*

Fifty minutes later Arnis arrived at the venue for the

Independence Day gathering. It was a large Georgian house on the edge of Regent's Park. He hurried up the steps through the dark green door which led into an oak-lined hallway. There was a long-cased clock to the right of the staircase. He stopped briefly to look at its delicately decorated face and was interested to see it had been made in Edinburgh, the city where he had done his medical training.

The main hall was already filling up and he was relieved to spot his son sitting on the back row. 'Antons. You made it.' He made no effort to cover up his surprise at his son's punctuality, but he was not best pleased to see that he was dressed in jeans with a flannel shirt and yellow T-shirt. On the point of asking him why he hadn't dressed in smarter clothes, he was stopped by a deep resounding voice from the back of the hall.

'Godu karogam.' Honour to the flag.

A young man appeared wearing a blue tunic and carrying the flag above his right shoulder. Accompanied by two pretty girls in full cream skirts, with bands of red embroidery above their hems and headbands to match, he walked up the aisle with quiet dignity and placed the flag in the recess on the right hand side of the stage.

Although Arnis didn't consider himself to be a Latvian nationalist, he had to admit that the sight of the the maroon and white flag filled him with pride. Yet without his mother at his side, he felt slightly awkward – almost as if his credibility in this tiny exile community depended on her presence. Without her he felt as if he didn't belong.

'Welcome to the eighty first Independence Day celebration,' said the ambassador.

The speeches began. Arnis let his mind wander,

thinking of Peter, of the letter from Quinn. The Trust seemed to have developed an almost crusade like-zeal against single-handed general practitioners. The letter would be the first of several more like it. Of that he was quite sure. But he had no intention of becoming a salaried GP, of being beholden to bureaucrats. Lost in thought, he listened to hardly any of the proceedings, until he remembered he ought to be because his mother would want to know exactly what had been said.

But it was too late. The ambassador finished his talk and the prize giving began.

'I suppose you've got this already?' Antons said as he returned to his seat without any great enthusiasm and showed his father the book he'd been given - *A History of the Latvians in Great Britain.*

'Yes.' Arnis nodded curtly as he spoke. He knew his son would never read it. It wasn't his *thing*.

That summer, Antons had obtained a degree in physiology from Manchester – an upper second in the end, better than anyone had expected - but it wasn't the Batchelor of Medicine or Batchelor of Surgery degrees that Arnis had always hoped he would get. To Arnis's great disappointment, and after a number of heavy arguments, Antons had left medical school at the end of his first Easter term and got a job in McDonald's. That lasted just a few months until he took off with a school friend to spend the summer in Europe.

Although it hadn't occurred to either of them at the time, a gap year might have helped him to develop a little more maturity, perhaps even enough to commit himself to the medical course. Arnis blamed himself and regretted it but that was the trouble with children: you had to learn far too much from your mistakes, by which time it was usually too late. Like his older brother, Henrijs, Antons was no sluggard and was definitely bright enough to have become a doctor. He might even have done it if his father hadn't made such a fuss about it.

'You expect far too much of both of them,' his wife had said more than once.

Perhaps she had been right, Arnis had reflected many times, and perhaps it was sadly fortunate that she had not lived to see Antons working at the local swimming pool. He was certainly a long way from finding his true niche in life but Penny never had to share Arnis's disappointment about their younger son's lack of achievement.

The official part of the evening's celebrations climaxed with another scintillating speech from the ambassador. Arnis dozed off for a few moments but woke with a start when he heard the first two bars of the National Anthem and realised he was the only person still sitting down. He silently thanked Antons for saving seats in the back row.

Moments later the young man in the blue tunic carried the flag down the aisle and the celebration was over for another year. Expecting Antons would not want to hang around too long, Arnis went to fetch his coat. When he got back from the cloakroom, his son was deep in conversation with a pretty girl wearing a short red skirt so he decided to eat a stick of cheese and pineapple and wash it down with another glass of wine.

The glass stopped barely short of his lips when he heard a voice behind him. 'Arnis?'

He spun round and saw a man with a moustache who was vaguely familiar but whose name escaped him.

'I thought it was you,' the man said, now with a smile

of recognition on his face. Then he turned and called to a woman.

'Solvita. Over here. Get Reina.'

As soon as Arnis heard the name Solvita, he realised who the man was. It was Jānis, Solvita's husband. Wasn't he a solicitor? Practising in North London somewhere? No doubt all would be revealed shortly.

But it wasn't. Jānis was more intent on introducing another member of his party. 'Reina, meet Arnis,' he said with a wide smile. 'Arnis, meet Reina. Reina is Solvita's cousin from Seattle.'

Arnis held out his hand to a slim woman wearing a green velvet suit and they passed the next few minutes exchanging social pleasantries and chatting about common acquaintances - people they all knew, who'd got married, who'd had babies, who'd passed their exams, and who'd been to Latvia recently. It was the sort of talk he found desperately boring, but could do very well when it when it suited him, especially when he knew he wouldn't have to speak to them again for at least another year. Even so, the conversation began to dry up after a few minutes.

Just when things were starting to become decidedly awkward with no more common interests, he noticed Reina was staring at him and he felt suddenly edgy. Reina's eyes narrowed and Arnis felt even more uncomfortable. Then she ended the conversational dearth when she lowered her voice and asked, 'Where are you from?'

For a moment he was thrown off balance, as much by the tone of her voice as the question. An odd question. Why would she ask that? Jānis and Solvita knew very well where he lived and the three of them had obviously been talking about him…

Arnis eventually answered with his customary directness. 'South of the river.' Not knowing where his answer would lead, he gave no more details but, intuitively, he felt this was not conversation for the sake of conversation.

'No, in Latvia,' she countered sharply, her narrowed eyes still watching him closely.

That wasn't something he was asked very often but he replied, 'Latvia? Oh, Kuldīga. I was born in Kuldīga.'

Most people who came to these anniversaries knew his mother well, and where they came from in Latvia, but few made a regular habit of discussing their past. Most, like his mother, wanted to erase it from their memories. Arnis began to feel more unnerved especially as Reina was now exchanging curious looks with her cousin.

Reina continued hesitantly. 'I ... rather, we did wonder about that.' She paused, as if to add suspense to uninformative statement, then she elucidated. 'The thing is, I'm also from there ... well, near there at any rate.' She lowered her voice still further. 'I actually went to school in Kuldīga.'

'School?' he repeated. The school in Kuldīga interested him greatly. For the first time, his nervousness eased and he returned her gaze full on. 'Really. When?'

'During the forties.' Reina's face coloured slightly and he could see she was beginning to feel unsure of herself.

'You don't look old enough,' he said deliberately.

Obviously flustered, she blushed even more, which was exactly what he'd intended, making it easier to conceal from her his growing interest in what she had to say. He had never met anyone from Kuldīga, he couldn't remember it because he and his mother had left when he was only three

16

years old, and his mother rarely, if ever, mentioned it.

But he soon found out it wasn't Kuldīga, as a place, she wanted to discuss. 'I think I knew your father ... Mr Vilks? Am I right?'

'Go on,' he replied without answering either of her questions.

Momentarily searching his eyes, she continued, 'Mr Vilks was such a wonderful teacher.' She was almost gushing now and, had Arnis not been so intent on her possible revelation, he might have found her conversation quite amusing. 'He was so patient,' she went on. 'He used to bring history alive.'

Arnis said nothing, but smiled encouragingly, wanting the woman to reveal more about his father without letting her know why. Perhaps she might be able to cast some light on the things his mother seemed so reluctant to divulge.

But Reina needed no encouragement. 'The thing I remember most is that he flatly refused to have a picture of Stalin in the classroom.' She lowered her voice again. 'Every classroom had to have a photograph of Stalin but ours didn't... not for long anyway,' she said proudly. 'Your father tore it down and ripped it into hundreds of tiny pieces. Right in front of us. We all clapped and cheered. Then at break time, my friend and I crawled on the floor. We wanted to piece together the bits. Why, I don't know. It was impossible of course. But I managed to find Stalin's nose. And my friend got an ear. We took them home as if they were trophies. My mother made me get rid of it. I'm not surprised looking back. She was probably terrified.'

Rooted to the spot, he willed her to go on. She was first person he'd met apart from his mother who had known his father. His mother had said hardly anything and, over the years, he had learned not to press her on the subject because he knew it upset her. As he was on the point of asking the woman how long she'd known his father, he was interrupted by Antons who, at that precise moment, came towards them pulling his jacket on.

'Dad, are you ready?' he said. 'Let's go and have something to eat.'

As usual, Antons's timing was completely impeccable. There was nothing Arnis would have liked more than to spend some time with his son, not least because he didn't often suggest it, but, although he wanted to say 'yes' he had no intention of leaving until he'd heard everything Reina had to say.

'Dad, are you OK?' Antons asked with a worried stare.

Arnis didn't like the thought of putting Antons off so he had to do it gently. 'Sorry, Antons, shan't keep you long but I'll be a few minutes yet.' Then he glanced deliberately at his watch. 'Good Lord, look at the time. I didn't realise it was this late. Why don't I call you tomorrow? We can arrange to have a meal when we've got longer to talk.'

Antons shrugged his shoulders, his expression of disappointment unconvincing, and disappeared into the hallway. Arnis watched him go and a twinge of guilty conscience almost prompted him to call Antons back but Reina interrupted his thought.

'I have something here that should interest you,' she said, fishing in her handbag. After considerable rummaging, she produced a time-weathered brown envelope and carefully undid the flap. A small sepia-tinted photograph slid into her hand and she turned it round to show him.

It was a picture of a passenger steamer tied up at the side of a river, its upper and lower decks crowded with people.

'Your father's on there,' Reina said excitedly.

Arnis stared hard at the tiny people in the photograph. He had never seen a picture of his father so he wouldn't have recognised him even if he could have made out the features of any of the passengers.

'There,' Reina said pointing to a man on the top deck.

'That's Mr Vilks. And that's me on the deck below … with the black beret and the pale coat. It was pale blue, I remember. I was so proud of myself wearing that.'

Her self-description didn't register as Arnis pulled his spectacle case from his inside pocket, put on his glasses, and stared intently at the man standing next to the life belt. Short of seeing he was wearing a dark jacket and a white shirt, perhaps a cap, little else was discernible.

As if sensing his disappointment, Reina delved into her handbag again. 'Sorry, I should have realised you can't really make out much detail on that picture. I only knew where I was because I recognised the coat.' She pulled out yet another brown envelope and opened it, this time producing a picture of a smaller group of people, actually taken on board. 'Is that better?' she asked as she handed over the picture. 'My father took it.'

Arnis stared at the picture for a few moments and then asked, 'Which one is Mr Vilks?'

'You don't know?' Reina asked, with a disbelieving frown.

Now he had to give up the pretence and just hope she could tell him more once she knew the truth. 'I never actually saw my father. He was taken away before I was born.'

Reina nodded sympathetically and pointed to one person in the photograph. 'That's him.'

The other faces in the picture instantly receded into the background as he tried to focus on what bit of the man's face he could see under the cap. What he really wanted to see was a likeness; any facial features that they had in common. But, though the photograph was clear enough, it was difficult to tell.

Staring hard, he searched the man's face and something his mother had once said came back to him. His father had a firm chin. The man in the photograph certainly had a firm chin and also the same type of burly build as himself. So there was a likeness - not too discernible, but it was there.

Reina's voice broke into his thoughts. 'Look, I'll get a copy done for you before I go back to the States. Solvita can put it in the post.'

'Thanks. I'd really appreciate that,' he said, wishing he could take it away with him. Reluctantly, he handed it back. 'Do you remember anything else about my father?'

Reina thought for a moment. 'He was a big man. Quite strict, and,' she added almost apologetically, 'he always gave us lots of homework.' She stopped and Arnis assumed there was nothing more to learn. Then she said, 'My father thought the world of him. 'You can trust Mr Vilks with your life is what he said.'

She stared at the picture as if she was trying to derive additional information but obviously it yielded no further clues.

But there was one thing she surely would know. 'Did

you ever see the puppets he made?' Arnis asked her.

'Puppets?' Reina frowned. 'I remember once seeing a puppet show in the town square but I don't recall it having anything to do with your father. Did he actually make puppets?'

Arnis nodded proudly. 'Yes, we still have one of them … Sprīdītis. It's exquisite.'

CHAPTER 2

An hour later Arnis arrived home and opened the door of the three-storey red brick detached house. His mother was in the kitchen preparing plums for jam.

'Hello, love,' she called in her deep guttural accent. 'I could have come with you tonight. My cold is much better. I wish you hadn't made such a fuss.' Then she looked at his face. 'You look dreadful,' she said. 'What's happened? You have been to Independence Day?'

'Yes,' he snapped, but he had no desire to talk about that immediately. The road accident was bothering him more than anything else that had happened that day; more than seeing a photograph of his father. He felt guilty for not doing more, and though he didn't want to upset his mother, he needed to talk. So he sat down at the kitchen table and told her everything. 'I can't get that boy's face out of my mind,' he said. 'The despair, the anguish in his eyes; I felt it all for him and there was nothing I could do. That was the worst of it. If only I could have done something.'

Margarita sat next to him and and calmly placed her hand on his white-knuckled fist that had been angrily pounding the table-top. 'I'm sure you did everything you could,' she said.

'But the way he screamed ...'

'God sometimes moves in mysterious ways and we

have to accept that.'

He looked at his mother and knew she was right. These things happened and there was nothing you could do about it.

Margarita kissed the back of his hand. 'Come on,' she said. 'Let's have coffee in the living room and talk about Antons. How did it all go?'

Minutes later, she joined him in the living room and put two mugs of coffee on the glass-topped table. Unwilling to talk any more, Arnis switched on the television and flicked through the channels, eventually settling on a programme about the Great Barrier Reef. Though his eyes stared at the TV screen, his mind's eye saw totally different images of small boys living their lives in a part-empty void; boys who didn't have fathers to play with them; boys whose fathers' bodies were mangled by hurtling missiles in the shape of motorbikes and boys whose fathers were left behind somewhere in countries that were disappearing over the horizon. Boys like Peter … and himself.

His thoughts were interrupted by his mother's voice. 'Switch off the TV,' she said anxiously. 'I don't want to see this.'

Arnis's eyes refocused on the screen. No longer were there vibrant pictures of the Great Barrier Reef, resplendent with its myriad of vividly-coloured fish. Instead there was a row of corpses lying exposed in an open grave. It was Kosovo.

'Arnis … turn it off!' she repeated and reached to snatch the remote from his hand.

Arnis pressed the off button before she could take it away. 'Sorry, Mum, I was miles away.' He felt guilty knowing she could never cope with scenes like that. It brought back bad memories of her parents after the Russians shot them and left their bodies in the farmhouse.

She was visibly shaking as the screen blanked and Arnis got up to make her a cup of tea. It was only when she had finished her drink that she calmed a little, and then she announced she was going to bed. 'You can tell me about Independence Day tomorrow,' she said.

Arnis decided to turn in himself a few minutes later, convinced that a sleeping nightmare could be no worse than one you had when you were still awake. Before switching off the living room light he went over to the fireplace and lifted one of the photographs from the mantelpiece. His wife's favourite, a photograph of the two of them taken on their wedding day thirty-five years ago.

He and Penny had met in the local library at the bottom of the high street. He'd spotted her immediately at the information desk; her long auburn hair parted in the middle, falling loosely round her shoulders over a bottle green polo neck jumper. Her smile was open and friendly, her green eyes direct and unwavering. Few were the evenings after that when he didn't visit the library.

His mother approved of the number of the books coming into the house until she found out the reason. She didn't like Penny at all, using every excuse she could think of to dissuade him from seeing her. It didn't help that he had split up from Ingrīda six months previously. Ingrīda was a beautiful Latvian girl whom Margarita had liked very much. 'A sensible reliable girl who would have made you a good wife,' was the way she had expressed it. By contrast she thought Penny was frivolous and too keen on enjoying herself. 'She'll spend all your money,' said his mother.

But her efforts were in vain. As Arnis got to know

Penny better, it was her sense of fun, her boundless energy for life which drew him to her. Opposite to him in some ways, but with an underlying sensitivity that was a mirror image of his own and to which he responded. And she was British. By the time he met Penny, that is what Arnis wanted most – to be British. Though his interest in his birthplace and his father would surface in the years to come, what he wanted at that point was to be British. To be part of a country that had been strong enough to have an empire, rather than one that was part of an empire. To be part of a nation that was confident, not one that was persecuted.

Penny represented all of this. Within a year they were engaged.

After that, Margarita kept her counsel until the week before the wedding when she said rather dolefully to Arnis. 'We shan't be a Latvian family any more.' To which he'd replied firmly, 'Our children will still have your family name. Your grandchildren will be called Rozenvalds.' It wasn't until then that he'd realised how upset his mother was. Penny having a cat called Pushkin didn't help matters.

But the wedding went ahead and they soon settled into their first home, a two-bedroomed terrace house, about a mile away from where he and his mother now lived. When Henrijs and Antons were born, Penny gave up her job at the library and immersed herself in their upbringing. Having children was all she'd ever wanted, but soon after the boys started school, her mother died and she became increasingly depressed. It took her a long time to come to terms with her loss, but three years later she decided to become a hairdresser. Though Arnis was not enthusiastic about her going out to work, he was relieved at the return of her cheerful spirits and in the end he even found some premises where she could open a salon.

During the next five years she built up a very successful business and Arnis had not seen her so happy since the boys were small. She began to get enthusiastic about going on holiday, moving house, the boys' schooling. They hardly ever talked about Latvia, there was nothing to say, except as the years went by, Arnis began to think more and more about his father. What happened to him? Was he still alive? Had he married again? Had his father had more children? It was the last question that filled Arnis's mind more than the others. Perhaps he was not an only child after all. Perhaps he had brothers and sisters. Occasionally he would voice his thoughts to Penny, but he sensed that it made her anxious.

Not wanting to disturb her happiness he tried to put his father out of his mind, to crowd out his growing list of questions with his responsibilities for the practice and his family. For a time, he managed to do this, until one night in the summer of 1989, he came home from the surgery to find Penny flicking through the channels on their new television.

Eventually she stopped on the CNN news to reveal a scene which took Arnis completely by surprise. It was Rīga. People lined a broad tree-lined avenue holding hands.

Then came the slow deliberate voice of the reporter. 'On this, the fiftieth anniversary of the Molotov-Ribbentrop pact, a treaty between Josef Stalin and Nazi Germany, which gave the Soviet Union control of the Baltic states after Hitler's take-over of Poland, Latvians have appeared on the streets of Rīga with posters exposing the still-existing Nazi-Soviet agreement. Two million people linked hands across the Baltic States from Tallinn to Vilnius, demanding freedom from

Soviet rule. In protest of the Soviet-Nazi pact, the Baltic people have sent a document to the Kremlin which reads: The USSR has infringed on the historical right of the Baltic nations to self-determinatioon, presented ruthless ultimatums to the Baltic republics, occupied them with overwhelming military force, and under conditons of military occupation and heavy political terror, carried out their violent annexations.'

Arnis blinked. It was the first time he'd seen Rīga on the television. Then a couple of banners flashed in front of the camera: 'How long will the Red Army Be Master of Our Land?' and 'Moscow! Hands off Latvia.' He could not take his eyes off the screen. Little had happened in recent weeks and months to prepare him for such scenes. The Berlin wall was still intact. Though there had been some reports of unrest in Prague, another three months would elapse before pictures from the Brandenburg Gate, Wenceslas Square and Ceaucescu's Palace filled the world's living rooms on a nightly basis

He continued watching until the next news item appeared, after which he phoned his mother repeating the story twice before she began to believe what he had seen. But she did not share his excitement. 'The Russians won't give up. I've lived it, remember,' she said in a quiet matter-of-fact voice.

Penny had been quiet for the rest of the evening. He sensed that the pictures had disturbed her, and they never mentioned it again. Every time he turned to CNN, which happened with increasing frequency over the following months, she always left the room, and he felt torn between watching out for news of Latvia and Penny's unease. But Latvia didn't feature again for over a year until five people, one of whom was a cameraman, were killed during the storming of the Latvian Ministry of the Interior in Rīga.

Though he discussed it with his mother regularly, still not a word passed between him and Penny until after the failure of the coup attempt against Mikhail Gorbachev, when one morning over breakfast she looked at him with a slightly wooden expression and said, 'So, the Soviet Union has disintegrated.'

That had hurt. Though they'd never talked a great deal about Latvia, it upset him that she could be so distant about something that she knew was so important to him. He felt as if he was living with a stranger, as if his marriage had been a lie.

Then a few days later, Latvia declared independence for the second time in its history, and without saying anything to Penny he bought a bottle of champagne and took it round to his mother's. As they watched the scenes on the television – the BBC was covering it now – Arnis had one thing in his mind. That was to get on the first plane he could to Rīga.

The next day he called the medical locum agency, but as it turned out, his plans didn't get very far; because later that same week he found Penny doubled up on the bathroom floor with severe abdominal pains. Intuitively he felt it was serious. Penny had hardly ailed from anything in her life. The only time she'd ever been in hospital had been to give birth to the boys.

'How long have you been having these pains?' he asked anxiously.

'Oh, on and off, a few months,' she replied.

He called the gastroenterologist at the local hospital who arranged immediately for a colonoscopy. It was worse than he had feared: end stage cancer of the colon, which had spread to the liver. She was only forty five. The cancer was inoperable and though she had radiotherapy, it didn't help and within two months she had lost three stone in weight.

Her last moments would stay with him always. It was a Sunday evening and his mother, who had moved in to help, had taken the boys out to the cinema.

'Carry me up to bed,' Penny had said. 'Before I take my morphine.' By then she weighed no more than five stone and he carried her up the stairs without any effort. When he had settled her down under the pale pink and beige bed cover, she smiled and murmured, 'Kiss me good night.'

Squeezing her hand tightly, he leaned over to kiss her lips. At that moment, she opened her eyes and tried to say something more. Arnis couldn't make out what it was and turned his head slightly so that his ear was closer to her mouth. Her voice was almost inaudible but this time he heard and understood.

'Latvia … You must go back,' she said.

Then her eyes closed for the last time.

*

After a night of fitful sleep, most of which he'd spent worrying about the future of young Peter, Arnis stirred thankfully as the first rays of morning sunshine filtered through the bedroom curtains.

He staggered downstairs and prepared the coffee machine to dispense his first dose of caffeine. As it gurgled, he still could not get Peter out of his mind. Thinking of his own mother, he began to wonder whether Peter's mother would remarry. Margarita had never considered the prospect of marrying again and Arnis had often wondered why.

When he had eaten his breakfast and dressed for the day, he dropped the car in at the garage for its MOT and walked from there to the surgery. The rain was pelting down and a crowd had massed at the bus stop; sodden school children in their badly fitting anoraks and leaky trainers poured into the newsagent to stock up their daily rations of fizzy pop and sweets. A couple of teenagers sheltered from the deluge and shared an illegal cigarette in the doorway of a video shop long since padlocked by the bailiffs. Everywhere Arnis looked he saw litter, a depressing reminder of the growing neglect of the south London borough where he had lived and worked for twenty five years.

When he took over the practice in the early seventies it had been a different world. The long economic boom of the fifties and sixties had come to an end but most people still had stable jobs and beer was more prominent than heroin. Reports of child sex abuse were rare though violent muggings and gang wars were just becoming a reality. In those days there had still been six general hospitals in the district, each with its own casualty department. He never saw posters in the pharmacy saying 'Save our hospital' but now yet another hospital was due for closure and would soon be on the market for its land value; land that would be used for rent yielding apartments or small industrial developments.

But there had always been the dump estates and he still remembered the shock of making home visits to places like Rhodesia House with its threatening graffiti, feuding neighbours, cooking smells and cacophony of noise – mostly shouting. He had replaced a much-loved GP who had practised on the High Street for more than thirty-five years. Arnis had stepped into his shoes with ease and soon felt at home amongst the growing population of Indians from East Africa and ex-merchant seamen from Barbados who had become bus drivers. Many were people who had crossed the seas either to find refuge from dictators or simply to improve their lot.

One day he'd been called out to see an unemployed docker with a collapsed lung, a dodgy liver and two months to live; on another occasion to a woman whose jaw had been broken in a domestic fight, which she'd concealed for three weeks. Every new day brought new problems and, in those early days, he'd loved it.

There had also been many other GPs in the locality. Arnis rarely mixed socially with them but they were characters, most of whom, like him, were fiercely independent. Their patients loved them and relied on their individual skills, always expecting to see the same doctor whenever they needed one - day or night. Now Arnis was one of the few remaining single-handed practitioners. Most of the others had retired and gone off to the country or the south of France. He didn't blame them for that. At the same time, he had no intention of working in a large practice, under the thumb of a practice manager, constrained by budgets, being told how many hips he could have done and what he could prescribe – being unable to care for his patients in the way he was used to.

As he continued his walk to the surgery, he passed a small shop that he remembered as a haberdasher's, a hardware shop and a shoe store. It now sold mobile phones and all these changes had taken place within the space of three years. When he reached the scene of the previous day's accident, the people queuing for their bus were engrossed in their newspapers and personal stereos. They were oblivious to the huge bouquet of flowers tied to the nearby lamp post. If any of them had even spotted the spray of red and white carnations, it would merely have signified a road traffic accident in which someone, presumably, had died. They wouldn't have given a second thought to the misery and grief the death left behind.

Morning surgery turned out to be busier than usual that day, but lunchtime brought a welcome lull and Arnis decided to sort out the pile of medical journals under his desk. He knew Latvian doctors had limited access to western journals and he intended to get Dawn to parcel them up and send them to the new drug information centre in Rīga where they could be used to produce information bulletins.

As he was going through the journals, he spotted a name he recognised. He had met and worked with John Sugden when he was a junior house officer at UCH and was intrigued to see that John had been working with the World Health Organization on a primary care project in Skopje, the capital of Macedonia. The article described refurbishing a clinic, training doctors in appropriate use of antibiotics, and setting up a nurse triage system. None of this was surprising given the circumstances in Macedonia but what struck Arnis was John's enthusiasm for the project. And this touched a raw nerve – Arnis's own enthusiasm had waned alarmingly in recent years.

The next day he called John and was surprised to find he was in. He was back in London for a month before he returned to Skopje for a longer stint. They arranged to meet for lunch in Windsor the following Sunday.

*

As soon as John appeared outside the restaurant where they had arranged to meet, Arnis was struck by how well and relaxed he looked. Over lunch, John explained that he'd left general practice five years previously to work for an agency that recruited doctors to work on training projects in other countries. 'I love the Balkans,' he said to Arnis, explaining that he was expecting to go to Belgrade for three months in the autumn. 'It's great and I'd had my fill of working here. What about you? Aren't you sick of working for the National Health Service?'

'You can say that again,' Arnis replied honestly. 'But times change. It's a new world. What else can we do?'

'What we can do, matey, is jack it in and go where we're appreciated.'

Arnis nodded dolefully. He accepted the sentiment but the reality was something else. 'If only it were that simple,' he said.

'But surely there must have been many times when you've thought about quitting.'

'Many times indeed,' Arnis told him. 'But thinking is as far as I get. I've found it so difficult to make decisions about anything these last few years. Even the simplest things like throwing away a pile of newspapers. Ever since Penny died.'

'Yes, I heard about that through the grapevine. I'm really sorry.'

Arnis swallowed as he recalled that awful day, then he brightened as he remembered something else. 'It's funny, John … well, not funny, exactly, but ironic. Penny's dying words were that I should go back to Latvia.'

John spread his elbows on the table. 'Then what are you waiting for, man? How long has Penny been dead? Good

God! You can speak the language and you probably understand the customs. That's a head start on me. I didn't speak a bloody word of the native tongue when I first went to Macedonia. I had to get by with translators and sign language.' He laughed as he imitated an injection into the arm.

Arnis smiled but said nothing. Yet his mind was working overtime.

'Have you been back to Latvia lately?' John asked.

Arnis nodded. 'Yes, twice during the last year. Medical conferences.'

'Then you must know something about practices out there?' The statement was both a question and an assumption. It demanded no answers so John continued. 'I guess there must be many similarities with the Balkans. Arnis, these places haven't had GPs since before the war. To call their systems of primary care embryonic is doing them a favour. Think of the contribution you could make and think of the satisfaction that would give you. Satisfaction, my friend … that's what it's all about. I wouldn't work in London again if I was offered twice the money.'

*

During the weeks that followed, events conspired to push Arnis closer to a decision. It started when he took his mother to meet her old friend, Vieda, for lunch. Unexpectedly, Vieda brought along her cousin, Miks, who was visiting from Rīga. Miks had recently become a consultant to the growing privatisation industry. He told them life in Rīga was getting better all the time. He told them the government was encouraging Latvians abroad to return to their own country where their skills were desperately needed.

Arnis was not wholly convinced. He knew his own skills would be invaluable but he had little expectation of any welcoming arms from the Latvian medical community. Returning ex-patriots were not universally popular, especially after so many years. And there was a chance that his way of doing things might cause resentment. They'd probably be very quick to tell him he didn't belong.

*

As the days passed, the words of John Sugden and Miks took root in Arnis's mind. He often drifted off in silent thought. Weighing up all the options.

His days of being being an independent practitioner in Britain could certainly be numbered. He did not like the way the health service was changing. He ran the risk of becoming a very small cog in a very large wheel – a wheel that was constantly growing in size; bureaucratic spokes that knew everything about nothing and nothing about everything.

The boys were off his hands and made contact infrequently – usually by telephone. They had their own lives to live. Since Penny had died, there had been no woman in his life except, of course, his mother. But if he were to make plans to work in Latvia she might not want to go. Would she, at eighty-seven, want to uproot and resettle in a homeland that had changed out of all recognition? She had always said that one day they would return to Latvia but had they left it too late? For the first forty-five years after they fled, there was no way she would have returned to a land occupied by the Russians but Latvia had now been independent again for eight years. As Miks had said and Arnis had seen for himself, things were getting better.

Maybe he could persuade her now. The more he thought about it, the more he realised he didn't want to stay in London any longer. He wanted a new challenge as a doctor but more importantly he wanted to find out about his father. Not that he had any idea where to start. Though he was fluent in Latvian, he didn't imagine it was going to be an easy task. Then one day he read in *Brīva Latvija* that more and more of the KGB records were becoming accessible to the public. His mind was made up.

LATVIA, 2002

CHAPTER 3

Waiting in queues, particularly those that consisted of a thronging mass assembled in haphazard order, had never been one of Arnis's favourite pastimes. So the idea of waiting at Rīga airport for an unknown length of time did not fill him with amusement. Antons's flight should have touched down more than forty minutes ago and the passengers should have cleared customs by now but the last time he checked, the arrivals board indicated a twenty minute delay to landing time. He squinted again at the board; it still said twenty minutes. That meant there was another five minute delay.

'Hi, Dad.'

The voice was undisputedly one he recognised instantly and he spun on his heel. 'Antons. How…?'

Antons dropped his luggage on the floor and threw both arms around his father's shoulders. 'How what, Dad?'

'How did you get here so quickly?'

Antons laughed. 'Simple, Dad. I couldn't find my flippers so I caught an aeroplane … you know, big metal thing with large wings and jet motors.' He imitated a take-off with his hand and made the appropriate accompanying noises.

'But how did you gain the time?' Arnis asked.

'Gain the time? Don't understand you. What time?'

'The arrivals board said the flight was running almost

an hour late.'

Antons was puzzled and glanced up at the board. 'Nope. We landed bang on time and that's what it says on the board.' Then he laughed uncontrollably. 'The board says the flight below the Heathrow arrival is running an hour late …you didn't read that by mistake, did you?' He didn't wait for an answer. 'Yes, you did, didn't you? God, Dad, you've got to get over this vanity hang-up about wearing glasses in public. It's pathetic!'

He was still laughing as he picked up his luggage. 'Come on, let's go. I want to see Gran.'

Arnis felt the warmth creeping up from his collar, spreading rapidly up to his hairline, and glanced round nervously to see if anyone else had noticed it. Each person he looked at stared back at him, making him feel more self-conscious than ever. He quickened his pace and caught up with Antons, anxious to leave this place of utter embarrassment.

As he pushed through the crowd, his face aimed more towards the ground than ahead, a hand grabbed his arm, and a shrill voice from behind said, 'Hello, Arnis.'

As soon as he turned he was kissed on both cheeks by a hefty middle-aged woman with dark blonde hair and gold-rimmed glasses. Then she gripped him in a firm embrace. He groaned inwardly. This was all he needed.

'What a lovely surprise,' she said, taking a firm hold of his arm, steering him towards the exit.

Ella was the daughter of an old friend of his mother's. A Latvian by birthright, she now worked as a London tour guide. Arnis was surprised to see her in Rīga at this time of year because September was the height of the tourist season in

London. Though he didn't particularly want to engage in conversation, he knew that if he didn't Ella most certainly would. 'What are you doing over here?' he asked.

'I've come to see Pēteris for a few days.'

Pēteris was her son and an estate agent, who was apparently doing very nicely in Rīga refurbishing flats and renting them out for increasingly extortionate prices. They weren't even nice flats, as Arnis had discovered when he'd been flat-hunting last winter. With their marbled floors and gold-plated bath taps, they looked brash and cheap, and stripped of their original character. He had no desire to live in such a place.

'But isn't it your busy time? Back in London, that is.'

'It's always busy,' she responded, 'but I have to have my time off and they don't object because I'm one of their most popular guides.'

Arnis though it rather strange that a Latvian could be a more popular guide than a native Londoner but he didn't get a chance to pursue the matter...

Ella continued, 'I know what you're thinking but the fact is I make the tours more interesting because I tell my flocks of tourists about the Latvian connection.'

'What Latvian connection?' Arnis asked.

'Well I tell them about famous Latvians who came to London with Karl Marx. I tell them about the famous Latvian doctor who saved many Londoners' lives during the great plague. I even use your name for that.'

'But that's dishonest, Ella.'

She winked. 'I know ... but the tourists don't.'

'But these are facts that could be substantiated, or not, in your case,' Arnis said, a slight hint of despair in his voice.

Ella bounced straight back. 'Americans don't check facts. They're just fascinated because a tiny little island like Britain has such close links with the Baltic countries, and has had for so many years.'

This time words failed Arnis.

Unfortunately, they never failed Ella. 'Changing the subject slightly, I almost asked your mother if she had a spare bed for me on this trip because I didn't really want to stay with Pēteris. It's a bit awkward with his new girlfriend around.'

This was worrying news. His mother had never made any secret of the fact that she thought Ella would make him a good wife. Heaven forbid! The idea filled him with horror.

'You said 'almost'?'

'Yes, I didn't ask in the end because she told me Antons was coming over for a few days. Where is Antons by the way?'

A good question. Where was Antons? Arnis had some important questions to ask him – the trouble is, he couldn't remember what they were. He racked his brains for a few seconds, but it was no good – they had gone. He glanced round the arrivals hall and eventually spotted his son skulking by a refreshment area, half turned away probably hoping Ella would not recognise him. Somehow, Arnis knew he had to ditch Ella.

But Ella was not instantly ditchable. She produced a yellow wallet from her handbag. 'Look, I must show you Sandra's wedding pictures.'

He took the photographs, one by one, making a few polite grunts as he briefly scanned each one. He knew Ella wanted to remind him that she hadn't forgiven him for not bringing his mother to Sandra's wedding. His mother hadn't forgiven him either. But it had coincided with the move to Rīga and he had been very glad of an excuse not to go.

But there was no escape now. 'Do you remember how Hannah set her cap at Antons all those years ago? She insisted she was going to marry him. Oh come on, you must remember that. I know they were only eight at the time, but…'

The incessant appetite women had for weddings both amused and irritated him; they were something he avoided whenever he could; Saturday morning surgeries came in very useful at times.

'No sign of your two taking the plunge yet? Henrijs must be in his late twenties now. No one serious yet?' Ella chattered on and Arnis knew he might have to be rude if he wanted to get rid of her. Then, much to his relief, she spotted Pēteris, kissed Arnis on both cheeks and ran off to greet her son.

The next week, or however long Ella intended staying in Rīga, was likely to be bad. If she wasn't round at the flat visiting his mother, she'd be knocking at the surgery on the pretext of some minor ailment – a corn on her little toe, some slight snuffle, or anything else she could dream up.

Penny would have accused him of rather enjoying it all; his female admirers had been something of a joke between them. Women had always adored him for his kindness, his charm, his old-fashioned politeness and his protectiveness.

*

Arnis and Antons stepped outside into the cool damp air. At one time they would have encountered Russian border guards. On Arnis's first visit, the airport had been swarming with them. Surly and bad-tempered, they had stared at his British-issued Latvian passport with great suspicion, making him feel as if he was the one with no right to be there. But with Latvia newly independent, they had no legitimate reason to be there. Thankfully, they had long gone.

Once outside the airport building, Arnis looked for a taxi. The gloom of a few years back hadn't quite been replaced by blazing lights but the strong smell of cheap petrol had long since evaporated. He took a sniff, just in case, but no, there wasn't even a faint whiff.

Disappointed? Yes, he had to admit it, although part of him felt guilty for mourning the passing of such palpable signs of grime and imperfection. Knowing full well that had he had to stand in the bread queues, cope with the shortages, the encroaching shabbiness, he would have hated it, just like everybody else.

A battered looking Merc crawled up to the kerb and the driver climbed out.

'Paldies,' Arnis said as the man put Antons's bags in the boot. 'Vecrīga,' he added, easing himself into the front of the taxi.

The driver grunted.

There would be no conversation with him. The man probably didn't know more than a few more words of Latvian, if that. Four months had passed since Arnis and his mother had moved back to Latvia and Rīga was full of Russians – not soldiers, but Russians all the same. At times it made him feel like a minority in his own country and his mother was angry. She told him the country didn't feel Latvian, except in the old town, which is where they now lived. She said she could still feel Latvian there. Being a minority in Britain was one thing.

That hadn't been easy, especially at first. But in Rīga, it was quite a different matter. If anything, the fear of miscegenation and dissolution was as great, if not greater, than anything she had felt in Britain.

Welcome to Latvia, Arnis thought grimly as he turned to look at his son.

*

Arnis fumbled in his coat pocket for his mobile so he could let his mother know they were on the way. He immediately spotted a missed message and was surprised to find it was from her. He realised it must have been fairly pressing because she hated using phones, and she hated voicemail services even more.

'Hello, it's Mrs Rozenvalda, here,' she said in her soft guttural tone. Arnis smiled. She always started on a formal note, as if she wasn't sure who would pick up the message, and waited for an acknowledgement. Then, as if remembering it didn't work like that she added quickly, 'Arnis you won't forget to make sure Antons has brought the PG Tips, will you?' After that there was a brief silence before she gave a slight cough and put the phone down.

The tea bags. That's what he had been trying to remember to ask Antons back at the airport. And if he hadn't got tied up with Ella he would have checked his voice mail earlier. Stupid woman!

'You did remember the PG Tips, didn't you?' he asked Antons.

'PG Tips?' Antons enquired.

'For God's sake please tell me you haven't forgotten,' Arnis snapped angrily. The boy had a memory like a sieve and now it was too late to get his mother some other sort of English tea at the airport; probably not her favourite, but it would have been better than nothing. Better than that Liptons stuff, as she called it, which she never tired of grumbling about, maintaining it tasted more like dishwater than tea.

'Calm down, Dad,' Antons said, a broad smile stretching across his face. 'You'll give yourself a heart attack. Of course I haven't forgotten.'

Arnis felt a momentary sense of relief before remembering something else. The oat cakes. He'd be in even worse trouble if Antons had forgotten those. She ate one every night before going to bed, a habit she'd developed when she worked at the sanatorium in Edinburgh. She'd had a stomach upset and one of the nurses had recommended them. From then on, she'd developed a taste for them, much preferring them to the doughy white bread, the only variety they could get in Scotland at that time. Even after they'd moved to London where she could get proper black bread, she still liked an oatcake with her cup of tea at bedtime.

'And the oat cakes?' Arnis asked.

'What oak cakes? You didn't say anything about oat cakes.'

Arnis nodded smugly. 'Ok, Antons. Joke over. Will you ever start taking things seriously?'

'No, seriously, Dad. You never mentioned oat cakes.'

Sometimes Antons took things too far. It was unlikely Arnis would give himself a heart attack, but Antons might.

'Enough is enough,' he said, his voice now showing signs of impatience.

'Dad, I'm being deadly serious. I haven't got any oat cakes.'

Arnis glanced down at the two bunches of flowers on his lap – one each of yellow and orange lilies. His mother was particularly fond of those, and they would look lovely in her green glass Iļguciems vase. Thank goodness he had bought them at the airport. They might just help to smooth the path when they got home. 'Buy some as soon as you get back to England and stick them in the post,' he ordered. At least they should be here in a few days, he thought to himself.

The taxi cruised along towards the city, passing a string of all-night filling stations, a flood of neon lights unimaginable only a few years ago. The advertising hoardings, far more numerous than they had been, looked incongruous, standing in total isolation in the middle of otherwise empty fields. Latvia was catching up quickly, of that there was no doubt, but she wore her new free-market clothes like a gawky teenager getting ready for her first grown-up party. But that was something Arnis had come to relish during the last few months: playing his part in the first act of a brand new play. In spite of the hundred and one irritations of daily life, he was relieved to have left South London, where shops were being boarded up as fast as new ones were opening in Rīga.

Leaving the neon lights behind, the road began to narrow, threading its way through the outskirts of the city, where the cloak of dilapidation was still all too evident. Putting right the damage of half a century would not happen overnight; it would take many years to repair the peeling plasterwork, the broken window ledges, the rotting doors, the cracked green paint and muddy puddles. Gloomy lamps, strung out across the street on thin wires, some working, some not, added an air of mystery to the things they were supposed to illuminate. Covering it up. Concealing a grime that had become privatised, almost effortlessly, except for those who had to live with it. All caused by decades of indifference and a system which had finally worn out at the seams.

The taxi took a hard jolt as it bumped over the tram tracks. It wasn't far to go now. The road swung round to the left, and sure enough, there were the cables of the suspension bridge straight ahead.

'Bljad!' Arnis looked sharply at the driver who, sticking two oily fingers in the air, swore as he swerved, narrowly missing a blue Peugeot that had appeared without any warning from a side road. People here always drove as if they'd come up from the country, never seeming to notice they'd joined a busy road. More and more traffic was beginning to choke a city that had never been built for cars and hadn't prepared for them. Much as Arnis enjoyed driving, he avoided using his own car in the city centre. Ten years earlier one could have parked anywhere, but not any more.

As they approached the bridge, he looked ahead waiting for his favourite view of the city – that long narrow view which had hardly changed since medieval times. A grand parade of mammoth churches, their fine spires and green steeples vying for attention, were dominated still, as they had been for almost seven centuries, by the huge Dom. With a tiny light shining from its bell-like tower, it bore more than a passing resemblance to the tower of Big Ben. On the far left of the picture, the creamy-coloured castle flew the maroon and white flag from one of its squat, round towers. To the right, a more recent and less wanted acquisition – that great hulk of a building, the Science Institute, one of Stalin's more visible gifts to Rīga, gradually faded from sight as the taxi sped over the bridge. A single tram trundled across the stone bridge under the watchful eye of a half moon slowly disappearing behind a bank of thick cloud. The river looked completely still, expectant almost.

A few moments later, the taxi turned sharp right into a tangle of narrow, crooked streets, bumping over cobbles still wet from the rain. His heart warmed at the sight of the wrought iron lamps casting a golden glow over the centuries old houses, flooding arched doorways into cellars and warehouses. The shouts of merchants trading their wares in amber, grain, hides and furs had long been silent – replaced by the clink of wineglasses and the strains of Mozart or Gershwin in restaurants where business was still conducted. By now most of the deals were over for the day and the streets were almost deserted.

The taxi rounded a corner, nosing its way out of the medieval muddle into an open triangular square. The driver finally drew to a stop on the corner under a turn of the century building. Arnis got out and fumbled in his pocket for his bag of change.

'Eight lati,' growled the taxi driver, lifting Antons's suitcase out of the boot.

'What?' Arnis scowled at the Russian.

'Eight lati. You heard!' the man repeated.

'You must be joking. That's robbery. Four's plenty.' He pushed a five-lati note into the driver's hand.

The Russian grabbed hold of his tie and pulled hard.

'Eight lati.'

'Who do you think you're threatening?' Arnis shouted, his breath coming faster by the second. 'You've got at least one more than it's worth. 'Ejiet prom!'

The driver grunted, let go of his tie, slammed down the boot lid and got back in the car. Arnis glared as the tyres rattled over the cobbles and the Merc's red taillights disappeared down the street. Breathing more freely, he realised he'd got away with that pretty easily. He felt in his pocket to check for his keys then picked up Antons's bags.

A few yards away, a linden tree rustled, gently waving its leafy shadows over the edge of the pavement. Two dark figures scuttled across the square and vanished into the medieval maze. Feeling calmer, he glanced up to the second floor of the pale pink building where a pair of stucco cherubs held up the semi-circular wrought iron balcony. The light in the corner window was still on and they made their way round to the main entrance.

Arnis tapped in the code then led Antons across the entrance hall to the lift. There was no response when he pressed the button. It would have to be tonight that the lift got stuck. He rammed the handle down on the suitcase, accidentally jerking his phone out of his top pocket from where it fell with a clatter to the granite floor, narrowly missing a black cat which had chosen that precise moment to weave round his legs.

'Damned animal!' he cursed. He disliked cats intensely; they always seemed so sly and disloyal. He hadn't seen one in the building before and he was wondering where it had come from when a door opened and the creature rushed into the ground floor flat beyond.

Arnis took a deep breath as they started to climb the curving wrought iron staircase. It was heavy going but at least it would help to keep him fit. Not that he'd lost any weight since they'd lived here – his mother's cooking was far too good for that. Trying to make as little noise as possible, he put his key in the lock of the first floor flat and immediately heard the sound of snuffling, followed by a quick excited bark. Chuckling, he pushed the tall double doors open and was greeted by two huge paws, one on each shoulder, a mound of black and tan fur obscuring his vision; a long tongue round his ears, wetting his hair, and a cold black nose nuzzling his cheeks.

With another bark and a string of delighted yelps, the Alsatian skidded along the parquet floor, using Margarita's homemade rug like a snowboard. Within seconds he was back, carrying a chewed brown slipper, which he promptly dropped at Arnis's feet. He looked up at Arnis, his brown eyes hopeful.

Chuckling again, Arnis bent down to pick up the slipper and felt a soft mouth round his hand, gently tugging him in the direction of a large living room. With its freshly painted primrose yellow walls, polished floor, walnut dining table and soft green leather sofa, its appearance had changed dramatically from ten years previously when it had not only been a living room but also a bedroom and study for an entire family consisting of a mother, father and two children. The other two smaller rooms in the flat had formed the living quarters for an elderly couple and a young couple with a baby. The kitchen and bathroom had been shared by all nine inhabitants.

'Hello,' his mother said as Reksis led the way to where she was sitting near the corner window, her feet resting on a large black beanbag.

Antons went straight to her and pulled her gently to her feet, kissing her on both cheeks. 'Ah, that's better,' he said. 'I really miss my old Gran.'

'Less of the *old*,' she said, her smile showing that the admonition was to be taken seriously but lightly. 'You've done well,' she added, glancing momentarily at the clock on the sideboard. 'No delays, I take it.'

'No, everything was fine,' Antons replied. 'Apart from the taxi, that is...'

She looked curiously at him. 'The taxi?'

'Well, the driver rather than the taxi ... a Russian. I thought Dad was trying to get us killed.'

'Don't tell me,' Margarita said, smiling her knowing smile, 'your father was arguing about the fare.'

Arnis butted in to a discussion where he was clearly outnumbered. 'It's a matter of principle,' he argued defensively. 'Why should we have to put up with ...' He gave up at that point.

His mother had no intention of listening to a tirade about taxi drivers – even if they were Russian taxi drivers. 'Can you fix these for me?' she asked, passing him her reading glasses and the right lens that had fallen from the frame.

'Mum, I do wish you'd use your bifocals,' Arnis said, knowing he was wasting his breath because she refused to wear them long enough to get used to them.

He went out to the hall to fetch a small screwdriver thinking it was high time she had her cataract sorted out. Twelve months ago the optician in London had agreed that it wasn't getting worse, and she needed no further encouragement to leave it at that. She hadn't ailed much in her life and for her to ask for, or receive, any help was almost to admit defeat; to feel she'd given in.

'These are perfectly good,' she said as she put her old glasses back on after the lens was firmly screwed in place yet again. 'Now I can get on with my needlework.' She smiled, looking at him fondly, deep lines fanning out from her almond-shaped grey eyes. She put a few more stitches in the cushion cover, tied a knot on the underside and smoothed it out on her lap, obviously pleased with the progress she'd made.

'This will do nicely for the chair,' she said, glancing at the round high-backed dugout chair on the far side of the room.

Almost as soon as she had put her needle away, the wet slipper landed on her lap, making the cushion cover damp and sticky. She glared at the Alsatian who stood at a safe distance with his tongue hanging out. 'I do wish you'd train that dog properly,' she said peering at Arnis over the top of her spectacles. 'He's into everything. Do you know, I left half a dozen eggs on top of the fridge this morning, an hour later they were everywhere. Lucky we haven't got fitted carpet. I spent the best part of the afternoon on my hands and knees with a scrubbing brush.'

As she was speaking, Reksis sat down in front of her and put a paw on her lap, nudging the slipper impatiently.

'You indulge him too much, Mum. What do you expect? He behaves perfectly well with me.'

'Indulge him! You should talk! I don't spoil animals ... you know that.'

Having been raised on a farm, she had no time for unruly dogs. It wasn't that she disliked dogs, she just thought they should be tied up outside.

Reaching into her apron pocket she withdrew a block of dark Laima chocolate. Reksis sidled up to her putting his nose on the curved arm of her wicker rocking chair. She removed the silver paper and the dog moved to sit close in front of her. Slowly, but deliberately, she removed the wrapping and placed a small square neatly on the Alsatian's nose.

'No,' she said. 'No,' she repeated firmly, with a smile in her voice. Raising her index finger, she watched Reksis intently for a moment. 'There. Now you can have it.' On the cue, Reksis tossed the chocolate into the air and caught it deftly in his jaws as it fell.

'You never miss, do you?' she murmured, burying her hand into the dog's thick coat.

Despite all she said about animals – dogs particularly - Arnis was pleased she had become so fond of the Alsatian, and in such a short space of time. Reksis had only been with them for a month.

'Reksis and I are good friends. Aren't we?' Leaning over, she picked up the slipper and tossed it to the other side of the room. 'Anyway he's here more than you are,' she continued teasingly. 'Good dog,' she added, as the Alsatian crawled under the dining table where he proceeded to make loud sucking sounds on the slipper. 'Better than that awful woman upstairs. She came down this afternoon when I was having my sleep and hammered on the door, moaning to me that the water had been turned off. As if I could do anything about it. Stupid woman!'

It was always the same when she hadn't seen him for a while. There would usually be something that wasn't quite right and she always managed to make it sound as if it was his fault. But she had been like that for years and he had got to the point where he would have worried if she hadn't greeted him that way.

'Then Mrs Bilmane came,' she continued. 'Asking me if I was all right. She said she'd heard a thump from my bedroom. I suppose she thought I was dead or something. I was only shifting that chest of drawers from under the window. I'd piled the drawers on my bed and one of them fell off. Honestly, there's no peace round here. Your life's not your own…'

'Ready for your tea?' Arnis said, suppressing a grin and winking at Antons.

'Yes, please,' Margarita answered. Then she looked at Antons. 'Did you remember to bring some tea from London?'

Arnis prayed his son wouldn't wind his grandmother up the way he had wound him up.

He didn't. 'Course I did, Gran,' he replied.

Arnis went off quickly to make a pot of tea. If his mother was going to continue her 'You didn't forget…' routine the kitchen was the safest place. Antons could carry the can.

Arnis rummaged in the cupboard and found, much to his relief, an unopened packet of oat cakes. He put one on a plate and took in her tea on a small silver tray.

'And while I think on,' Margarita resumed, 'that girl you call your receptionist … Maija … said she'd been trying to contact you to confirm an appointment for Alīna. She said she couldn't get through on your mobile. I really don't know why you have a mobile if it's never switched on. And I don't know why that girl doesn't use her initiative … if she has any. You'll have to get rid of her.'

Much as it irritated him when she meddled in anything to do with his work, he knew she was right about his receptionist. Maija would have to go. Looking back, he was never quite sure why he'd taken her on in the first place. His gut instinct normally served him well and, when he'd first met her, she'd seemed pleasant enough though her qualifications were not ideal. She'd previously had a job as a cloakroom attendant at the local polyclinic but she was the only one of the fifteen applicants to have had any experience of working in a medical environment. As it turned out, heaving coats across a counter didn't prepare her for dealing with patients and she could be downright rude at times. Like hundreds of others, she still expected to earn a salary without having to work for it.

It annoyed Arnis when people – usually foreign visitors – said that communism had ended. Sure, the faces of the politicians had altered, the maroon and white flag now flew proudly from scores of buildings, monuments of Lenin and Stalin had been torn down and Russian street names replaced with Latvian ones. But communism was more than an ideology or a system of government. It was a state of mind, infiltrating people's personalities and ways of thinking, which would take years to change. Maia still had the mentality. But Arnis didn't relish the idea of sacking her and it didn't help that her father and mother were unemployed. Their jobs at the Ogres woollen factory had come to an end some weeks ago.

When they had finished their tea, Margarita went to bed. Arnis and Antons talked for a couple of hours then, feeling pretty tired himself, Arnis decided it was time to turn in. Antons also.

Reksis, asleep on the beanbag, jumped up as soon as Arnis switched off the light. The Alsatian followed him to his bedroom and settled himself on the white rug at the side of the bed. Arnis undressed and then went over to his chest of drawers and opened the top one. He took out a brown envelope and opened it sliding out the photograph of his father on the boat that Reina had sent him after the Independence Day celebration.

Since then he had carried it everywhere but today he'd inadvertently left it behind. Not that his mother would have disturbed it. She didn't know it was there and he hadn't told her anything about it, or that he was aiming to find out what had happened to his father. Deep inside he was sure she didn't really want to know.

CHAPTER 4

During the next few days, Arnis enjoyed playing the tour guide. He showed Antons the Dom with its magnificent organ and also the newly restored House of the Blackheads, which with its ornate stepped gable was easily Arnis's favourite building in Rīga. They climbed up to the belfry of St Peter's Church to take in the panoramic view over the red-tiled roofs, towers and church spires of the Old Town, and round to the park where Arnis pointed out the Freedom Monument, telling his son that the locals called it Milda. On their way to the castle, they turned into Anglikāņu iela and stopped at the English church where Arnis explained that it had British soil for its foundation and the bricks, also from England, had been brought as ballast in ships.

Though museums held little interest for Antons, Arnis was keen that he should see the Occupation Museum where they spent an hour silently walking round the exhibits: a reconstructed gulag barracks, prisoners' clothes, cutlery, spectacles, letters and photographs. Items crafted by Latvians in captivity: embroidered handkerchiefs, bookmarks, a chess set, greeting cards. This was Arnis's third visit to the museum, but by the time they were ready to leave, his head was thumping between his eyes and he could tell that Antons had been affected by it too. Longing to talk to his son about what they'd seen, he spotted a bar and they went in and ordered a couple of beers. Arnis felt for his wallet to show Antons the photographs of his grandfather. But he couldn't bring himself to do it. The harsh reminders of the Siberian labour camps they had just seen made it impossible to even mention his father. He could not find the words.

*

The fragrance of warm apples and cinnamon greeted Arnis as soon as he opened the door of the flat and he was a little surprised. It wasn't usual for his mother to cook pastries in the middle of the afternoon because he always snacked on the way home from morning surgery and didn't eat again until he returned from evening surgery by which time she had cooked him a dinner. So this had to be something special.

And he found out how special it was when his mother emerged from the kitchen wiping her floury hands on her pinafore. 'Ah, I'm glad you're home in time,' she said brightly. 'Ella's coming to tea.'

Arnis's heart sank. The prospect of an afternoon spent listening to Beethoven before he went back to the surgery was suddenly shot to pieces. 'Sorry, mother, but I have to go out,' he said trying to disguise his annoyance behind softer tones.

'Out? Out where?'

Arnis suddenly developed an irritating cough as he walked to his bedroom to pick up his car keys. It gave him the few seconds he needed to think up a plausible excuse. 'I have to do some research at the Institute so I thought I would do that first and then take the dog for a walk.'

Reksis immediately sped off to grab his lead from the hook in the coat cupboard.

'I took him for a walk this morning,' Margarita said,

59

glancing at Reksis who was now sitting by the door thumping his tail on the floor. 'He doesn't need to go out again.'

'Another walk won't do him any harm,' Arnis assured her. 'He's getting flabby laying around the flat all day.'

'What time will you be back?'

'Difficult to say … later.'

She gave him one of her exasperated looks. 'Arnis … how late is later?'

'I'll be back in time to drop Reksis off before I do evening surgery.'

'So you won't have time for tea?'

'Doubt it.'

'Ella will be very disappointed, you know. I think she has a bit of a soft spot for you.'

He ignored her remark. 'Sorry, mother, but no doubt you two will find plenty to talk about,' he said dryly.

His mother glanced again at Reksis. 'Well, at least he won't be here when she arrives. Ella can't stand dogs.'

'All the more reason for having one,' Arnis muttered under his breath, grinning to himself as he slipped the chain over the Alsatian's head. Reksis immediately dragged him to the door, hooked it open with his paw, and rushed down the stairs, winding his chain around the scrolls and swirls of the wrought iron banister.

As Arnis crossed the street to his car, a small boy raced across the square towards him. Tālis always managed to appear at the most opportune moment and this time he was joined by another boy Arnis hadn't seen before, staggering along with a bucket of water and a dishcloth. Without asking, both boys set to work on the car, so Arnis walked off with Reksis to buy a newspaper and get some cash from the 'hole in the wall'.

As he began to wander back towards his car, he became aware of someone walking quite closely behind him. He turned his head to one side and just within his field of vision there was a woman with thick, shoulder length auburn hair. He could hear her heels tap the cobbles and he kept up his pace not wanting her to pass by too quickly. As she drew level with him, he got a glimpse of her face, long enough to catch her eye. She gave him a half smile, which he returned.

But it was her hair that his eyes were drawn to – that lustrous blend of deep red and brown. He hadn't stopped to gaze at a red-haired woman for years though he always gave them more than a passing glance, particularly the attractive ones. But this time it was different. Unlike the other red-haired girls who passed him in the street, this one disturbed his equanimity. There was something about the way she walked – focused and determined, and most uncannily of all, he could hardly believe it. A silk scarf was tied to her handbag.

Penny had always done that.

He watched as she walked into the square, her herring bone jacket and charcoal grey trousers fitting her slim figure to perfection. She turned off in the direction of the castle, and he did not take his eyes off her until she disappeared through the doorway of a terracotta building a few doors down the street.

*

The car was straight ahead and Tālis was standing on the bonnet in his bare feet, chamois leather in his hand. Arnis opened the door to let Reksis jump in then he waited until the other boy finished wiping the hubcaps. Normally, Tālis did a pretty good job but today he had left it smeary with the wheel

61

arches still coated in sand.

Tālis obviously sensed Arnis's disappointment and provided a solution without prompting. 'We'll do it again tomorrow,' he promised, looking hopeful.

Arnis considered the proposal briefly. 'You'd better. Here you are.' He tossed him a couple of coins reckoning the money was still going to a better cause than it might if he went to the local car wash.

Both boys grinned; Tālis with a row of even white teeth, the other with a less perfect set, some of which had turned quite black.

'What's your name?' Arnis asked him.

'Jēkabs,' the boy replied, eyes flashing.

'He's my brother,' Tālis interjected.

With their dark hair and green eyes, the two boys did indeed look alike yet in other respects they were quite different.

'Where do you live?' Arnis asked Jēkabs: a question he'd asked of Tālis many times before without ever getting an answer.

The brother was equally uncommunicative and merely shrugged his shoulders before he turned his attention to Reksis. The Alsatian was now sitting on the front seat and Tālis knocked on the glass. Reksis started barking at him, not in anger but in playful recognition.

On a similar day a few weeks earlier, Tālis had, as usual, appeared from nowhere as soon as Arnis approached his car. But on this particular occasion he was towing a decidedly unkempt Alsatian on a piece of string. 'Do you want a dog?' Tālis had asked.

At that time, there was nothing Arnis wanted more.

Throughout his married life, he had always wanted a dog. The boys also wanted a dog but Penny disliked dogs, so they had never had one. Arnis squatted to stroke the manky fur behind the dog's ear as it rested its haunches on the cobbled street with its head on one side and its tongue hanging from the corner of its mouth. Apart from the matted coat there was an obvious eye infection but otherwise it didn't look too bad. Clearly it was a young dog yet it appeared to be fully grown.

'Where did you find him?' Arnis had asked.

Tālis had replied without hesitation, 'Near the hospital. Wandering about on the rubbish dump.'

'How much?'

The boy had shrugged his shoulders. What *was* the value of a dog that scrounged its food on a rubbish dump? He didn't know.

Arnis had given Tālis a couple of lati then he took him to the vet for a check-up. Apart from the red eye and a bad dose of worms, the Alsatian had been pronounced fit and healthy so Arnis had taken him home. After all, it was unlikely anyone would claim him. Since then, he had settled in with Arnis and his mother as though he had been born to life in a comfortable flat with food that was prepared regularly for him. For Reksis, as his new master called him, there was no more scavenging on rubbish dumps and Tālis was the person who had brought about this new-found luxury. That's why there was always recognition in his eyes and his playful bark.

After saying goodbye to the boys, Arnis climbed into the old black BMW and pushed Reksis over to the passenger seat. The car was something else Arnis had fallen in love with. Although the BMW was slightly worse for wear, there was only one other car he had driven which had given him quite the same enjoyment – a green MG he'd borrowed many years ago from a fellow student to take his girlfriend on a trip to Loch Lomond.

As the car approached the forest, Reksis began to whine softly; sitting bolt upright in the front seat, his body quivered in anticipation. The whine changed to an excitable yelp as a familiar spot came into view and Reksis raised his body on to all four feet, no longer able to contain himself. When Arnis stopped and opened the passenger door, the dog sprang out and rushed along the grass verge. Arnis followed, entering a quiet pedestrian street with small, bright shops on either side. He paused to look in the Lego shop and decided he would buy some on his way back for children at the surgery to play with. As he continued along the street, his mobile phone started ringing. Without looking at the display, he figured it would be his mother. She would want to know where he was, when he would be back, whether he would be in time to catch Ella before she left …

He raised the phone to his ear.

'Hi, Dad,' It was Antons. 'Just to let you know I've put the oatcakes in the post. And some more PG Tips.'

Arnis grinned. 'Good on you. Thanks,' he said, thinking that his son must have some other reason for calling. 'You sound cheerful.'

'I am. I start my course next week.'

Suddenly, this didn't sound like the Antons Arnis knew. He had decided to train as a paramedic but courses involved studying - and studying was not Antons's forte. But Antons's next words made it all clearer. 'I've got to go on a driving course in December,' he said.

Arnis smiled to himself. 'You'll enjoy that.'

'Yeah. It'll be cool. Anyway, must go. Bye.'

Now that was the Antons Arnis knew very well. Communicate only the briefest facts on a need to know basis. Short, succinct, and to the point - then goodbye and click before his father had a chance to develop the conversation. Still smiling, Arnis switched his phone off and ambled on. A love of driving was one of the few things he and his son had in common and he couldn't help thinking it was that aspect of a paramedic's job that had most probably attracted Antons to it in the first place.

If Margarita had just heard Antons's words, she would have given Arnis one of her I-told-you-so looks. Many times she had expressed an opinion that Arnis should show some pride in her grandson. 'Okay,' she had said, 'so he never finished his medical training ... so what? He wanted to do something useful with his life but training to be a doctor wasn't right for him.'

Which was all very well for Antons, but if Arnis had left university without his medical degree he would have been in big trouble! Failing at anything had never been an option for him. Even though he'd always had a natural inclination to laziness, which he had obviously passed on to Antons, he was always glad his mother had pushed him to achieve his goals – and hers. Now it appeared there were dual standards: The *De Facto Book of Parental Academic Guidance* clearly came in two distinct editions – one for sons; another for grandsons, and this either amused or annoyed him depending on the mood he was in.

He took a right turn and followed a track that wended its way through the pine trees. It was a lovely day - one of those days only late summer can bring; warm without being uncomfortably hot, the sky washed by the previous night's rain into hints of blue intermingled with the palest shade of grey. As he walked, the remains of a hotel came into view. Its windows were smashed and a few shreds of cheap floral curtains flapped raggedly behind the frames. The woodwork on the once grand house was now barely covered by the flaky remnants of dirty blue paint; its front door was lying amongst the weeds on the overgrown garden path where it had been cast aside many years previously. The total dereliction scarred the otherwise beautiful scenery.

Strolling on, his hands behind his back, he wondered how Antons was finding it being back in England. It had been his first trip to Latvia. Arnis could remember very clearly the first time he'd returned to London from Rīga. The lights at Gatwick airport had been an assault on his senses. The choice in the shops – even the corner shop at the bottom of his street – had overwhelmed him. Then he'd felt guilty for his irritation at not being able to find his favourite chocolate orange biscuits. But that was ten years ago. Rīga had changed enormously since then. Though drabness and shabbiness were still evident in the suburbs, the new out of town supermarkets were almost bigger than those in London.

He was sure Antons had enjoyed himself, but he was equally sure his son would not leave London permanently. Though Arnis was beginning to appreciate being in a smaller city, Antons would not. Bureaucracy still ruled in many aspects of Latvian life, a malignant hangover of the communist times, but when the cracks appeared, as they did with increasing frequency, Arnis relished the feeling that anything was possible. Even simple things like being able to walk into the Department of Health without having to run the gamut of security checks and having to sign himself in and out. The sheer joy of being able to see someone quite senior without an appointment. It reminded him of something his friend, Michael, had said about Ireland: being able to speak to his publisher in Dublin without having to go through a switchboard. Living in a small country had many advantages.

Straight ahead, the houses had a less derelict appearance. A number of them were now being renovated. The smell of fresh paint mingled with the scent of the pine; muted colours of primrose yellow, powder blue, mint green, and butterscotch provided a welcome contrast to the sad-looking houses further back. The echoes of tapping and banging hand tools filled air that might once have resounded to the noises of wandering musicians who strolled in the woods playing trumpets, trombones and clarinets at the turn-of-the century. Or the shouts of peddlers with barking dogs rushing at their heels.

When Arnis reached the end of the town he turned down a woodland track that led to the beach. The sounds of workmanlike activity faded into the distance and soon he heard only the noises of pine needles crunching beneath his thick-soled brown shoes. A short while later, the forestation ended and he walked into bright sunlight bathing the sand dunes. People were ambling along the beach in groups of half a dozen or more, linking arms, some of them singing, a sight which always made Arnis smile, used as he was to the beaches of Britain with their solitary walkers or couples.

Reksis charged down to the water's edge to paddle. Arnis laughed as the dog ducked its snout into the gently lapping surf and snorted through its nostrils. He jumped back as the bubbles surfaced in front of his eyes. On their last visit, there had been quite a swell and the Alsatian had stood at the water's edge, biting at the foam, barking at the waves, advancing and retreating as the tide ebbed and flowed. Today great mounds of seaweed marked out the edge of the beautifully calm sea and Reksis took chunks of it in his jaws and tossed it in the air, catching it again as it fell back to earth.

To the south, a slight mist obscured the promontory like a wispy trail of cotton wool stretching vaguely out to sea. From behind, the sound of a siren drifted slowly over the bay as the Stockholm ferry made its way out to sea. He stopped and sat down on the edge of the dunes, letting a handful of sand run through his fingers, watching Reksis rolling on his back, thinking of a similar beach, about a hundred miles from here, where he had waited with his mother over half a century ago. He was only three years old at that time so he could remember little of the detail, but what he could recall was his mother asking him to watch out for a rowing boat.

Earlier that day, they had not been alone. Others had been waiting for small boats to carry them out to a German troopship. Hundreds of them – men, women and children but mostly women and children – all of whom had decided they had to leave Latvia because the Russians were coming back. Several boats had worked in relays and when one reached the shore close to where they stood, people thronged forwards in a tangled mass, all trying to climb aboard at once. Arnis remembered that the overcrowding crush on the beach had been suffocating and the sea got rougher as the boats left the shoreline. Water appeared to be engulfing the tiny boats as they battled against the waves. At one stage, they were in danger of sinking and some of the passengers started throwing their bags into the sea. Looking back now, and knowing what he now knew, he realised the pressures to lighten the boat must have been enormous - the survival of twenty or more people depended on it. And yet, for some, it had all been in vain.

When they were about midway between the beach and the ship, the air was suddenly filled with the noise from the screaming engines of two Russian Polikarpov fighter planes. The tracers from their machine tore a path through the water and many people died as the bullets hit their targets. The planes roared on and aimed their 20mm cannons at the troopship. Most of the shells missed the target but there were at least two direct hits. The loud sounds of the explosions were followed immediately by flames and smoke at two points on the ship's deck.

The terrified survivors on the rowing boats watched in horror as more German seamen appeared on the decks. Some ran to their gun positions and returned fire at the attackers who were looping back for another strike; others started to tackle the fires on the ship. Then the looks of horror turned to dismay as the survivors and German seamen manning the small boats heard the throbbing noises of large propellers and saw the churning waters at the ship's stern. The large troopship gradually distanced itself from the shoreline, and the rowing boats. When the oarsmen realised they were being abandoned, they did the only thing they could: they turned the boats around and rowed towards the beach, anxious to reach land before the fighters swooped in again.

Looking out to sea now, Arnis realised how fortunate his mother had been to find another means of escape so quickly – a small sailing boat on which they had sailed with six other Latvians from Liepāja, eventually landing on the

Scottish coast at Dunbar. From there they had made their way to Edinburgh where Margarita got a job as a cleaner in a sanatorium. When that came to an end, she found work as a domestic in Oban, which is where they lived until Arnis qualified as a doctor. He could only admire the way his mother had been so resolutely determined to get them both to a safer land. He also understood why she hated boats so much. The journey across the North Sea had been terrible.

A train rattled through the forest on its way to Rīga, breaking into Arnis's reverie. He glanced at his watch and then looked towards the sky. The light was beginning to fade and the clouds were forming a quilted grey canopy overhead. It was time to go. Reluctantly, he strolled back to the car. Reksis ran ahead, dragging a huge piece of driftwood. When Arnis caught up with him, the Alsatian was looking hopefully at the car door, the piece of wood still clenched in his jaws.

'You don't want that,' Arnis said firmly. It took considerable force to wrestle it from his grip and the dog was reluctant to get into the car without it. Eventually he released it and Arnis laid it carefully alongside the wheels out of the dog's sight.

*

It was late afternoon by the time Arnis got back to the city. He parked the car in the Dom square and cast his eyes upwards to his flat. Though he was ready for a cup of tea, he would not go in yet. Ella was bound to be there. He looked along the cobbled street towards the castle, thinking of the auburn haired woman, wondering whether she was still inside the terracotta building. He stayed in the car for a few seconds, staring through the windscreen, willing her to come back towards the square. Naturally, she did not.

He locked the car and wanting to kill some time, he strolled in the direction of St Peter's Church then into Strēlnieku laukums. Ahead there was a huge sculpture, commemorating the Latvian Riflemen, Latvians who had sided with Lenin in the Bolshevik Revolution: a part of history that Arnis was not proud of.

As he continued walking, Antons came into his mind again, and he regretted that he had said nothing about his father to him. He had hoped it would be easier to talk to his son when they were in Rīga together. But it hadn't been. Then another thought occurred to him. Would the Occupation Museum have any information that could help him to find out what had happened to his father? It seemed unlikely, but the building was straight ahead so it was worth a try. He pulled open the door and went into the entrance hall. 'I wonder if you can help me' he said to the woman behind the desk. 'Do you have any information here about people who were deported or imprisoned? I'm trying to find out about my father.'

She gave him a sympathetic smile. 'I'll call someone,' she replied.

Within a few moments, another woman appeared and Arnis explained again.

Her reply made his heart leap. 'We do have some records here. Where did your father live?'

'Kuldīga.'

'I'll have a look. Sit down. I won't be a minute.'

She re-appeared in no time at all with a thick ledger. 'These records aren't complete,' she warned. 'We've collected information wherever we can, but it's not comprehensive by any means.' She thumbed through the register and quickly

71

found a section marked Kuldīga. 'Have a look.'

Arnis pulled out his glasses and ran his index finger down the relevant pages. With every line his hopes faded. His father's name was not there. Just to be sure, he looked again. But there was nothing.

'I'm sorry,' she said, obviously sensing his disappointment. 'But don't give up. There's more information appearing all the time. If they release all the KGB records, they may help you.'

'Thank you,' he replied, fully intending to make further enquiries as soon as he could.

He stood up and was about to leave when a group of youngsters came in, filling the entrance hall. Unable to get to the door, he could not help but listen as their English-speaking guide gave a brief explanation of the museum and its exhibits. After she had finished talking she invited them to follow her, but before climbing the stairs, she added, 'What you must understand is that this is a country where the past is more uncertain than the future.'

A good way of describing Latvia, Arnis thought, at the same time wondering whether the youngsters would understand what she meant.

*

It was getting quite late when he arrived back home but he was not entirely surprised to hear Ella's voice when he opened the outer door into the flat. Dreadful woman! But it was too late to duck out again and anyway she had already seen him.

She was standing in the hall next to his mother admiring the painting he'd bought earlier that summer - a Latvian country scene with a farmhouse standing next to a river. 'This is nice,' said Ella turning to face him. 'Do you know where it is?'

'No,' he replied sharply, barely attempting to disguise his annoyance.

Obviously not sensing it, she continued. 'I thought it might be somewhere near to where you came from.'

He shrugged. 'It could be anywhere. I've no idea.'

'We should find out,' said his mother. 'When I get the chance, I'll go to the art gallery to see what I can find out about the artist.'

Ella turned to his mother. 'It's strange. Despite the number of years we've known each other, I have no idea where you actually came from.'

'It's not a secret,' his mother replied. 'We lived in Kuldīga.'

'Kuldīga! That's a pretty place.' She turned towards Arnis. 'So is that where you were born?'

He nodded. 'You obviously know it.'

'Yes, my son ... Pēteris ... took me there one day last summer. We had lunch at a lovely restaurant by the river.'

'Nice,' Arnis said impatiently, at the same time thinking, 'Why don't you go, woman?'

Going did not appear to be Ella's priority. 'I guess you've already been back ... since you returned to Latvia, that is.'

'No, we haven't,' Arnis replied curtly. Being polite to Ella would only encourage her.

Ella frowned. 'Why ever not? You should.' She turned to his mother again. 'You really haven't been back since you left? He hasn't taken you?'

'No,' his mother replied.

Ella again turned to face Arnis 'Well, it's about time you did,' she said. 'I would have thought it would have been one of the first places you would have visited.'

'I would like to go,' said his mother in a quiet voice.

Arnis was astonished. He had suggested it several times before yet she'd never seemed very keen – which he could understand. Now Ella had mentioned it, it seemed to be his fault they hadn't been.

'That's settled then,' said Ella. 'That takes care of your next day out.'

*

Lying awake that night, Arnis was puzzled but, at the same time, delighted at his mother's apparent change of heart about going to Kuldīga. Having had every intention of going on his own, he was glad that they could now go together, though he was apprehensive about her reaction to the little country town she hadn't seen for fifty-eight years.

He turned over and thought again of the woman with the auburn hair, her silk scarf trailing from her handbag, and the way her gaze had fleetingly held his. He closed his eye lids tight shut, trying to picture her face.

Was she Latvian? His mother said she could distinguish between a Latvian, a Russian and a Baltic-German. But she knew what she was looking for. She trusted her senses. Arnis was not so sure. Only occasionally could he tell a Latvian from the others. But as he couldn't bring the woman's face to his mind, the question was pointless.

CHAPTER 5

A few days after his trip to the seaside, Arnis met his mother for lunch at a café on Vāgnera iela. She liked the chicken soup there, and although he wasn't fond of soup, the omelettes were tasty, and they both enjoyed the ice cream.

'Ella went back to London yesterday,' his mother remarked as she scraped out her bowl. 'I don't suppose we shall see much of her for a while.'

'Oh, why's that?' he replied hopefully. Ella usually came to Rīga three or four times a year.

'Her daughter, Sandra is expecting a baby. It's due in March, she told me.'

Excellent! Arnis thought. If that really was enough to keep Ella in England for a while it would suit him. And it would certainly help to keep his mother occupied, knitting baby clothes for the new arrival. Not that she was a person who ever felt the lack of something to do. She could never understand people who said they were bored and she always maintained sloth was by far the worst of the seven deadly sins.

They shared the last slice of black bread and, not having to get back to the surgery for an hour or so, he ordered another beer and they sat and chatted for a few moments more. The sun flooded past the tiled windowsills and the strains of a violinist drifted in through the half-open door. It was another beautiful day, and autumn still seemed far away.

'Do you fancy going to a concert later this week?' he said, thinking they could take a look at the programme at the Wagner Hall on their way back to the flat.

'Yes, why not?' she said, beaming a smile at the waitress as she put a slice of chocolate cake in front of her.

Looking at her watch, she said quickly, 'Have you time to call in at Centreks before you go to the surgery? I want to buy a shovel and spade.'

'A shovel and spade? What for? We don't have a garden.'

'I thought you wanted to go to Kuldīga,' she said mystifyingly.

There was no obvious connection between a spade and shovel and Kuldīga. 'Yes, I do want to go,' he replied. 'But what do we need a ...'

She held her hand up to stop him completing the sentence. Looking around furtively, she lowered her voice. 'I want to search for something.'

'What?' he said, still mystified.

Margarita tapped the side of her nose as she leaned across the table. She was beginning to act and sound like a conspirator. 'Something your father and I buried many years ago.'

'Mother...' He stopped himself from telling her she was crazy if she thought she'd find anything buried all that time ago because he didn't want to do anything to put her off the idea of going to Kuldīga.

Without another word, he swallowed the last of his beer and paid the bill. As they made their way to the store, she explained that they had buried whatever it was a few weeks before the Russians occupied Latvia in 1940. Then she dropped a clue - it was a family heirloom given to them by her maternal grandmother. Delighted that the idea had furnished her with a more definite reason for wanting to go to Kuldīga, even though he was sure they wouldn't find it, he decided they should go as soon as possible in case she changed her mind. Apart from that, it would soon be winter and the ground would be far too hard for digging if they delayed the trip.

Shopping completed he went back to the surgery. What on earth had his mother buried? She obviously had no intention of telling him, perhaps because she didn't want him to be disappointed when they didn't find it. He was sure they wouldn't. But there was nothing she loved more than creating a mystery, and he had not seen her so animated in the four months they'd lived in Rīga.

The first patient came in for a repeat prescription and when she had left, he went over to the filing cabinet to search for Mrs Ozoliņa's test results. Seconds later, the door opened again. Assuming it was another patient, he didn't turn round for a few moments but, when he did, he was astonished to see the auburn-haired woman he had spotted in the street a week ago. Close up, she looked even more like Penny and he began to be aware of his heartbeat.

'Hi,' she said simply. Her generous smiling lips revealed a row of even white teeth. 'I'm Anita Celma,' she added, stretching out a slim, lightly-tanned hand.

'What can I do for you?' he asked, automatically thinking she wanted to sign on as a patient.

But that was not her reason for calling. 'I'm writing an article for *Diena*. I'm hoping you can help me.'

He groaned inwardly. A journalist.

Perhaps if she had not been so good-looking, he might have told her he didn't talk to journalists and asked her to leave. But she was absolutely stunning and, on this occasion, he had time to study her properly.

Her breasts were round and full and her straight navy trousers showed her slim waist and thighs to perfection. He wondered, as he had on the day he'd first seen her, how old she was. It was difficult to tell but he guessed she would be around forty - forty-five at most. Her skin was perfect with no telltale lines at the corners of her eyes – eyes, he realised now, that were exactly the same green as Penny's.

For the next few moments she held his gaze, obviously enjoying it, then she continued, 'It's about the new system of family doctors. Someone told me you'd practised in England before coming here, so I thought you'd be the ideal person to talk to.' Her voice was smooth and seducing. It held his attention effortlessly. She continued, 'I know how strong general practice is in Britain and I'd be interested to get your reaction to the new developments in Latvia. Would you be happy to talk to me? I've got time now, if you've got a few minutes. It won't take very long.'

He thought quickly. General medical practice was a contentious issue in Latvia right now so, if he talked to her at all, he would have to play it carefully. But it was a long, long while since he'd had the opportunity to spend time with such a stunningly beautiful woman. 'I would be happy to talk to you but unfortunately not right now. I have a busy evening surgery,' he said, hoping his excuse would not rule out another meeting.

It didn't. 'Fine,' she said. 'When would suit you?'

'Afternoons are best.' Arnis did his best to sound

casual.

'How about Sunday? We could meet for a cup of tea and discuss it.'

'I'm afraid not.' Sunday was the only free day he had to go to Kuldīga.

Her face flickered with annoyance. 'Monday?'

'Yes, OK.'

'Monday it is then,' she said. She thought for a few moments. 'How about that café on Barona ... Osīris. You know which one I mean?'

He nodded, now stuck for words.

'Two o'clock OK for you?' she suggested.

He nodded again and she smiled and left. A few moments later, he heard the outer door shut. And he heard his heartbeat echoing in his ears. He was not entirely surprised to find he felt a little light-headed.

*

The following Sunday, Arnis and his mother left Rīga, shovel and spade in the boot of the car, and headed due west. Leaving the old town behind, they crossed the river and drove along a narrow road with old wooden houses on either side. After a couple of miles, the houses thinned out and the countryside opened up.

'Look at the land. Just look at it,' his mother said plaintively.

Arnis could tell she was upset and he could see why. Huge hedgeless fields surrounded a few scattered farmhouses. Barns, long-empty, their roofs caved in, stood sad and forlorn; pieces of rusting machinery were lying outside. Collectivisation and half a century of Soviet rule had taken its toll, leaving in its wake a trail of scrap iron and ruin, draining the land of colour. But no one, neither the tsars of Russia, nor the commissars of communism could take away the love of these people for their land, their soil, their forests. They were a rural people, and hard work was in their blood.

After an hour he stopped to look at the map. 'We'll take the back roads, Mum. Can you keep an eye open for Kandava?'

They left the surfaced road behind and joined a track through the forest. Margarita began to look happier. She opened the window and the scent of pine filled the car. 'Wonderful,' she murmured appreciatively. She had always loved trees, which was why he had suggested coming this way.

Approaching a bend, they passed a dumpy little woman wearing a brown coat and a pink headscarf, trudging along the road carrying a bag in each hand. Despite the distance from the nearest bus or shop, she wasn't unique by any means: they saw several more like her before they got to Kuldīga. Setting off at first light, they went to gather potatoes from an allotment and took them back to little houses in the forest.

'Poor old soul,' his mother remarked. He could tell what she was thinking. Perhaps this could have been me. Had I stayed in Latvia, this could have been me. Though Britain had never felt like home to her, materially, she had been comfortable after he had become a doctor. In Latvia, with her husband deported to Siberia, her life would have been difficult unless she'd become an ardent Party supporter.

He glanced at her, asking himself the question he had asked many times over, but they had never discussed. What would she have done if they had stayed in Latvia? What would he have done? Would they have been amongst the people who spied on their neighbours? Would they have stood in line at the post office, shamelessly peering over shoulders at people's phone bills ready to inform if they were spending too long talking to goodness knows who? Making lists of people arriving at neighbours' parties in order to pass their names on through the system. Would he have done that? He hated the idea of it, but he couldn't be sure what he might have done to ensure his sons got a university education or a reasonable job.

As he continued to drive on through the forest, his mother turned to him and said suddenly, 'Can we stop for a few minutes. I know you want to get on, but...'

Smiling, because he realised she wanted to walk amidst the pines, he stopped the car at the side of the road and they got out. She set off, and he followed, plunging into the forest straight away. A few feet in, it was chilly, very chilly. Only the heat of mid summer could bring a vestige of warmth to this deep, dark, impenetrable world. Yet, in an odd sort of way, he thought it had a comfortable, lived-in feel too, as if people had been here for thousands of years. He could feel the people who had made their home there. Worked the land. Even though the forest had taken over again. This was no virgin land; it had been cultivated for a long, long time.

They stood together for a moment. Rejoicing in the stillness. The absolute silence. Looking upwards, they were barely able to see the sky. He saw the lump in his mother's throat, her eyes alive with tears. Gently touching her arm, he lead her back towards the car in a different direction. Approaching a small clearing, they were greeted by the sun, a few rays scything between the silver birch, turning the last traces of morning mist into a magnificent violet haze.

'Thank you,' she said, when they got to the car. 'I've needed to do that for a very long time. When we lived in Britain and I thought of Latvia, this was it. I always thought of the forest.'

They sat quietly for a few moments, neither of them saying anything, until she broke the silence. 'You did bring the flask, didn't you? I could do with a cup of tea.'

Although there was nothing he disliked more than drinking tea out of a vacuum flask, he reached on to the back seat, unscrewed the top and she held the cups while he poured out the slightly greying liquid. He took a few sips from the smaller cup, while she drank from the other. Half way into her second cup, she stopped drinking and then threw the rest out of the window. 'I do hate these pills,' she said, crossly. 'I can't even enjoy a cup of tea.'

They set off once more and a little further on the forest thinned out. He was struck immediately by the change in the landscape. The flat countryside of the earlier part of the journey – and so typical of much of Latvia - had given way to gentle hills with copses of deciduous trees and wide valleys. 'Little Switzerland' some of the guide books called this part of the country but it reminded Arnis of the lowlands of Scotland. They approached a small settlement where he took another track which led over a medieval stone bridge and up a gradual hill towards a disused manor house. With an oak tree slumped against its faded ochre walls, it was in a sorry state, much like several others they'd seen already that morning.

'My mother worked in a place like this once,' Margarita said. 'It was an awful place. She hated it.'

'You haven't mentioned that before. How long was she there?'

'Oh, two or three years, maybe. Until she met my father.'

'What was he doing when they met?' He had no idea what his grandfather's job had been before he built the farm.

'He was a labourer … at the same house. That's where they met,' she continued. 'Dad always wanted his own land. Land and books … that's what he believed in. He said if you had those you didn't need anything else. He hated being beholden to someone else.'

'I can understand that,' Arnis empathised.

'But,' Margarita continued, 'he was lucky to be alive.'

'You mean … after the revolution?'

'Yes, but don't ask me how he was involved. It was seven years before I was born. Mother never said much, except that he was fortunate not to be shot.'

Twiddling her handbag straps between her thumbs and forefingers, she fell silent and looked straight ahead. Her normally pink cheeks had turned pale and he began to wish they hadn't come.

'Anyway, he settled down for a while when he got married,' she carried on. 'Until the war started. Then he joined the army. We saw little of him for the next few years. That's what mother said. I can't remember. But I can remember him coming home.'

A smile came over her face as she explained how her father had re-appeared one day, quite unexpectedly. After being demobilised, he had walked all the way from Rīga. Sleeping in the forest and eating mushrooms and wild berries, he had been travelling for more than a week.

'He was exhausted. I can see him now standing at the door. Mother was so happy. Then she got upset because all she had to feed him on was potatoes and turnips. But we had such a celebration that night. I can remember being allowed to stay up late ... falling asleep in front of the fire. Dad picked me up and carried me to bed. Then the next day ... oh yes, I remember ... Granddad came to visit us. He brought a huge salmon.'

Her voice caught in her throat and, as they joined the main road, she fell silent again. Arnis struggled to find something to say, but as usual when his mother was upset, he found himself speechless.

Half an hour later they reached a signpost for Kuldīga and drove down a long straight bumpy track with single-storey dwellings on either side. Wood smoke drifted from the chimneys. Arnis slowed down to let a woman cross the road with a few chickens and some goats.

At the end of the row of houses, the view opened up to reveal a wide red-bricked bridge. 'The river,' Margarita said, suddenly breaking the silence. 'Stop! I want you to see this.'

She climbed out of the car as quickly as she could, and hurried over to the side of the bridge. 'There it is,' she said, her finger pointing to a low waterfall forming a gracious curve from bank to bank. A fine cloud of spray rose above it, obscuring the birch trees on the far side.

'I used to stand there,' she explained, her voice brightening as she pointed to the right bank where, amidst the red and yellow hues of the autumn foliage, a fisherman was preparing his bait. 'I held the basket while my granddad went to collect the salmon.'

She went on to explain how her grandfather had

fishing nets attached to long poles, criss-crossed like scaffolding and wedged under the rocks at the side of the waterfall. 'He caught a huge one once. It weighed nearly thirty pounds. We used to go to the restaurants selling them. I loved that. I felt ever so important. My, it *was* a wonderful life.'

Arnis put a protective arm round her and gave her a long hug. At that moment he wished more than anything that she hadn't had to leave Latvia. The horror of it struck him in a way it hadn't before. Then, as if she'd remembered something else, she broke away from him and started to walk along slowly in the direction of the town.

'What are you looking for?' he asked, wondering why she stopped every so often to look at the stone work.

'Oh, nothing,' she sighed. 'I was just thinking what a lot of tales this bridge could tell…'

Trailing her fingers along the stone, she walked on, continuing across the bridge until she reached a wrought iron double lamp immediately above the parapet. She gazed up at it for a few seconds then, casting her eyes downwards, she smiled, as if she'd recognised something. She leaned over the edge to stare at the waterfall.

Arnis went up to her and touched her elbow. As she turned round to face him, he was dismayed to see a tear at the corner of her eye. 'What is it, Mum?' he said gently.

'Oh, nothing. Come on, let's go.'

Not wanting to press her, he took hold of her arm which, unusually for her, she accepted straight away. As they walked towards the car, the photograph of his father on the boat came to mind. It must have been taken somewhere near here and, now they were actually here, he couldn't think why he hadn't shown it to her. It seemed so silly to keep it from her and he wished he'd brought it with him.

'Did boats used to sail from here?' he asked, wondering if she too had been on the boat that day.

She sounded surprised. 'Yes, they did. I don't remember telling you that. Yes, they went from down there,' she said, pointing to a small promontory downstream.

'Did you go on them?'

'Not if I could help it. You know I don't like boats. We had to go on school trips, of course. Down to Ventspils.'

'What about Dad? Was he on those trips?'

It seemed to him as if she was taken aback by his question, but she replied quickly enough. 'I suppose he must have been. But he was a lot older than me. We weren't at school together.'

She sounded almost dismissive and he felt hurt. He gazed at the promontory, imagining the landing stage; his father accompanying a class full of children on a day out. Taking charge, keeping them all in order. From the photograph, his father looked to be a man who wouldn't have stood any nonsense. Then he imagined the steamer, smoke billowing from its funnel, like the steamers in Oban; a connection between the two of them that hadn't occurred to him before. It made him think of the puppet again and he wondered if his mother had brought Sprīdītis to Rīga. He was sure she would have done but he couldn't recall seeing the familiar suitcase in which she kept him. On the point of asking her, he noticed her staring at the wrought iron lamp again.

He went up to her and, as he touched her arm, she jumped. Puzzled, he opened the car door and, as they drove over the bridge, she glanced at the lamp yet again.

'I'll bet that's where you used to meet your boyfriends,'

he suggested teasingly.

'We weren't always out enjoying ourselves,' she replied with an anger which took him by surprise. 'Even in those days. There was far too much to do,' she snapped. 'You don't know the half of it!'

'No, and I shan't unless you tell me. At least you had a father till you were thirty.' As the words left his lips, he wished they hadn't.

They drove towards the town in silence, a nervous pulse flickering under his eye. He had never felt he needed his mother more than at this moment but she had suddenly become so distant. Like those occasions when, as a small boy, he used to watch her baking bread. Sitting on a stool, he watched her as she stared through the kitchen window at the dry stone wall, pummelling the brown dough on a wooden board. What she was thinking on those occasions, he never knew, but it was as if she was in another world – a world in which he didn't belong. Sometimes, she sang; beautiful, melodious songs; but it made him sad inside and he never knew why. But he remembered it again now. Remembered how part of him had wanted to run away and play outside. Until she came back to him. But he could never take his eyes off her and somehow he couldn't be happy. Not when she was far away. It didn't feel right. He had to stay with her; to be near her in case she disappeared altogether. And so he would sit, glued to the stool, until she finished kneading the dough.

Then she would turn round to him and smile, not realising he'd been watching her. There would have been trouble if she had, especially if he was supposed to be doing his homework. Her reverence for education was enormous. It came from her father and the fact that her own bright intelligence had never been harnessed by any formal education after she left school. So she'd pushed him hard, telling him he had to get good qualifications.

'You can lose everything,' she'd told him. 'Family, friends, house, job. Everything. But not qualifications. No one can take those away.'

As they approached the edge of the town he began to realise, more than ever before, that this was the town where she had lost everything; everything and everyone who had ever meant anything to her – her mother, her father, her sister, his father. Everyone except him.

Looking at her again, he noticed how pale she'd gone, her grey eyes vacant and staring. 'I think we should eat first,' he said gently.

'I'm not hungry,' she replied with a weak smile. And then, getting her customary grip on herself, she spoke again, with a brightness she clearly didn't feel. 'You're right. You need a break.'

A large white church came into view, its red roof visible through the yew trees, then the road narrowed, leading into a cobbled street. Old timber-framed houses in dusty shades of burnt ochre, banana yellow and sage green blended contentedly in the afternoon sun whilst wood smoke curled lazily from red chimney pots, too sleepy to make the effort to climb up towards the milky blue sky. It looked to him as if it hadn't changed since he and his mother had left.

But this was not Margarita's opinion. 'Oh, it's so different. How shabby it is."

He was used to this, her acute disappointment when nothing was quite as she remembered it. It had been the same in Rīga but here, in the town where she'd spent the first thirty-two years of her life, he knew she would feel it so much more. Suddenly, his son's joke about Granny's virtual Latvia didn't seem at all funny.

'Well, I suppose we'd better get out and have a look. Seeing as we're here,' she said reluctantly, making him think she would rather have gone straight back to Rīga.
But worse was to come.

As she opened the door, another car came from behind, splashing her shoes and stockings with muddy water from a nearby puddle as it passed.

'You didn't used to need Wellington boots to walk along here,' she muttered. 'Cars!' she said, glaring at him, making him feel as if it was his fault. 'There were hardly any cars then. It's a good thing my poor mother isn't here now. She would have been terrified. She was scared to cross the road if she saw a horse and cart coming.'

This was not a good start. Knowing that some food might improve her spirits, he looked round hoping to spot a nice café.

But she was already halfway across the square. 'Come on. Come and stand here,' she said. When he caught up with her in front of a big green building with yellow shutters, she explained proudly, 'This is where we had our stall. Right next to this window.'

'So this was the market,' he said, relieved that her anger, which he invariably took far too much to heart, had evaporated so rapidly. In any case, he was delighted to see the market place for real at last although it was nowhere near as large as he'd expected.

'Yes, this is where we brought our produce. Butter, eggs, cottage cheese ... potatoes as well if we had some to spare. In the summer we used to sell fruit too. Apples, cherries, strawberries and pears. Every Monday, Wednesday and Friday. It was a wonderful sight. The women would bustle about in their white shawls and long thick skirts. Children played hide and seek behind the stalls. The horses would be over there with their noses stuffed in a bucket of hay or a pail of water. And there was an open air theatre. That always drew a crowd. Happy days,' she said sadly, looking across the square, which was now silent and deserted. 'We didn't appreciate it then. Not until it was too late.'

'Come on, Mum, let's get something to eat,' he said, anxious not to see her distressed again.

Slowly, they ambled towards the main street. 'You don't remember Princis, do you?'

Arnis shook his head.

'No, of course you don't. What am I thinking of? You were too young. Princis was the black horse who used to pull our cart to the market. We grew up with him. We were so disappointed if dad wanted us to take the brown horse instead,' she said.

When they reached the next corner, she stopped for a moment, a frown on her face. 'What's happened to that lovely shop? That's where we used to buy chocolate.' Then she gave a slight giggle. 'There was always a policeman standing outside. We used to dodge round the back of him, hoping he wouldn't see us. I don't suppose he bothered about us at all but we were always scared of him.'

She was beginning to sound considerably more cheerful and they continued down the street. The shops were bright and the sunlight bathed their old doorways, showing off their intricate decoration to perfection. It had a nice warm feel, Arnis thought.

But as they carried on walking, he began to feel surrounded by apparitions. Perhaps they were amongst relatives. What about the descendants of his father's family, of his mother's family? He knew she was convinced they were all dead, but surely they had some blood ties in the town or surrounding area. He began to feel uncomfortable, as if some of the passers-by knew who he was. Despite his liking for the place he didn't feel at home here. Part of him had expected to, perhaps even hoped to, though he knew it was silly when it was fifty-eight years since they'd left. It was too long ago.

Now he was seeing Kuldīga for the first time, he began to wonder what it would have been like to grow up here. Would he have become a doctor in this small country town? Country practice in England had never attracted him and much as he still loved Scotland he'd had no desire to work there. Back in the sixties, with a foreign sounding name, it had been easier to work in London, where very few of his patients questioned where he was from. That's what he had liked about being in London: the feeling of not having to apologise for who he was. But here, he might not have been a doctor at all; during the Soviet times most of the doctors had been women. Medicine had been considered to be a menial task and as a man he might well have worked in the local factory.

A few steps ahead walked his mother. What was she thinking? He couldn't bring himself to ask her, but he wondered if she could remember the last time she'd walked this street. How different it must have looked when she was a young girl. A cobbled street perhaps, sounding to the steady clip clop of a horse and the creak of a cart, no pot holes, but well-laid pavements, the men in their caps and suits gathering in twos and threes to discuss the price of chickens and butter. Headscarfed women hunting for bargains. Discussing the local gossip: far more interesting than fiction. The sour smell of black bread mingled with the sweet smell of cakes and buns. Every type of shop, each with their creamy coloured awnings casting shadows across the sunlit street. An odd bicycle, a dog or two maybe; probably nothing like as quiet as it was today.

Then he began to think of his father and he realised they had not seen a school. On the point of asking his mother where it was, he noticed that she was staring at a book shop casting her eyes upwards at the pale yellow façade. Looking puzzled she said, 'This was the chemist shop ... I'm sure it was. Mr Schmidt's. He left here before the war started and said we had to look him up if ever we went to Hamburg. I've often wondered what happened to him. Such a nice man.'

There was a café next door, which looked clean and bright so they went in. Margarita went to find a table while Arnis hung their coats on a peg. Then the waitress took their order - fried pork and boiled potatoes with dill for him; brown beans and a plate of black bread for his mother. While they were eating, Arnis noticed an old man in the far corner, staring at them, especially at his mother.

When they'd finished their meal, the man came across to their table. 'Excuse me. Were you married to Mr Vilks?' he said to Margarita.

She looked quite startled and Arnis couldn't work out whether she recognised the man or not. And she didn't respond to his question.

Looking embarrassed, the old man scratched his beard. 'I'm sorry if I'm mistaken but Mr Vilks taught me at school and you look so like his wife.'

'Mum?' Arnis said gently. Feeling torn between her anxiety and his own excitement at meeting someone who appeared to have known his father, he didn't know what to say, either to her or the old man. And again she didn't respond.

'It is you, isn't it?' the old man insisted.

Margarita turned to Arnis, her eyes wide. 'I don't know who this is.'

'Fēlikss Siliņš,' the man said, introducing himself. 'Fēlikss Siliņš,' he repeated loudly, as if he thought she was deaf.

'You say my husband taught you?'

'You are Mrs Vilka then?' the old man replied.

She nodded. 'I don't remember all the pupils,' she answered defensively.

Siliņš pulled up a chair to sit beside her. 'I knew it,' he said, ignoring her excuse. 'You haven't changed at all. He was a lucky man. We all said he'd married the prettiest girl in town.' Flattery was in his words but his tone and expression were serious.

Arnis wanted to talk to the man but he could see his mother shifting uneasily in her seat. He was anxious lest she was going to have an attack of angina, so he called for the bill.

The old man smiled, a wide toothless smile. Fixing her with his clear blue eyes, he leaned towards her on his stick and said, 'I've seen a good few people come back. Those that left. Coming to have a look.'

Margarita stood up and Arnis went to fetch their coats. They shook hands with the old man and made their way to the door.

'Come and find me if you're this way again,' he called

after them. 'I'm usually in here. Or at the brown house on the corner.'

'Are you all right, Mum?' Arnis asked anxiously as they walked back down the street.

She looked at him as if she couldn't leave fast enough. 'Yes. It was unexpected, that's all. And I really don't remember him.'

Feeling puzzled because she seemed more on edge than the occasion warranted, he took her arm again. 'He looked older than you. Still, a lot of people do,' he said, trying to cheer her up.

'There's no need for you to flatter me either,' she said with a weak smile.

They ambled back to the medieval market place. As they approached the car, she paused to look at the creamy coloured Renaissance style town hall. 'We had some good times in there,' she said wistfully. 'New Year's Eve especially. The dances were tremendous.' She gave a long sigh. 'Do you know, I haven't given it a moment's thought since we were in Edinburgh. But I remember the first New Year's Eve we were in Scotland. I went out to post a letter and had a walk round. You were starting to get better but you were still coughing. Morag was keeping an eye on you that evening. You remember her, don't you?'

Arnis nodded as he recalled the round-faced nurse, who had looked after him when he had TB.

'Well, it was a lovely night and I walked along Princes Street. There was a full moon and the castle looked lovely. I was really enjoying it. Then a huge gaggle of people poured out of one of the hotels. All laughing and joking. The women wearing long dresses. I remember thinking we used to be like that in Latvia … going out enjoying ourselves. I don't think it was until then I realised what had happened. Not really. But I remember thinking I should be doing that. I stood and watched them for a few minutes. Piling into their big black cars.' She gave a long sigh, then composed herself. 'Oh, come on, this won't do.'

CHAPTER 6

Margarita fished in her handbag, fumbling amongst her handkerchiefs, purse and all the other things she kept in there. She retrieved a small bottle, opened it, and slipped a couple of white tablets in her mouth.

'Mum, are you sure you want to do this?' Arnis asked anxiously. Over the last couple of hours, he had become painfully aware of the enormous gulf between her life here and her life after they'd arrived in Britain. More than that, he was finding it difficult to keep up with her rapidly changing mood.

'Of course I am! What are we waiting for?' she replied crossly.

'Mum, you know it won't...'

Looking astonished, she snapped, 'Yes, I know the farm won't be there. You don't have to tell me that. The Russians smashed everything ... razed it all to the ground.' She looked at him as if he was stupid. 'You've seen what they've done. The countryside. They've ruined everything. Everything.' She started to fidget with her necklace, grinding the amber beads against each other.

He could sense her turmoil. Seeing Kuldīga again was one thing. But to see where she'd been brought up, the land her father had farmed, to find the house where she'd grown up, gone - probably without a trace - that was quite another thing.

He was glad he couldn't remember the house but it made him think of the first proper home he could recall – their tiny white two-roomed cottage in Oban. He knew he could go there anytime to see it looking the same as it always had done, with its dark green front door. The same wispy-haired woman still ran the corner shop and she had still tried to sell him a quarter of chocolate limes the last time he went back.

'Come on,' Margarita said. 'It's already past two. You know how quickly the light goes at this time of year. You did bring the shovel and spade, didn't you?'

He nodded and much as he would have loved to have found his father's school, they set off immediately taking a southerly direction out of the town, As they approached a crossroads, he said, 'Which way, now?'

'Straight on, but wait a moment,' she replied.

He looked as she pointed to a narrow track on a low embankment with bushes either side.

'That's where the railway used to be. So they destroyed that too,' she said sadly. They couldn't leave anything alone! I can remember the day the first train came. The engine was covered in flowers. Everyone turned out. What a day that was. I took my little nephew to watch. Toms.' She smiled. 'He'd just had his fifth birthday. He was terrified. The platform filled with smoke. The engine whistled. He'd never seen a steam engine before.'

'How old were you then?'

'I can't remember.' She scratched her chin. 'It wasn't long before the war. A few years, maybe.'

Arnis put the car into gear and drove off. As they approached the edge of town the houses became shabbier, more neglected. They were all in need of a coat of paint. It was such a shame for a town that had known better times.

Then, for no logical reason, he suddenly recalled the old man in the café. What had he said his name was? Fēlikss Siliņš? A name he should make a note of before he forgot. Glancing at his mother, he realised he'd done the right thing not to question the old man. Much as he'd wanted to find out what Siliņš knew about his father, his mother seemed to have been unsettled by the encounter. He didn't know why but he didn't want to make it any worse. The day was passing quickly. He hadn't intended to pack so much into it and the thing his mother most wanted to do – to dig something up – hadn't even been started. But it had to be done now because the frost would come in a few weeks time and the earth would be impossible to dig until spring.

At the edge of the town the road curved to the left. 'Where are you going?' Margarita said. 'We've passed it.'

'Yes, Mother,' he replied, with a half-smile, because she seemed to have forgotten he had no idea where to go.

'You think I don't know where I am, don't you?' she said, as he reversed to the fork in the road. Then, in a quiet voice, 'I remember this road very well. It's like it was yesterday. When I came along here with the horse and cart, one half of me was thinking we were going to the market to sell vegetables, but I knew really that we weren't coming back. Benita came with us as far as the crossroads...' The words choked in her throat as she remembered the sister she never saw again.

Benita's husband owned a nearby farm and they stayed on after the Germans retreated. When Soviet domination was re-established, farming was collectivised.

Benita's farm was destroyed and her husband and their two sons were deported to Siberia. Benita ended up working on one of the huge state-run farms that sprang up during the early 1950s.

Over the next few years, Margarita had received a number of letters from her; letters that said nothing other than she was all right and enjoying her work. But Margarita could read between the lines even though she had little idea what was happening in Latvia.

Then there was a long silence.

No more letters came until the day Arnis learned he had won a scholarship to medical school in Edinburgh. The postman brought an official-looking envelope and Arnis had to call for his mother to sign for it. She'd taken it to the kitchen where she was finishing clearing away the breakfast dishes. A few minutes later, Arnis found her sitting on the stool, the opened letter in her hand, sobbing. He had never seen his mother crying like that and it was some time before he could get her to talk.

'It's Benita,' she said between sobs. 'She's dying of cancer.'

The official letter from Latvia contained an invitation to return to the country to see her sister. Margarita mulled over it for the rest of the morning, then phoned a friend in Leicester.

'Be very careful,' Silvija warned. 'Other people have received letters like that. Who knows if they're telling you the truth? I wouldn't go if I was you.' Torn between anxiety for Benita and fear of returning to Latvia, his mother wrote back asking for more news.

Another long silence.

Several months passed before she got a reply and by then Arnis had started at medical school. In one of her weekly letters to him, she told him there had been another official letter. Benita had died. Two or three years later she heard through another friend that her sister had died several months before the first letter arrived.

She never spoke about Benita again after that.

Back at the junction, Arnis took the right-hand fork and drove along a narrow bumpy track through an avenue of birch trees. He felt more and more apprehensive and neither of them spoke until they came to an open stretch of land.

'Slow down. This is the wood.' Margarita pointed to a side road heading towards a pine forest. The car jolted along an even narrower track through the forest until the view opened out once more.

'Stop,' she said, frowning. 'Let me think for a minute. We came through the woods. And then … it wasn't far. I'm sure it wasn't.' She scanned the open ground to the right. 'The fences have all gone. It looks so different. There were more trees. Oh dear, it's difficult to remember.'

Suddenly, Arnis spotted a slight rise in the ground a hundred yards further on. 'What's that lump?' he questioned.

She stared at it for a moment then she put her hand to her mouth and let out a small moan. She covered her face with her hands and the tears started to flow like beads down her face.

He felt helpless. As on all other occasions when he felt like that, a string of useless ideas floated through his mind, one after the other. He wanted to give her a cup of tea but the flask was empty. He longed to go out in the garden to pick her a bunch of flowers but there was no garden to pick them - no daffodils, no lupins, no roses, no lilac bush growing next to the front door; not even any buttercups or dandelions. Just the bare flat earth overlaid with the mulch of a regime which had destroyed everything she had lived for.

Everything was so bare, so silent. No cackle of geese, no cows to milk, no farm hands wielding scythes, no stacks of corn. How Arnis wished the mound had also been flattened - it would have been better if it had completely gone rather than seeing the obvious remains covered by a thin layer of turf.

'Mum...' he said and she turned to him with a look of helpless emptiness on her face. Leaning back in her seat, she stared at the mound of earth for a few moments and then found her handkerchief. She dried her eyes then she opened the car door and started up the track. Scared she might fall, Arnis quickly caught up with her and they stood side by side staring at the mound.

'Yes, this is where it was. I'm sure now. See, look,' she said, drawing his attention to a pool a few yards beyond the mound of earth. 'I couldn't see that from the car.'

'You had a pool next to the farm?' he asked.

'Oh yes. Most farms did,' she replied as she started down the bank towards it. 'Ours was right next to the bath house. At the end of the day, the men would come in from the fields and scrub themselves down. Then they'd go in the pool.'

Arnis shivered. 'All the year round?' Much as he loved the sea, he had never learned how to swim. Getting cold and wet had never been his idea of fun and the thought of plunging into freezing cold water was horrible.

'Yes. Even in winter ... after breaking the ice, of course.'

She smiled. 'I can hear them now, shouting and laughing and splashing each other.' She went to the edge of the pool and knelt down, ruffling the reflection of the white clouds with her hands. Faint ripples fanned out to the other side.

After the pool became still again, she got up gingerly and walked towards him searching his face. 'Don't upset yourself,' she said gently. 'It wasn't all bad. Not till the end. We had some wonderful times here in the early years ... when Dad first built the house.'

He could tell from her expression that she knew he was upset. He was feeling this more than he'd expected. Over the years, when she'd talked about the farm, it had seemed so distant and so unreal. But now, standing here on the land his grandfather had owned and fought for, a lump came to his throat, and he scraped at the earth with the toe of his shoe.

His grandfather had bought this plot of land after the First World War, when Latvia became independent for the first time. Land belonging to German barons had been divided up and his grandfather had bought a fifty-acre plot – a 'two horse farm' was the way his mother sometimes described it. Not that you could tell where the fifty acres began and ended now. Within a few years, his grandfather had built a house and tamed the land, turning it into a good going concern and raising a family. Then the Russians came back only months after he finished paying off his loan.

It was difficult now to tell what had happened to the land after his mother had fled. It gave the impression no plough had turned it for several years. There was no sign of any other buildings, no obvious indication it had been taken over to become part of a state-run farm. Arnis looked at his mother again, feeling angry and protective at the same time. This was her land. No one else's.

As if reading his thoughts, she said, 'I couldn't live here now. But I can remember it as it was.' She started to talk about the house. 'It was small to start with … just three rooms. Benita and I slept in one room, Mother and Dad in another. We had straw mattresses for the first few years, and we did our homework by the light of kerosene lamps.'

'The third room was the kitchen, presumably?'

'Yes, that was the biggest room. There was a stove at one end of it and we used to keep our toys behind that. At the other end there was a trough for kneading bread. That was next to the oven.'

'You really loved it here, didn't you?'

She nodded, her eyes again filling with tears. 'We were always so warm. It was cosy. I often used to think of it after we arrived in Oban and were up in that tower room without so much as a paraffin stove. And that dreadful woman used to call it Siberia. I'm not surprised looking back. But Siberia! How I had to bite my tongue!'

She then explained how, after a few years, her father had extended the farmhouse to make an upstairs with three small bedrooms, leaving room downstairs to create a large parlour next to the kitchen. 'Mother kept her spinning wheel in there. I can see her now, sitting under the window in one of Dad's home-made chairs spinning flax. You didn't go out buying furniture in those days,' she added. 'Not unless you had a lot more money than we did.'

'I suppose your Dad wanted to put everything he could into the farm.'

'Yes. They had to work very hard. Mother and Dad were always up at five, even in the winter. We all had our tasks. I helped Mother to hoe the potatoes and gather the flax.

That's why I thought I could do some weaving when we arrived in Britain. I thought I would be able to work in a linen factory.'

As she got older, she helped with the ploughing, following her father and throwing manure into the furrows. And she helped with the milking. They'd had half a dozen Latvian Browns and another of her jobs had been to take the milk to the creamery. 'It was a long journey,' she said. 'At least it seemed so … three hours there and back, I seem to remember. I had to bring back the cream to feed the pigs. Woe betide me if I forgot that. We made some of it into butter, but most of it went to feed the pigs.' She smiled, remembering something else. 'That was nice. We all used to share our pigs. Every spring Dad bought half a dozen and when we slaughtered one we'd let the neighbours know. When they killed one they'd do the same.'

'It must have been a good way of making sure you all had plenty of fresh meat.'

'Yes, it was.' Then she continued. 'Scrubbing the yard. That was some job. I used to get out of that as often as I could. My mother did it most of the time. It was spotless. You could have eaten your dinner off it. Except when we had the geese. Dirty things. They made such a mess. You won't remember, but you took a liking to one of them. You learnt to walk following that goose round the yard. Then you started to let it in the house. And then, right at the end…'

He heard the tears in her voice before he saw them in her eyes. Feeling helpless, he turned to stare at the mound again and a flock of starlings drifted up into the darkening sky, settling on the branches of birch trees where they cackled and quarrelled, a cacophony of sound amidst the otherwise silent landscape.

Regaining her composure, she went on, 'You knew something was happening that day before you saw me pack the farm cart. But you wouldn't go without the goose. It was the only one we had left by then. You screamed blue murder. Anyway, Benita said we should take it. It travelled all the way to Liepaja in the cart. Then we had to sell it, along with the pony and cart. '

'What are you looking for?' Arnis said, noticing her gazing in the direction of the pine trees.

'The oak tree. It must be over there somewhere.' The furrows in her brow deepened. 'The house faced away from the wood and the oak tree was over to the right.' Without another moment's thought, she set off across the grass.

'Careful,' he said. The ground was rough and stony and he had visions of her falling, breaking a hip. Ignoring him, she strode off in the direction of the wood. Then she stopped for a moment, looking round again, obviously unsure.

'Mum, put your scarf on if you're going to go in the woods. You know the ticks are bad this summer.'

She scowled. 'Don't distract me. You didn't hear about ticks when I was a girl. We never had them then. Not before the Russians came. They brought them. Like everything else bad.'

This wasn't the time to point out it was more to do with the warmer summers of recent years so Arnis changed the subject. 'Are you sure we're in the right place? Either that or the tree has gone.'

'No one could have moved that tree. It was one of the oldest oaks in Latvia. Huge. It's a bit more to the right, I'm sure.' She narrowed her eyes again trying to get her bearings in the middle of a landscape that was almost beyond recognition. 'There it is,' she exclaimed suddenly. 'It's further than I thought. Not as close to the house as I remember.'

They walked towards it. It was massive, its thick trunk draped in green lichen. Arnis touched it, almost reverently, then he walked back to the car to get the spade, shovel and a torch.

'It isn't deep,' Margarita said, beginning to sound excited. 'We didn't dig far down.'

Maybe, but Arnis reckoned it wasn't going to be as easy as she thought. All the same, he started to dig with the spade while she joined in with the shovel, clearing the soil to the side. Her energy never failed to astonish him, especially when she was doing something she really wanted to do. Already his back ached – no way would he be doing this when he was ninety years old. They continued for twenty minutes but found nothing.

Straightening himself for a moment, he leaned on the spade and looked at her. 'Mum…'

'No one knew it was here. Only your father and I,' she said firmly.

Daylight was fading fast. He tried another spot, and another, until the ground around the base of the tree was covered in holes. Impatiently, she took the spade from him and started to dig herself. Then she got down on her knees, scraping the earth away with her hands. 'I can feel something,' she said. 'Come and help me. And do be careful.'

He loosened the earth gently and they scraped away the rest of the soil with their hands. Underneath was a large canvas sack.

'This is it,' Margarita said triumphantly as he started to

lift it out of the hole. It was heavy and once it was clear of its grave he looked round for a smooth patch of ground on which to lay it. He shone the torch on it and brushed some more soil off with his hands.

'I'd forgotten it was green,' she said touching the canvas. 'Dad had that in his tool shed for a while. For a moment, I really did wonder whether…' She stopped in mid-sentence and he smiled wryly. She wasn't going to admit she'd had her doubts about finding it too. 'Come on, let's go,' she said. 'We can't unpack it here.'

She went to pick up the shovel and spade and, as he continued to shine the torch over the sack, he noticed a small brown bottle tied to one end of the thick twine seam. Crouching down, he took hold of it and shook it gently but he couldn't hear anything. Puzzled, he looked round for his mother. She was coming towards him with the shovel and spade. 'What's in the bottle,' he asked.

'What bottle? What do you mean?'

'The bottle tied to the sack.'

Arnis took his knife out, cut the twine, and held up the dark brown bottle. Margarita looked mystified. He shone the torch on it again. The glass was extremely dirty but there didn't seem to be anything in it. Yet, the top was sealed with wax. Why would anyone have tied an empty sealed bottle to the sack? It didn't make sense. He looked at his mother but she was obviously as puzzled as he was.

'I don't know. We didn't bury a bottle,' she said defiantly. 'Put it in your pocket. We'll examine it when we've got more light.'

They picked up the sack between them and carried it to the car. Arnis held the bottle under the light in the boot but could still see nothing. He opened the lid of his toolbox and banged the glass neck against the metal. It smashed at first attempt, and he shone the torch inside.

'Can you see anything?' his mother said, staring intently.

'Yes, it's a roll of paper.'

'Paper?'

He reached in his toolbox for a pair of thin-nosed pliers and carefully withdrew the piece of yellowing paper. As he unrolled it, she picked up the torch. It was small, six inches by four, and he smoothed it out in his hands to reveal several lines of brown handwriting. He put on his glasses and pulled the torch closer. The writing was clearer than it had looked at first sight and he was able to decipher it quite easily. It was a letter addressed to his mother. He read it out loud.

5.10.47

'Dear Margarita

'Shall we ever see each other again? I have tried to find out where you are. People tell me you left Kuldīga. Did you go to Germany to find Alberts? No one here knows anything so I may never find you. But wherever you are, try to be happy. I will always love you.

Kārlis'

Arnis looked at his mother. Her grey eyes were filled with anxiety. 'Let me see,' she said quickly. He passed her the note and his pair of glasses. Looking totally bewildered, she read it through several times.

'Mum, is it Dad's handwriting?' he said, his pulse hammering in his throat.

She didn't reply immediately. 'I'm not sure. It could be.'

'It looks quite distinctive to me,' he continued. 'Look at those loops on the bottom of each letter I. It's certainly a well-educated hand.'

'I really can't be sure,' she repeated.

He looked at her again, sensing a growing discomfort in her. Surely she must remember her husband's handwriting. Thinking aloud, he went on, 'How many other people knew you'd buried the ... whatever it is? Your mother must have known. And Aunt Benita? Perhaps they mentioned it to someone. Dad could have told someone. Maybe the whole thing was a trap,' he said, his words coming out faster and faster.

'What do you mean, a trap?' Margarita said.

'Oh come on, you know what the Russians were like! You know that better than I do. They tried it with Aunt Benita.' Noticing the look of growing dismay on her face, he continued more gently, 'You said you were on a deportation list. Maybe they wanted to trick you. Maybe they weren't sure you'd gone. But perhaps they'd figured you would try to find Dad if you thought he was still alive. That you'd go to the place where he hid in the woods. They probably knew where that was. Yes, I'll bet they were waiting for you. The whole thing could have been a trap?'

The minute Arnis finished his sentence he realised the idea was too crazy to contemplate. If the Russians had known there was something valuable buried in the ground they would have stolen it. There was no doubt about that.

'Maybe,' his mother said, but plainly looking as if she didn't believe that theory either. 'But we shan't find out now. Not after this length of time.'

He looked at her sharply. How could she be so

109

dismissive? Why wasn't she pouring over every word, wondering if his father really had written it. His father was thirteen years her senior so, whatever had happened, he would almost certainly be dead by now. But if he *had* written the note, it could mean only one thing: he was alive in 1947 - six years after he had been taken away on that fateful June night. She said he'd been sent to Siberia but, if that was true, maybe he had come back to Kuldīga. Perhaps he hadn't been sent to Siberia at all. Perhaps he had escaped from the truck. Perhaps he had hidden in the forest.

Arnis continued to stare at the note, turning over the possibilities in his mind.

'It's getting late,' Margarita said at last. 'There's nothing more we can do here.'

Arnis took one last look back towards the oak tree then they climbed into the car and set off down the track in silence. When they reached the crossroads, he opened the map but, as he looked up to switch on the overhead light, he noticed a signpost for Rīga. He took a right turn and ten minutes later they were on the main road home.

'Mum, are you sure you can't think of any other explanation for that note?' he enquired.

'I've told you. I've no idea. Do stop going on about it.'

Whatever she said, he felt certain she wanted to know as much as he did. But the more he thought about the note, the less was he able to make any sense of it. There had been no hint that his father had come back from Siberia. Unless…

Suddenly, an event came to his mind - an event which he hadn't given any thought to for a long time.

One summer he and his mother had visited London for a song festival. It had been many years since she had heard a

Latvian choir and, not wanting to miss the occasion, she had asked Mrs Nicholson for some time off. They had travelled south by train – he was eleven or twelve at the time – and they went to stay for the weekend with another Latvian family who lived in Finchley; someone his mother had met at one of the annual Latvian independence celebrations.

On the Sunday, there had been a lunch party and one of the guests had, quite suddenly, turned to his mother and asked if she'd been married to Kārlis Vilks, the school teacher from Kuldīga. Visibly startled, she answered in the affirmative and the guest went on to say she had recently heard from a friend of a friend that someone had seen him. Apparently this person had spotted him in Sydney a few months previously. She said they knew Mr Vilks because they had owned a shop in Kuldīga.

Gradually, it all started to come back. How anxious his mother had looked, how uneasy he'd felt, and how he'd wished he were somewhere else. There was an uncomfortable silence until the main course appeared then the topic of conversation changed. But his mother was very quiet during the remainder of their stay in London and he was relieved when they returned to Scotland.

A few days after they got back to Oban, he woke up one night to hear his mother talking in her sleep through the curtain which divided the bedroom they shared. He couldn't make out what she was saying but she sounded troubled. Linking it with the trip to London, he blamed the woman at the lunch table and wished they had not gone to the song festival. But he spent a lot of time that summer walking along the shore, thinking about his father and wondering if he really was in Australia. For a while, he had even thought he might

111

try to find him.

Now that he had seen the note, Australia didn't make a lot of sense. His father had assumed Margarita might have taken Arnis to Germany; a reasonable assumption as many Latvians had fled their country and ended up in displaced persons' camps in Germany. Surely, then, he would have started searching for them in Europe, not the other side of the world. But that, in turn, assumed that his father had actually written the note, and that idea held doubts of its own.

Suddenly Arnis started to shiver, more with shock than cold, and he switched the car heater on. It was now quite dark - too dark even for stars - and they cruised along in the inky blackness, passing few other vehicles. The birch trees massed along the side of the road, their silver trunks like gleaming intruders. Normally, he loved the silver birch but tonight he found them menacing; their endless brooding presence adding to the turbulence of his brain.

He reached across to the glove compartment and rummaged around until he found a tape. He glanced quickly at the label. Chopin's Nocturnes Volume Two was perfect for calming his troubled mind and he slipped it into the tape machine. In seconds, the lilting airs began to work their usual magic. The birch trees gradually receded, slipping back into the forest, disappearing like ghosts through the trunks of the pines. His shivering abated and he felt calmer.

His thoughts turned to Anita. They were due to meet tomorrow afternoon. He smiled to himself. In the morning he would buy a copy of *Diena*. To see the sort of thing she wrote.

He looked across at his mother. Her eyes were closed and her hands were tightly clasped on her lap.

But he knew she wasn't asleep.

112

CHAPTER 7

The next day started badly. Arnis slept through the alarm and dressed hurriedly, realising he was too late for a breakfast. He also remembered that they hadn't unloaded the canvas sack from the car boot but time was now against him. It would have to wait until later. He looked in on his mother and, relieved to find she was still asleep, left immediately for the surgery.

The bright blue sky of the previous day had vanished and sullen clouds spat angry drops of rain against the back of his head. Emerging from the confined streets of the old town, he entered the park and walked alongside the canal. A short way along the path was the spot where the Latvian camerman had been shot while filming the crackdown of Soviet troops in 1991. The television scenes came into Arnis's mind, scenes which he could not separate from Penny's death which happened later that same year.

Not wanting to dwell on either event, he tried to focus on the day ahead. He couldn't remember how full his appointment book was but the gaps between appointments were diminishing as the weeks went by. His reputation as a doctor who spent time listening to his patients and explaining what was wrong with them, had spread rapidly. Judging by the increasing numbers trying to get on his books during his first four months in practice, he would soon be turning patients away.

Spotting a newspaper kiosk, he stopped and bought a copy of *Diena*. He skimmed through it, looking for Anita's name. It did not take him long to find it. 'Counterfeit medicines flooding into Latvia from Azerbaijan' ran the headline of her article. He read it quickly. It was sharp, clear and to the point and urged the government to tighten up its controls. He was impressed. She certainly seemed to know what she was talking about.

Leaving the park behind, he caught a glimpse of the baroque façade of the Latvian National Theatre, where the country's first independence had been announced in 1918. After crossing the road into a wide avenue with enormous grey granite buildings on either side, he began to think again about the woman at the lunch in Finchley, trying to remember her name. But it was not just her name that escaped him, he couldn't even remember what she looked like. He knew his mother would probably know the name of the woman who owned the house, she might even know who the guest was, but he wasn't sure he wanted to ask her. He was pretty certain she had made no attempt to find out if his father was in Australia and, if she had, she'd never given him the slightest hint.

He walked past a large red-bricked building on his right and carried on past the traffic lights. The rain had stopped and a few oak leaves fell to the ground, weaving their way into the already rich fabric of red, burnished bronze, green and yellow leaves that carpeted the pavements. He waited as a trolley bus rattled by then he crossed the road and turned into the wide street that hosted his surgery.

The premises were in a two-storey wooden house

painted apple green with contrasting chocolate brown doors and window frames. Built in the late nineteenth century as a warehouse, the property had known many occupants. Its first owner had been a grain merchant who was eventually bankrupted, then it had become the home of a poet for a few years, then a jeweller had taken it over. During the Soviet period it had been one of those food shops with half empty shelves selling jars of sauerkraut, lumps of gristly meat, tins of plums and little else. More recently, it had been a bookshop. Then, two years ago, it had been reclaimed by a dentist, the grandson of the jeweller who had owned it before the war. Bruno practiced his dentistry on the ground floor and Arnis rented two rooms on the upper floor.

Arnis put his key in the lock and was about to go upstairs when the man himself emerged from his surgery looking as though his world was crumbling around him.

'Good morning, Bruno,' Arnis said, trying to lift whatever gloom had immersed his friend.

'I've got some bad news, I'm afraid,' Bruno said. 'We've got dry rot in the timbers. The owner of the shoe shop next door discovered it when he had some re-plastering done.'

Arnis scowled at Bruno. 'That's all we need.'

These old timber slatted buildings always needed something doing on them but they had plenty of character and that was what attracted him in the first place – with the added bonus that the rent was pretty reasonable. Rectifying the problem, Arnis knew, would make mess and he hated mess, especially at work. At home he was happy to live in a muddle but the surgery was different. Here he liked order and tidiness and he was not amused at the thought of the place being reduced to a builder's yard. Besides, the job would probably take weeks, if not months, depending on how bad it was.

He began to picture the whole thing from start to finish. The workmen not turning up when they should, taking three times the amount of time they actually needed to complete the job; the drilling, the dust getting everywhere, settling into every drawer and filing cabinet. Having experienced it all before in London, the idea of renovation experience here didn't bear thinking about. He had heard plenty of nightmare stories about the standard of local building work. Arnis shuddered and hoped by some miracle they wouldn't need to touch the rooms where he worked.

He trudged upstairs and turned the handle on the door. It was still locked so Maija obviously hadn't come in. The phone was ringing and he rushed to answer it. Had he known Mrs Dragunova was on the other end of the line he might not have made such an effort. She could be a tiresome woman at the best of times and this morning was no exception.

'Have you got me an appointment at the hospital yet?' she barked. Without waiting for him to answer, she went on, 'Because if you haven't, I'm going to go myself. I'm not waiting any longer. Six weeks is quite long enough. Besides it was your idea in the first place. It's not as if I care whether I go to hospital or not.'

'My dear Mrs Dragunova, I need to check with my receptionist. I'll call you back,' he said lamely, not knowing if the appointment had been agreed.

'See you do. And quickly,' she snapped.

He put the phone down, thankful she hadn't made more fuss, and went back downstairs to collect the post, hoping the consultant might have replied to his letter. He wanted Mrs Dragunova to have some tests – fairly routine ones, an ECG and some blood counts – and had written to the cardiologist a couple of weeks earlier. He looked through the post but Dr Rubenis still hadn't replied so he called his number.

'Hello, Rubenis here.'

'It's Rozenvalds, Doctor Rubenis. Sorry to press you but I need a reply to my recent letter.'

'What letter? I've had no letter from you,' the cardiologist said snappily.

Having had previous similar experiences with Dr Rubenis, Arnis was sure he was being fobbed off. 'Look I have a patient who needs an appointment straight away,' he said firmly.

'I'm too busy,' replied Rubenis with equal firmness.

'What, you mean you can't fit in an ECG?'

'No, I can't. Not until after Christmas.'

'Christmas! Don't be ridiculous. That's two months away.'

'I don't need you to tell me how to count, Rozenvalds. And I don't need any of your patients. Who do you think you are? You've only been here five minutes. I've had enough of your sort. Coming back from abroad, telling us what to do.' With that, the cardiologist slammed the phone down.

Arnis was furious. Although he knew that a bribe would easily have sorted out the situation he'd never made a habit of paying consultants to take care of his patients. He would sort this out his own way.

Maija still hadn't turned up and, judging by the pile of paper underneath the desk, it looked as if she hadn't done the filing for at least a fortnight. To make matters worse, he found the phone bill at the side of the waste paper basket. It was twice if not three times the amount he'd expected. Frowning, he scanned through the bill, and soon spotted the problem in the shape of a number of phone calls to Canada, which is where Maija's boyfriend lived. Well, his mother had warned him. Intending to have it out with her, he shoved the bill in his pocket. Then the phone rang again.

This time it was Maija herself. 'I'm locked out of my flat,' she said. 'I don't know how long I'm going to be but I'll try to come in this afternoon.'

'Don't bother,' he told her. In no mood for any more of her tearful yarns, the time seemed right to make the decision he knew he would have to make sooner or later. 'I won't need you any more, Maija. Just come in sometime to collect the rest of your money.'

The rest of the morning did not go quite so badly and after surgery finished, he made himself a coffee and re-read Anita's article. Turning over the page he spotted something else she'd written: a short piece about pollution affecting the fish catch in the Baltic Sea. He didn't think it was quite as good as the other one, but she certainly knew how to engage her readers. He swallowed the rest of his coffee and looked at the clock. It would take him about fifteen minutes to walk to the café so he ought to be on his way.

He locked up and walked towards Brīvības iela feeling anticipation and apprehension in equal measure. Excited at the prospect of seeing her, yet wondering what she would write about him. As he approached the traffic lights, he saw a crowd gathered on the pavement outside the Benetton shop and a trolley bus stopped in the middle of the junction. The pantograph had dropped off the overhead wire, and the queue of traffic stretched back as far as the Orthodox church. Arnis wanted to watch too, but it was already five to two. Though he didn't want to get to the café before her, he didn't want to be too late.

He quickened his pace and reached Osīris to find Anita sitting in the window at a table covered in sheets of writing paper, looking as if she'd been there all morning. No doubt she'd written her article already, he thought. All she would want from him would be a few quotes to say what she wanted to say. He went inside and hung his coat on the rack. She saw him and hastily gathered up her papers, stuffing them into a well-worn leather briefcase.

The waitress took their order and while they waited Anita explained she had spent the morning writing a medical news report for Reuters.

Having assumed she was on the staff at *Diena*, he was quite surprised. 'So, you're a freelance journalist?'

'Yes, I work for several publishers … Latvian and foreign. It's great fun,' she added. 'I'm off to Prague tomorrow to cover a meeting of the American Heart Association.'

'Have you been to Prague before?' he asked.

'I have. You?'

Arnis shook his head. 'No. But my son's got a Czech girlfriend.'

Surprising even himself, he went on to tell her more about Antons and Olga. He didn't usually talk about his family with people he'd just met but Anita was one of those individuals who had the knack of making you feel very comfortable, very quickly and she did it without saying very much about herself.

'So, what's it like being a GP in Rīga?' she asked.

It was not the opening question he expected and he had to be cautious. 'Patients are patients ... wherever they are,' he replied. 'They get colds, stomach upsets ... the same here as they do in England,' he added, amused at her look which said 'that's not what I meant and you know it'. Unless he had completely misjudged her, he thought she could do better than that. Besides, it was true, as his mother had never tired of reminding him – 'once a doctor, always a doctor. If we have to move again, you'll never be short of a job, wherever we go,' she'd said when he was growing up.

But Anita was not about to be put off by his evasive reply. 'You are one of the first GPs in Rīga, though, aren't you? You must feel like something of a pioneer. Everyone will have to register with a GP soon but we haven't been used to that here. Not since before the war, anyway.' She was referring to the fact that patients could see any doctor they wanted and they didn't need to see a family doctor to get a referral to a specialist. 'I'm not convinced it's the right way to go,' she added. 'I've read GPs in England are starting to specialise now, running heart failure and diabetes clinics and the like, so why reverse the situation here and make more doctors into generalists?'

He raised his eyebrows. This was getting interesting. She obviously knew what she was talking about even though she was slightly missing the point about family doctors. GPs were specialising in England – that was true - but they were still family doctors.

She continued: 'Why is having one family doctor supposed to be so good for patients when they've always been used to deciding which doctor they want to see? Why should they be made to feel like imbeciles who don't know what's

120

wrong with them? Because that's exactly what they do feel like.'

'And what makes you so sure you'd know the difference between a bad bout of indigestion and an attack of angina?' he retorted.

'OK. But that's an extreme example. My point is this: how can one GP know enough about every disease to treat any patient who comes into the surgery properly? Surely if you have angina you need to see a heart specialist?'

'In the first instance, yes. But it's up to the GP to manage the patient's routine care,' he replied.

Arnis believed passionately in general practice but never before had he been called upon to articulate his conviction so clearly and so thoroughly. Questions poured out of her one after the other and the time went so fast that it was almost dark outside when she finished.

She looked at her watch. 'I ought to be off,' she said reaching for her bag. 'I'm due at Reuters at half past four.'

He thought quickly. 'I'm going that way myself. I've got a book to collect at the shop on Aspazijas. Do you mind if I walk with you?'

'Not at all,' she replied, giving him a wry smile that told him she recognised a weak excuse when she saw one.

Outside, the temperature felt as if it had dropped several degrees and the turn-of-the-century buildings were silhouetted against the darkening sky. They walked towards the old town and as they approached the Music Academy, she slowed her pace and stopped to look at the programmes. 'I like to keep an eye on the concerts here,' she explained. 'The students are very professional. Have you been?'

'No, I haven't, he replied. The Wagner Hall and the

Great Guild had satisfied most of his passion for music since he'd been in Rīga. Besides, both were only a ten-minute walk from his flat. 'But that looks a very good programme,' he said.

Anita followed his finger. 'Prokofiev, Beethoven, Sibelius. Yes it is,' she agreed. She caught his eye and held his gaze for a few moments. 'Do you fancy going?'

He raised his eyebrows and smiled. 'Yes, why not?'

It was the first time he'd been asked out by a woman he'd only just met. Given the courage, he would have asked her, but he felt relieved, flattered even, that it was she who had done the asking.

'Don't sound so enthusiastic,' she said, looking at him in mock disbelief.

Was he really that transparent? Much to his annoyance he felt his cheeks begin to turn slightly pink. 'I'll get the tickets,' he said quickly.

'Actually, I think it should be my treat. I made you work pretty hard this afternoon,' she added with a twinkle in her eye.

He laughed. 'OK, I'm not going to refuse an invitation like that.'

'I'll give them a call.' she said. 'I'll let you know tomorrow.'

*

His mother's face lit up when he got back to the flat and she immediately jumped up to put the kettle on. Arnis spotted a box of PG Tips and a packet of oatcakes on the side. They had obviously arrived that day. Antons had timed it well.

Then he noticed the muddy green canvas sack lying behind the door and went through to the kitchen. The only new thing he could see was a china tea set laid out on the table. He picked up one of the plates and held it up to the light. It was extremely pretty - white with a pink floral design in the centre and a dark blue rim, edged with gold leaf.

'*This* is what you buried?' he said to Margarita.

'Yes,' she answered, looking at him in a way that suggested she knew he wouldn't understand.

'But it's just a tea service. Why would you bury that?' As he spoke he examined some of the other pieces. The gold leaf had worn on some of the cups but his mother had obviously washed everything and there was nothing to indicate it had been buried in the earth for more than half a century.

She cast aside her exasperation and answered his question. 'This tea service is extremely valuable and it was one of the things your father and I cherished most. It was something we shared every day of our married lives, short though they were.'

'But why bury it?' he asked again, still not understanding.

'Because we knew that, sooner or later, the Russians would come to take either, or both, of us away. They destroyed everything they got their hands on and we wanted to hide our most precious belongings.'

Arnis didn't really understand why a tea service should be quite so significant but he did at least appreciate the sentiment. 'I see,' he said calmly. He watched as she bustled about making the tea, envious of her ability to immerse herself in domesticity, but not taken in by her rushing about. Perhaps she was as bothered by the note as he was, even though she appeared to dismiss it.

'Come on, the tea's ready,' she said brightly, taking the tray into the living room. She poured two cups and started to drink hers straight away. 'What a treat. I didn't think I'd drink out of these again,' she said running her index finger round the top of the cup.

He smiled but, although he could see how pleased she was to find the tea service, he knew that her brightness was forced. He began to wonder if she really did know what had happened to his father. Perhaps she'd found out and never told him.

His mind flipped back across the years to a patient he'd met when he was working at the Royal Free in London. Hadn't she told him something just like that? He thought hard. Her husband had been a pilot in the RAF and his plane had been shot down in Belgium, although his body had never been found. A few years later she'd discovered he was living in South Africa with a new wife. Feeling ashamed and thinking her children might blame her for their father not coming back, she hadn't told them. But the guilt had tormented her. 'Do you think I should tell them?' she'd asked him.

'What do you think? It has to be your decision,' he'd replied. Then the ward sister had called him to attend to another patient and he never saw the woman again. Occasionally, he had wondered if she ever had told her children.

As he watched his mother gazing at her cup and saucer, he began to wonder if she was keeping things from him and began to feel slightly sick. The note had been a shock, but not in the way he had thought. Perhaps she knew all along that his father had returned from Siberia. And perhaps she was now troubled because he had seen the note and would suspect that she knew.

Margarita took the tea tray to the kitchen and started to prepare supper. Trying to push the note from his mind, he thought about Anita and of how well they had got on. He was sure she'd enjoyed his company as much as he'd enjoyed hers. The prospect of seeing her again filled him with a warmth he hadn't felt for years.

The next day he went to the surgery and though it was busy without Maia it felt easier. He had never found working on his own difficult. Though Dawn in London had had been a superb receptionist, he generally found himself able to work more efficiently when she had a day off. Today was proving to be the same, though with much better reason in the absence of Maia. Yet despite his ability to get on with his work, he felt inside him a tingle of anticipation, that at any moment the phone might ring and he'd hear Anita's voice. Why, he asked himself, was he longing to hear her voice? Why could he not get her out his mind? Why did he put the phone down with a heavy heart after every call? When the day came to an end and she had not phoned, his acute disappointment made him feel ridiculous.

That night in bed, he thought of the way her hair had glowed under the light of the lamp in the café, of the way she had undone the buttons on the cuffs of her crisp white shirt, of the way she had folded the sleeves back to reveal the fine paler hairs on her forearms. He replayed the conversation they'd had outside the Music Academy, of the way she'd held his gaze. Had she said *tomorrow I'll phone you* or *tomorrow I'll phone the ticket office*? The more he thought about it, the less sure he was. The concert was on the following Wednesday so perhaps she would ring him yet.

But she did not.

On Friday morning he picked up two copies of *Diena*. He found the article easily. 'Medical care: family doctors are the future' ran the headline. 'The Ministry of Health's push to get patients to see a family doctor is highly commendable, according to Dr Arnis Rozenvalds. 'Patients should not refer themselves directly to specialists. It is a waste of health service money and bad for patients.' A Latvian by birth, Dr Rozenvalds returned after fifty five years in Britain to set up in general practice in Elizabetes iela…' He read on down the two column article. It was fair and well-balanced and he felt quite pleased with what she'd said about him.

He arrived at the surgery and found his answerphone flashing. With a renewed sense of hope, he played the messages back. But there was nothing from Anita. He called the *Diena* office but they told him she wasn't due in that day. He thought quickly and left her a message to say that he was pleased with the article. Then he called Reuters. She wasn't there so he left a message there too. At lunch time he called the Music Academy to ask if there were any tickets booked in the name of Celma for the following week. There weren't.

With a heavy heart he resumed his day's work. By late afternoon he began to feel silly. Had he taken leave of his senses? Why did it matter so much? Why did he want to see her again? It was crazy. He'd spent less than a couple of hours with her.

*

That evening, as he was locking up, a pretty girl with fair hair and grave blue eyes turned up on the landing saying she had heard he was without a receptionist. Arnis had seen her before. She occasionally sat with Bruno's daughter in the café across the road. Impressed by her direct approach and air of quiet confidence, he chatted with her on the landing.

Sigita, as she introduced herself, had recently started a master's degree in history at the university and was looking for a day job to pay for her studies.

'Have you had any experience working as a receptionist?' he asked. 'Or anything similar?'

'No. But I have worked in an office ... for a property developer on Stabu iela. And I'm good with computers,' she offered hopefully.

Her confidence suggested she would also be good with people but after a bad experience with one receptionist, Arnis wanted to sleep on it. 'I'll let you know on Monday,' he promised as he followed her out.

When they reached the bottom of the stairs, she untied a tiny little dog from the banister. 'This is Artūrs,' she said proudly as he bent down to pat him.

'He's lovely,' said Arnis, and bent to stroke the dog's ear. As he stood up, he noticed a sticker on Sigita's bag – a picture of Mull. He touched it with his finger. 'Ah, Scotland,' he said. 'Have you been there?'

Sigita's face lit up. 'Yes, this summer. I went for a month with my friend. I worked on a stall on the sea front in Oban making sandwiches. I loved it.'

There was no more to be said.

His decision was made and Sigita began work on the Monday morning. Within a couple of days she had got the filing sorted out and started to get to grips with the computer database, setting up the patient records. The fact she couldn't always do Saturday mornings and needed to leave at half past five on Tuesdays and Thursdays to get to her lectures was a small price to pay. She was good with the patients and, best of all, she was always extremely polite to his mother on the telephone. Arnis was delighted with her efficiency, her conscientiousness, her pleasant manner. By the end of her first week, his memories of Maia were beginning to fade.

But his memory of Anita had not.

The night of the concert had passed and he was planning to phone the *Diena* office again. Then on Sunday morning as he was setting off to take Reksis for a walk, he spotted her emerging from a doorway along Pils iela.

She noticed him too, and without hesitating, she approached him and said in a matter-of-fact voice, 'You live near here?'

'Yes, over there, on the corner,' he replied, pointing to the ornately decorated pink building with the half moon balcony on the second floor.

'Mmm. You've got a good view of the Dom.'

'Yes.'

He sensed she wanted to go. 'You got my message about your article? It was good.'

She smiled but said nothing.

'Have you got time for a coffee?'

She looked uncertain for a moment, then nodded.

He put Reksis in the car, and they walked along Skuņu iela. A slight breeze combed the narrow little street, silent apart from the occasional shout of a seagull and the distant sound of a flute. They stopped at a café he was fond of. He'd been there on his first visit to Rīga ten years ago, when worn grey linoleum covered the floor, and he'd sat on a red Rexine seat opposite the bar, sipping a mug of hot chocolate from a huge cracked white beaker. Now it had been refurbished. Ochre coloured walls with painted ivy leaves round the edges of the windows, dark polished wooden benches, candles on the tables and a spotlessly clean red-tiled floor.

They took off their coats and he hung them on the stand by the door.

She sat opposite him – in black trousers and pale pink jumper, looking less elegant than when he'd last seen her, but still attractive. 'Did you go to the concert?' he asked.

'Concert?' When? Oh yes,' she remembered. 'No, I didn't. I had something I had to finish.'

He was not convinced. 'You were going to phone me.'

'Phone? I haven't got your number.'

He knew very well he'd given her his card.

'I'm sorry if you thought I was going to phone.'

'No, no. It's fine.'

'I've been so busy lately. I've had to work a lot of evenings.'

'How was the Prague conference?'

She looked astonished. 'You have a good memory,' she said. 'No it wasn't so interesting. Too many sessions about cytokines and immune function. Nothing very new. I wrote a bit for Reuters. That was all.'

'Do you find that kind of thing hard work?'

'No, not really,' she replied giving him a sharp look which he took to mean she did know her stuff on immunology. They both took a sip of their cappuccino. 'There was something that was interesting, though. Have you heard about this link between gingivitis and heart disease? she asked him.

'Yes,' he answered. He was being truthful, though he didn't know a great deal about it.

'I was reading something yesterday saying that brushing your teeth can prevent heart attacks.'

'I suspect it's not that simple.'

She looked at him quizzically.

'Heart disease is caused by inflamed arteries, and gingivitis by inflamed gums.'

'And there's a bacterial source for both?'

'Yes, though I can't remember its name.'

She laughed. 'No, nor can I. But I think what you're saying is that both can be caused by inflammation. So it doesn't mean that bleeding gums cause heart disease.'

'No, but a person who harbours the bacteria may be prone to both.'

Their conversation began to flow as it had the other day. All trace of awkwardness disappeared, and his inner excitement which had not been far beneath the surface began to flood his veins. They went on to talk about a piece she was writing about TB, which was a growing problem in Latvia, then about another article on the amount of new equipment lying unused in hospitals because of the cost of running it.

Eventually, she looked at her watch and gave a start. 'I have to be at a poetry reading in twenty minutes.'

'Where, can I give you a lift?' he asked.

'Juglas. Do you know where I mean?'

He nodded. 'Are you writing this up too?' He was sure this must be work too because she did not strike him as the sort of person who would enjoy poetry.

But he was wrong. 'No, this is pure hobby. I love poetry.'

It was a few minutes after twelve when they got to Juglas. 'Can you drop me at the end of the trolley route?' she said.

He pulled in at a lay by next to the terminal. 'I'd like to see you again for longer,' he said. 'How long does the poetry reading last?

'Till two. Except that I have dancing classes afterwards,'

'And tonight? Are you going anywhere tonight?'

'Yes. It's my friend's birthday. We're having a meal out.'

He was sure he could sense a tinge of regret in her voice.

She opened the car door. 'Thank you for bringing me all this way. I would never have been on time otherwise.' She gave him a card. 'Phone me. My mobile number's usually the best.'

He watched her hurry across the road in the direction of a block of flats. She disappeared without looking back. He wasn't sure what to think. She'd given him more than a hint of interest, but then she had the other day outside the Music Academy. At least now he had her phone number.

CHAPTER 8

The following day Arnis was writing a prescription for a patient, a man in his late fifties, when he decided to check his blood pressure. 'Very good,' he said as he removed the stethoscope. 'Do you come from a long-living family?'

The man looked surprised at the question. 'I wouldn't know,' he said sadly. My father and grandfather were deported to Siberia. We never saw them again. I don't know how long they'd have lived.'

Immediately Arnis's curiosity was raised. 'Have you found out anything about them? Where they went, what happened to them?

'Yes. They were sentenced to ten years in the mines of Vorkuta. They both died in 1954.'

Arnis nodded sympathetically. He wanted to encourage the man to carry on talking. It was clear he'd been able to find out quite a lot. 'Where did you learn this?' he asked.

'I went to the records office to start with. They're quite helpful. They're getting more and more information now. This year has made a big difference.'

'Because of the KGB records being released?'

'Exactly,' agreed the man.

Arnis felt he owed him an explanation for his questions so he told him about his father.

'I should go down there if I were you. I'm glad I found about my family. It was upsetting to find out for definite what had happened, but I'm glad I did. I don't think about it so much know. I feel I can move on.'

As soon as the man had gone, Arnis called the records office and made an appointment for the day after tomorrow.

Then he called Anita.

'I'm in a meeting.' she said. She sounded apologetic and promised to phone back about five.

Contemplating disappointment, he spent the next hour talking to Sigita about refurbishing the surgery. He wanted to make the waiting room more comfortable for the patients. Sigita proved to be very creative and by five o'clock they'd planned the décor – a parquet floor and off white walls; a semi-circular desk in one corner, a couple of sofas – she thought they'd look good covered in a dark maroon colour - a play area for the children; a couple of shelves for self-care books so that patients could learn more about their health.

At five to five the phone rang. He did not pick it up. 'For you,' said Sigita.

It was Anita. His heart smiled. 'I'm sorry I couldn't talk earlier,' she said.

'Do you want to meet?' he asked.

'Yes, I'd like that.'

'How about a concert? Immediately he wished he'd suggested the threatre – anything else – because he didn't want to make her feel uncomfortable about the last time.

But there was no trace of awkwardness in her reply. 'Sounds good.'

'The Latvian Philarmonic Chamber Orchestra is playing at the Wagner Hall on Friday evening. Seven o'clock'

'Yes, OK. I'll meet you there.' The firmness in his reply filled him with hope.

*

Two days later, at the end of morning surgery, he set off visit the state records office but, having promised his mother he would get her some kefir from the market, he decided to do that first. The days were getting noticeably shorter and it was one of those damp, joint-aching days when it never seemed to get light. Emerging from the underpass, he reached the edge of the market. There was the usual row of puppies, one already wrapped in a fur coat to protect against the autumnal chill, followed by an avenue of toothless babushkas selling pairs of tights, designer carrier bags and cheap floral dresses.

A freight train rumbled its way through the gloom towards the central station, its huge green locomotive making light work of the forty or so trucks loaded with timber. Arnis passed under the bridge, heading towards the vaulted roofs of the indoor market. He approached a row of fruit and vegetable stalls where headscarved women rummaged through bananas, grapes, oranges, kiwi - a variety unimaginable during the days when exotic fruit was limited to little other than an irregular consignment of poor quality lemons from Moscow.

A little way further, he came to a standstill at the back of a huge crowd. Impatient to get on, he stood on tiptoe to see what, or who, was holding things up. It was a stooped old man manoeuvring a low wooden cart laden with huge jars of pickled tomatoes. 'Dod ceļu,' he cried, a fragile scrap of humanity hemmed in on all sides by a convivial throng, pushing, shoving, elbowing its way forward.

In this place you could forget you were in a capital city. It was like everyone was up from the country for the day, all armed with steely determination, making good manners an expendable luxury. He reached the door of the Zeppelin hanger where a huge woman with a round, heavily-lined face was doling out steaming potatoes in white sauce on to a metal plate. Next to her, her companions chewed on hunks of black bread with slabs of white butter, raw onion rings and lumps of gristly meat, all washed down with gallons of tea from the nearby samovar.

Sidestepping a puddle, he made his way into the market hall, quickly finding a stall selling dairy produce. He handed his brown bottle to a white-coated woman with a drawstring hat and she promptly slopped half a litre of thick creamy kefir through a plastic funnel.

'Tak,' ('So') she said, uttering one of the few words of Russian he understood. 'Tak,' she said again, screwing the top back on and wiping the sides with a cloth.

As he gave her a one-lat coin, he noticed some sauerkraut. Sauerkraut was one of those things he got a real craving for at times. His mother hadn't made any since they'd lived in Rīga and he was beginning to get withdrawal symptoms. So, he bought a pot, and some halva for his mother. On the next stall there were some nice chocolates so he bought a box for Sigita.

He headed back towards the old town, crossing the road in front of the Opera House. He had only taken a few strides when a couple of youngsters appeared and fell in step beside him. 'Postcards. Rīga. Postcards. One lat,' they shouted.

'No thanks,' he said firmly.

'Only one lat. Only one lat,' they persisted, letting the

cards concertina towards the ground as they moved in front of him and ran backwards facing towards him.

'Go away. I live here,' he snapped at them, increasing his pace. It irritated him that they could still target him. Foreigners stood out like a sore thumb but he hoped four months might have made a difference. His accent was the giveaway, he was sure of that. All the locals could hear the difference. They said he spoke in softer Latvian, as in the old days before the war. Eventually, the boys gave up and he hurried on back to his flat.

He went upstairs and put his purchases in the kitchen table.

'You don't like nuts,' said his mother, glancing at the box of chocolates.

'True. But Sigita does.'

She gave him a wry smile. 'You never learn, do you? Last time we were out shopping it was a bunch of flowers.'

'Mother, if you'd had to work with Maija, you'd appreciate Sigita.'

'Maybe, but not enough to give her presents every week. She'll get the wrong idea.'

'For goodness sake, I'm old enough to be her father.'

'And when has that ever made any difference? I can see the way she looks at you. A few more bunches of flowers and the wedding bells will start to chime. You should know by now.'

'Oh, so that's how it worked for you, is it?'

She made no reply and he set off for his appointment at the records office. Checking to make sure he still had the piece of paper on which he had scribbled down the address, he made his way through the square towards the river. He wondered whether his mother could be right. He got on well with women, preferring their company to that of men, but they could be such a bother if you couldn't spoil them without they read something deeper into an innocent gesture of appreciation. So, much as he was flattered by the thought that Sigita might be just a little in love with him, he certainly didn't want to spoil his working relationship with her and decided not to give her the chocolates.

Deep in thought, Arnis walked along the embankment. Thick cloud hung low over the city, barring the last traces of daylight, confining the world under its damp grey blanket. He arrived at the tram stop as a number five loomed out of the mist. People were wedged inside it but he climbed into the back and found a few santimi to pay the conductress. The tram trundled over the bridge then rounded a corner past a disused factory.

He began to feel apprehensive, wondering what they would have to tell him at the office. Would they have any record of his father? Would they be able to say what had happened to him? Which camp he'd been sent to. Whether he'd died in the camp.

The more he thought about it, the more he realised that was the most important piece of information. If they could tell him his father had died in Siberia he would go back home and tell his mother. And she would say that's what I've always told you. And that would be an end to the matter.

Or would it? Could he really discount the note so easily? Could someone really have planted it? If the office were able to tell him anything, would it be reliable? Would he be able to believe it?

For the hundredth time he began to torture himself

with an endless string of questions, wondering whether he really wanted to know the answers. The day he'd made the appointment, he'd felt certain he did. Now he felt anything but.

'Don't be so stupid,' he told himself. 'Of course you want to know. This is one of the reasons you came to Latvia.'

He peered out of the tram, keeping his eye open for the clinic. As far as he could remember the records office was the stop after that. He noticed the roofs of some small wooden huts in the foreground. Those must be the allotments. After rounding a curve the tram approached a straight grassy stretch of road, passing an old mill. A row of gloomy shops appeared on the left, then a low brick building. The tram stopped near the clinic.

At the next stop, he got off and the tram rattled away into the gloom. Frowning, he looked up and down the street. It didn't seem right somehow and the mist didn't help. Hadn't there been a pharmacy opposite the tram stop? He looked in vain for the illuminated dark red 'A'. Then he spotted two figures emerging from a building that looked like a factory. There was a small wooden lodge just inside the gate and the window was lit. He knocked on the door.

'Yes,' answered a bad-tempered voice.

Arnis opened the door. 'Am I in the right place for the records office?'

'Next door,' muttered the man, not looking up from the hurricane lamp he was cleaning.

Arnis headed off along the street. As soon as he spotted the grey-stained concrete building he remembered it. He took a deep breath and went up the steps into the entrance hall where a huge woman was carelessly slopping a mop across the floor.

'The records office?' he asked her.

'On the right,' she grunted, pointing vaguely ahead.

He made his way down the gloomy, ill-lit corridor and tried the dark brown door at the end. It opened into a small room and he approached the first of two windows and knocked. Immediately, a green curtain shot across the glass and a fat hand stuffed a "closed" sign in front of the cloth.

Typical, thought Arnis, tightening his lips as he moved to the second window. This time, the frosted glass slid back and a woman with henna-coloured hair and green eye shadow appeared. 'Name,' she barked.

'Mine?' he asked.

'Yes,' she uttered contemptuously, looking at him as if she thought the cat could bring in better.

'Rozenvalds.'

'Relative's name?'

'Vilks. Kārlis Vilks.'

She ran her pen down the list of appointments, found his name and ticked it. Saying no more, she rammed the glass shut and he went to sit down on the Rexine sofa underneath the window. What an awful place. The room was lined with cheap, teak look-alike Formica and the floor was covered with brown linoleum. In the opposite corner sat a man of about his own age with a pelmet of grey hair and a suit to match. A young woman sat next to him. Wearing long black boots and a short purple skirt, she lit a cigarette and blew puffs of smoke towards a ceiling that didn't look in need of another coat of nicotine.

The glass crashed back and the henna-coloured woman scowled round the room. 'Juris Bērziņš,' she bawled.

The man and woman got up and disappeared through another dark brown door. The window slammed shut again. Arnis scowled in disgust. People had put up with this sort of behaviour for fifty years but he had never come across a woman who relished her power quite as much as this one. She reminded him of Maija. Thank goodness he had got rid of her. With her as a receptionist, why worry about hostile consultants? It was a wonder he had had any patients at all.

But there was a difference. In this place they didn't have to be polite. You couldn't go anywhere else and they knew it. It was like the post office, but worse.

Before long he began to feel uncomfortably hot and he took off his anorak, at the same time loosening his tie. That was the worst thing about central heating. It was either on or it was off. With Soviet heating, there was nothing in between: a good work horse with no finesse. Longing for some air, he went out into the corridor where the woman was still busy with the mop. After slopping water along half the corridor, she gave up and waddled away.

Glad to be on his own, Arnis wiped the condensation from the window and stared outside to a small disused courtyard with leaves congregating in huge sodden heaps and weeds growing between the cobbles. The few trees were almost bare, their blackened trunks branching into fine silvery twigs, drifting towards an uneasy winter's rest. He felt their desolation, hemmed in on all sides by a greyness they couldn't escape, rooted in a soil they wouldn't have chosen. Imprisoned in this bleak courtyard, devoid of their sage green clothing that would not return until it again quivered in the spring breeze; a breeze that might bring a breath of hope for seeds to scatter and take root in less dismal surroundings.

140

Anita came into his mind and he pulled out his wallet to look for the concert tickets. They were there in the back pouch exactly where he'd put them. He wished there weren't so many appointments this Friday. It meant he would have to go straight to the Wagner Hall from the surgery. What was Anita doing now? He pictured her sitting at her desk: probably with a large mug of coffee next to her computer and listening to music. He could imagine that she liked to write with music playing. Where she worked he didn't know. Presumably at home some of the time. But he didn't know where she lived.

The man in the grey suit emerged from the room at the end of the corridor with the young woman in tow. The man looked as if he'd been given a death sentence and, feeling an apprehension bordering on panic, Arnis went back into the hot airless office. A few moments later, the frosted glass crashed back again, and the henna woman shouted his name. 'Rozenvalds. Second door on the left.'

He found himself in another room, gloomier than the first, with only out of the four fluorescent tubes lit, a huge wooden desk across one wall and a fireplace to the right. He sat down on the single high-backed chair and a middle-aged woman wearing a plain grey skirt and a blue jumper came in and sat behind the desk.

'What's the name of your relative?'

'Vilks. Kārlis Vilks.'

'Mmm, mmm' She took a sip of coffee from a cup on the mantelpiece, then disappeared.

He took a deep breath and pulled his tie from under his collar. The door opened again and in came henna woman carrying his anorak. His mobile phone was ringing. In no mood to talk to anyone, he took it out of the pocket and was about to thumb the off-switch when he noticed the familiar six-figure number from the surgery. He put the instrument to his ear.

'Dr Rozenvalds. It's Sigita. Can you call Mrs Dragunova? I tried to get her to call back tomorrow, but she wouldn't. She sounded really angry... Can you hear me? Did you get that?'

He thought quickly. Since speaking with Dr Rubenis the other day he hadn't done anything further about Mrs Dragunova. He had hoped the consultant would have calmed down by now and replied to his letter, but it must be nearly a month since he'd written to the man. 'Sigita, can you phone Dr Rubenis...'

'I've got her number,' Sigita said, ignoring him. 'It's right here in front of me,' she said insistently.

A few moments later, the door opened again, and the bespectacled woman re-appeared with a thick black ledger.

He had no intention of dealing with any patients now, no matter how urgent. 'Sigita, I'll call you back in a minute or two.' He pressed the end button and switched off the phone.

'Kuldīga, you said. Your father lived in Kuldīga?' asked the bespectacled woman.

'Yes, that's right.'

'Mmm, mmm.' She turned the pages, separating them carefully between her thumb and forefinger. 'Yes, here we are. Kuldīga. Address?'

'Raina iela. Number seven.' He leaned over towards the desk, longing to get hold of the ledger, to go through the names himself.

'Mmm, mmm. Vilks. Kārlis. Here we are. Raina iela.

You did say number seven?'

He nodded and she turned the ledger round, sliding it to the front of the desk so he could see it. 'There,' she said, pointing to the entry right at the bottom of the page. Feeling his pulse race slightly, he leaned over the ledger.

Case number 357. Vilks, Kārlis. Kuldīga, Raiņa 7.

Born April 16, 1899. Detained on June 14, 1941.

Sentence, ten years. Destination Krasnoyarsk. Bandit.

'Bandit!' he burst out, making the bespectacled woman drop her teaspoon on the floor. 'What's that supposed to mean? My father was a schoolteacher. How dare they put that! He was not a bandit!'

'Oh, that word appears all the time,' the woman replied carelessly. 'See, look,' she said, pointing to a couple more entries on the same page. 'They used it to mean a guerrilla fighter. Anyone who was against the Soviet state was a bandit.'

Arnis took off his glasses and rubbed the lenses over the edge of his cuff. Bandit! He felt very angry. Putting his glasses on again, he re-read the two-line entry. It was clear enough. He stared at the destination - Krasnoyarsk. Over the years, he had scrutinised maps of Siberia so often that he felt he knew them better than a London tube map. He was sure Krasnoyarsk was somewhere in the middle.

He looked at the record again. It made no mention of his father's death but, from what he had gathered from other people, few of those deported in 1941 ever came back. He frowned. A ten-year sentence; if he had been released, that meant 1951. What year was on the note? Not for the first time that day, he wished he'd brought it with him, but he was certain it was 1947. He began to feel slightly calmer, wanting

143

to believe anything that could prove his father hadn't written it.

He was about to pass the book back to the woman, when, for some reason, his eye moved on to the top of the next page. It carried just a single phrase. When he read what it said, he felt his blood freeze in his veins.

Released July 15, 1947.

Released! The page blurred slightly for a moment. His throat tightened and he read the whole thing again.

'This ... here,' he said, pointing shakily at the line topping the next page. 'It does relate to Mr Vilks?'

'That's what it says.'

He scrutinised the words again and rooted in his inside pocket for a pen. 'Have you got a sheet of paper?' he said, in a voice he didn't recognise as his own. She found a small pad and carefully tore off a quarter of a sheet. He copied the entry down, checking it carefully several times, wanting to be sure he'd got it right.

He had hardly any time to recover before the door opened again. Another woman appeared, much younger than the bespectacled one, prettier, with short dark wavy hair and very blue eyes. Carrying another thick black ledger, she spoke to her colleague who by then was standing at the window, lighting a cigarette.

'I've found the rest of it,' she said.

'Leave it on the desk.' The older woman opened the ledger and leafed her way through to the page that the dark-haired girl had marked with a piece of paper.

'Can you read Russian?' Giving him a look that said she already knew he couldn't, she called down the corridor, 'Olga, can you come back?'

The dark-haired girl returned. 'You'll have to translate,' said the older woman irritably, nodding towards the ledger.

Motioning him to draw his chair up to the desk, the young woman flicked through the pages of the second ledger with her right hand. 'This file is very long. It runs to nearly fifty pages.'

In a calm, matter-of-fact voice, she explained that the file contained a record of Mr Vilks's interrogation. It had taken place in the Cheka headquarters in Kuldīga, the place he had been held before being deported to Siberia.

Despite her measured tone, he had difficulty taking any of it in, his mind still fixed on the half-line phrase. *Released July 15, 1947.* What was the date on the note? He was now more certain than ever it was 1947. The room began to swim and he took hold of the edge of the desk with both hands.

The woman read the first of the interrogator's questions. 'Tell me about your background.'

Then came his father's reply. 'I was born in Kuldīga, the son of a middle-class bourgeois family.' He tried to focus on her index finger as it moved along the lines of Cyrillic script. 'My father was a foreman at the mill,' she went on. 'He was a Latvian nationalist. He punished the workers and sacked any that did not have the same views as him. He never renounced his nationalist views. He was anti-Soviet the whole of his life.

My mother did not work. She was also from a middle-class bourgeois family. She too was a Latvian nationalist and anti-Soviet…'

Arnis's mouth felt like sandpaper. 'May I open the window?'

The girl nodded and carried on reading. 'My cousin Modris and Uncle Emīls were also Latvian nationalists and anti-Soviets. They supported the Latvian nationalist movement and killed Russian soldiers in the woods.'

She continued her monotone delivery turning the pages one by one. 'What was your work?' she said reading another of the interrogator's questions.

'I was a schoolteacher in Kuldīga,' was the response. 'I taught all the pupils to hold Latvian nationalist, anti-Soviet, bourgeois views. I punished them if they did not hold Latvian nationalist, anti-Soviet views. I taught the history of Latvia from a nationalist anti-Soviet viewpoint. I brainwashed all the pupils into a Latvian nationalist, anti-Soviet way of thinking. I punished them if they believed anything else.'

'Just a minute!' Arnis said, angry again. Whether his father had abandoned them or not, he was still his father. 'My father wouldn't have said that.'

Ignoring him, the girl recommenced her reading, obviously wanting to press on quickly to the end. The words of the interrogator again. 'Tell me about your anti-Soviet activities after the German capitulation.'

'After the capitulation of Germany, I remained an anti-Soviet bourgeois Latvian nationalist. I did not renounce my nationalist views. I took part in meetings and incited others to do the same.'

'Where did the meetings take place?'

'I met in the woods with other bourgeois Latvian nationalists.'

'What happened at those meetings?'

'I read aloud from the sayings of Kārlis Ulmanis.'

'Who else was at those meetings?'

'There was Balvis Taurens, Guntis Ozoliņš, Zigrīda Stranga and myself. We all read aloud from the sayings of Kārlis Ulmanis. We were all bourgeois Latvian nationalists. We did not like Soviet literature. We all admired Kārlis Ulmanis...'

The woman stopped for a moment to get her breath before continuing again. More of the same, page after page. This was ridiculous. In fact so ridiculous as to be unbelievable. Not that his father wouldn't have admired Kārlis Ulmanis. Of course, he would. But to say all of that; it was impossible. His father was an intelligent man. Who could have written this rubbish? No one in their right mind could say those things. More likely the whole lot had been falsified by some hack paid a few roubles to make the boss look good.

'I am a Latvian, middle-class, bourgeois, nationalist.' The woman's voice stopped. It was the end of the file. The silence brought him back to a level of reality and he took hold of the ledger to scan through the pages. The record was meticulous all the way through. There were no smudges, no marks; page after page of perfect copy. Then he looked at the last line. There were two signatures. He wished he'd got a magnifying glass as he tried in vain to make out the handwriting. He couldn't even be sure it was his father's name, much less his signature, and he kicked himself again for not bringing the note. The other signature was just as undecipherable, but whether it had been written by a different hand or not, he could not tell.

He pushed the book back towards the young woman and leaned back in the chair. She got up, picked up the ledger and left the room without saying another word.

Henna woman came back carrying a large bunch of

keys, making her intentions plain. 'We're closed now,' she said coldly.

Feeling quite sick, he scraped his chair away from the desk and started towards the door and the street. Spotting an Aldaris sign opposite he went to the bar and ordered a whisky. Soon, he began to feel as if the black ledger had been a dream, as if he'd never been in that poky office, but to make doubly sure he ordered another drink. He was halfway through it when the woman behind the counter started to fiddle with the radio knob, shattering his brain with loud western music. Disliking that at the best of times, he swiftly downed the last of his whisky and stepped outside.

Relieved to feel the cool air on his face, he decided to walk home. After half an hour it began to drizzle but he tramped on, his feet on automatic. The only thing he could remember clearly now was that three-word phrase: *released July 1947*. Had his father really been released? He didn't want to believe it but the words in the ledger made it look real enough. But was it reliable? How much credence could he attach to it? How were these records compiled? It could easily be inaccurate. How would he have felt if he and his mother hadn't found the note? He wasn't sure but he still didn't think he could have ignored what he'd seen that afternoon. So what about the woman who said his father had been seen in Sydney? Did it all add up or not? Or was it a series of coincidences? So-called sightings of missing people were not unusual.

Still in a daze, he arrived home and opened the door. Reksis gave a string of delighted yelps, hurling himself at Arnis in an excited frenzy.

'What's the matter, lad?' he said, trying to calm him

down, not having seen the Alsatian quite so pleased to see him before.

'Where have you been?' his mother asked anxiously. 'Sigita's been on the phone. I told her to try your mobile.'

There had been few occasions in his life when he'd longed to tell his mother to shut up, but this was one of them. Delving in his pocket, he found his phone. Sigita had left three messages. What was the matter with the pair of them? It was only ten past five. He thought quickly then called her.

'I think I might have sorted it out,' she said brightly.

'Sorted what out?' he said, not having a clue what she meant.

'Mrs Dragunova. I called Dr Rubenis's secretary. I know Valda. We were at school together. Anyway, she called me back and Mrs Dragunova is going in on Monday. I let her know straight away. She thinks you're wonderful.'

'Sigita ... thanks...' He wiped his hand across the top of his head.

'That's OK. It only took two minutes to save your life. May I go a bit earlier tonight? I've got an essay I want to finish.'

'Yes, of course.' Take the rest of the week off, he wanted to say. But he didn't.

He put his phone on charge then went to look at the note which he had put on the chest of drawers in his bedroom. He'd been right. The date was 1947. October 1947; three months after the file said his father had been released. The muscles in his stomach contracted. Why did it all have to point in the same direction? Even though his father would be long dead by now, there was no way he could let the matter rest.

He went into the living room and his mother followed

carrying two cups of tea. 'You do look bedraggled. Where have you been?' She looked at Reksis who had curled himself into his usual contented semi-circle round the bottom of the blue and white-tiled stove. 'He made me feel worse. He howled like a banshee. Anyone would think he'd been abandoned.'

Arnis gazed at the dog. Had Reksis sensed his torment? It made him think of the night they'd got back from Kuldīga after finding the note. Then Reksis had insisted on crawling into bed with him, rather than sleeping on the rug as he always did. It had occurred to him then that Reksis knew he was troubled but he had quickly dismissed the idea and assumed the dog was upset because he'd been left on his own all day. But now he was not so sure.

As they were finishing their tea, the phone rang. 'Say I'm out,' he snapped as his mother went to answer it.

She picked up the receiver and covered the mouthpiece. 'It's Michael,' she said with a smile. She'd always been fond of Michael and she'd been sad when he'd gone to live in Ireland because she knew they wouldn't see him so often, if at all. 'Talk to him. He'll cheer you up.'

Had it been anyone other than his old school friend, he would have shaken his head, but he hadn't spoken to Michael for several months.

'Hi, how's things?' said Michael cheerily.

'OK.'

They chatted for a few minutes, Michael talking about the house, how he was getting it rewired, central heating put in and so on. How his mother had lived in it the way it was he didn't know.

Arnis was happy to let him talk. He didn't want to talk

about himself at all. It felt too painful, though he did eventually fill Michael in with a few details about the practice and Antons's ambulance course.

But Michael wasn't taken in. He'd known Arnis for too long. 'You sound down,' he said.

'I'm OK.'

'Any news of your father?' Michael was the only person he'd told about the photograph.

'Yes.' He took a deep breath. 'I can't talk now. I haven't got my head round it yet. How's the book?' he asked, wanting to change the subject.

Michael gave a deep groan. He was writing his first novel - a three-generation story about an Irish family who had settled in Tennessee. 'It's worse than rowing the Atlantic,' he replied. 'You see the Statue of Liberty, land on Ellis Island, only to be turned away. That happened to my great grandfather. But he made it twenty years later.' He laughed. 'I'll let you know if I ever make it to Fifth Avenue.'

Arnis couldn't help but smile at that. They chatted again for a few minutes before saying goodbye, and he put the phone down. He wondered how far across the Atlantic *he* was. It didn't feel as if he'd reached the Azores, never mind the Statue of Liberty. But one thing was certain. It was no time to turn back.

CHAPTER 9

The next day, Arnis was standing in front of the mirror, combing his hair and adjusting his tie, when Sigita brought him a letter to sign. Her reflected image showed a look of bright amusement on her face.

'Someone important?' she said.

By now, he was well used to her teasing and merely smiled. After she left, he washed his hands and switched off the computer. Then he signed the letter and put his head round the door to tell her he'd see her tomorrow. Sigita was rummaging in her desk drawers and didn't seem to have heard.

But she had. 'Don't go yet,' she said, looking up.

Expecting she had found something else she wanted him to do, he went across to her desk. To his surprise, she handed him a clothes brush. 'That's the trouble with dogs. You can't go out looking smart.' She laughed.

He looked down at his dark grey trousers and saw what she meant. 'Thanks,' he murmured, taking the brush and ridding himself of the tan-coloured hair. 'Do I look OK now?'

She eyed him seriously for a few moments. 'You'll do,' she said with a mischievous grin.

He left the surgery and hurried down Brīvības, passing the Freedom Monument into the park. As he approached the floodlit Opera House, he heard a familiar voice calling from the car park. 'Hello, Doctor.'

Tālis, complete with red bobble hat, was sitting on the roof of a white Mercedes, his legs draped over the edge of the windscreen.

'Hey, you haven't done mine for a bit. It could do with a wash,' Arnis said playfully, relieved the lad looked less unkempt than when he'd last seen him.

'Tomorrow,' the youngster promised. 'See, I've got a brush now,' he said proudly and, with that, he continued washing the roof of the Merc.

At ten minutes to seven Arnis reached the Wagner Hall. There was no sign of Anita. Again preparing for disappointment, he waited outside on the pavement. A fine drizzle began to dampen the cobbles and he pulled the collar up on his anorak. A steady stream of concert goers made their way up the steps into the entrance. Noticing three of his patients amongst them, he moved a few steps away. Though he was gradually getting used to the inevitability of being recognised outside of the surgery, he did miss the anonymity of a bigger city.

He checked his watch. It was a minute before seven. With a heavy heart, he made his way across the street to the antique shop. Samovars of every design and size filled the left hand window and as he moved to look at the other window, he spotted Anita hurrying along the street.

'I'm so sorry,' she breathed. Without any further explanation, she added, 'Come on, we don't want to miss the beginning.'

They made their way up the stairs, and as they entered the hall, the crystal chandeliers were already dimming so they quickly found their seats. The orchestra was ready and he scanned the programme. Vivaldi's Symphony in B minor to start with. Good, he liked that piece. The rest of the first half consisted of some Bach and some Sibelius, and he was delighted to see that second half was devoted to the Latvian composer Pauls Vasks.

He had a quick look round. 'It's full tonight,' he whispered. Each of the polished wood chairs was taken apart from two or three on the back row. 'But not surprising given the programme.'

'No,' she replied. It's always the same when the Latvian Chamber Orchestra is playing here. But if they can't attract a crowd when they're playing in their home concert hall, when can they?'

'Any music sounds good in here,' he replied. 'The acoustics are superb.' During the next hour and a half the orchestra surpassed itself, exceeding Arnis's expectations.

As the concert came to an end with a flourish of the strings, Anita turned to him with an enormous smile on her face. 'Thank you for suggesting this tonight. I did enjoy it.'

'They certainly live up to their reputation,' he replied. 'It was a novel interpretation of Vivaldi.'

'Yes. I really couldn't fault them except on the Vasks quartet. I thought they were a bit slow.'

'Maybe,' he replied.

She laughed. 'You think I'm being too critical, don't you?' Without waiting for him to reply, she added, 'You're probably right. We're spoiled in Rīga. The music is of such high quality. I shouldn't take it for granted, but I do.'

They made their way out of the hall and down the cast iron stairway. There was a strong cold wind blowing along the dimly lit street and they quickly crossed over into a small courtyard where he knew there was a bar. The entrance was crowded so they went straight down the steps. There were half a dozen low oak tables with benches either side, but all were fully occupied. An old brick archway led into another part of the cellar where, after a few minutes wait, they managed to find a table next to a wood burning stove.

They hung their coats up and sat down opposite each other. Anita wanted Chardonnay so he ordered a bottle and decided to forgo his usual Aldaris. As they waited for the glasses, he took in again the deep richness of her voice, the colour of her lips, her pale pink cheeks, the strand of auburn hair resting against her collar bone. He had not met a woman who had captivated him quite so much and so rapidly.

Suddenly it struck him that she could see it and would think he was ridiculous, but she seemed relaxed enough and her conversation soon turned again to Prague, which she confessed to liking more than Rīga. When he asked her why, she thought for a moment before explaining that she loved the mass of baroque architecture, the restaurants right on the river bank, the castle on top of a hill with the city down below.

He laughed when she said that. There were no hills in Rīga.

'I guess it's just the joy of being somewhere new,' she said. 'Especially as I never travelled anywhere much till I was thirty. You couldn't.'

'Presumably you could have gone to Prague though?'

'Yes, but even going there was not so easy. It took for ever to get your papers sorted out. My dad was going to take us in 1968, but the travel agency stopped all visits to Prague that summer. We were so disappointed. Before 1990, I'd only ever been to Poland. And Moscow. It's still strange seeing coaches here heading for Brussels and Frankfurt. It's wonderful. It's great to feel you're a part of something bigger that's not the Soviet Union. I know joining the EU won't solve all Latvia's problems overnight but…

'So, it's more important to you to be European than Latvian?' he said teasingly.

She laughed. 'I wouldn't say that.'

'I thought not.' He dropped his eyes as she pushed up the sleeves on her shirt. He didn't know why but he found her arms incredibly sexy. 'Did you ever want to live anywhere else?' he asked her.

She thought for a moment. 'Quite honestly, no. Sure, you dreamt that things could be different, without having any expectation that they ever could be. Actually, when everything did start to change, it was quite frightening. What had seemed so permanent suddenly falling apart. It wasn't a pleasant experience. Not at first. But, no, right through my life, I don't think I ever wanted to be anywhere else. I didn't want to leave Latvia.' As soon as she'd spoken, she looked at him sheepishly. 'I'm sorry, I didn't mean…'

He smiled. 'Don't apologise. It's fine. Anita, you may find this strange but there were times as a child when I really wanted to live in Latvia.' He went on to explain to her that he'd hated being accused of being Russian one minute then German the next because his classmates did not understand. 'I longed to be Latvian, to be able to live in Latvia, where I thought I could be myself.' Seeing the look of incredulity on her face, he added quickly, 'As I got older I knew it wasn't like that, but as a boy… that was my dream.'

She took hold of her glass, running her slim fingers up and down the stem. 'I remember the first time I went abroad properly. It was my birthday and a friend and I went to Stockholm on the overnight ferry. First thing the following morning I went up on deck and saw the land ahead. I was so excited and I thought to myself so - Sweden really does exist. It sounds so crazy now looking back. But I have never forgotten it. My first sight of somewhere outside of the Soviet bloc. I don't think I shall ever take travel for granted. That's what freedom means to me.'

He nodded and began to ask her about music. He was delighted to find they had similar tastes, though she wasn't quite as keen on Beethoven as he was. He ordered another bottle of wine and she became more animated, talking about books she'd read, theatre, opera, ballet, much of which he hadn't heard of. Not that he minded. His earlier worries that she wouldn't turn up at the concert hall or that she wouldn't like the programme he'd chosen had completely evaporated. He thought he could see her in eyes that she was enjoying the evening as much as he was.

Then quite suddenly she stopped talking and an awkward silence fell between them. She took a few more sips of wine then looked at her watch. 'Oh, no. It's ten o'clock. I'm supposed to be meeting a colleague outside the opera house. To pass on a disc with some pictures for Monday's paper. Arnis, I'm sorry I'm going to have to rush.'

He did not know what to say. 'Shall I'll wait for you?'

'No,' she said quickly. 'I'll phone you. After all I have your number on my mobile now.'

With that she grabbed her coat and ran up the cellar steps so fast that he was lost for further words. He was stunned. This was the second time she'd rushed off and he felt hurt. Why was she doing this? Looking round for the waitress he became aware of the people sitting at adjacent tables. He began to feel embarrassed, as if they were staring at him having seen what had happened. He paid for the wine, retrieved his anorak from the wooden stand and left.

Outside he felt the force of the wind, blowing even stronger, nipping at his fingers and ears. He walked back towards his flat, going over their conversation again in his mind, wondering if he'd said something silly. But he could not think of anything and she'd seemed to enjoy their conversation as much as he did. But the way she'd rushed off and not offered to come back – the opera house was only minutes away – made him wonder again if she'd sensed his feelings for her and found them unwelcome. Or perhaps she was seeing someone. Perhaps the colleague was a boyfriend. He felt angry at the thought that she could be with someone else.

*

By the next morning he had convinced himself that he would not hear from her, but as he was walking up Valdemara iela, his mobile rang. 'Hi, it's Anita.' His heart lifted as he heard her voice. 'I'm so sorry about last night. I really am. It was so rude of me. Please forgive me.'

'Forgive...It's fine.'

'No, I at least owe you an explanation.'

He made no reply, at the same time thinking, yes you do. He waited, expecting her to justify her need for meeting her colleague.

But he was mistaken. 'I talked too much. I had too much to drink,' she said.

Taken aback because he didn't think she'd talked too

much at all, he said. 'Forget it. It doesn't matter.'

'I was sure you must have thought….'

'Thought what?'

'That I was stupid.'

'Stupid. Now you're being daft. Look, can we forget this?' he said firmly.

He thought he could sense relief in her silence. But he wasn't absolutely sure until she spoke again. 'Salome is on at the opera house. Do you fancy going?' she said.

He replied without hesitation. 'Yes, that would be lovely.'

'Wonderful. Thursday OK?

'Yes.'

He continued walking with a definite spring in his step.

*

The following afternoon, Arnis decided to join his mother for a cup of tea before going back to work. With an hour to spare before evening surgery, he arrived at the flat, went up in the lift and put his key in the door. 'Hello, Mum,' he called.

There was no reply and knowing that she was not usually asleep at four o'clock he felt quite panicky. But his fears were unfounded. She was in the living room, standing with her back to him, ironing next to the window.

'What are you doing here at this time?' she quizzed. She seemed to be alarmed and he felt puzzled. Then she brightened. 'The kettle's just boiled,' she added without looking up from the ironing board.

He raised his eyebrows and went off to the kitchen wondering why the ironing was suddenly so important. These days she tended to do it a bit at a time interspersing it with other jobs like mending. Increasingly arthritic knees combined with occasional spells of dizziness made it difficult for her to stand for more than ten minutes at a time. Not that she ever admitted that. The idea of sitting down to do the ironing or, worse still, letting him do it – in her mind a sign of decrepitude – would have been rejected out of hand so it was not something he even suggested. Doing everything the way she had always done it had almost become an obsession and she took any offer of extra help as personal criticism, accusing him of treating her like a geriatric.

He carried the tea tray in. Curious to see what she was ironing, he went to look over her shoulder.

'Get out of the light,' she said crossly.

It was a tiny yellow shirt with puffed sleeves.

'What is it?' he asked feeling mystified. The shirt was hardly big enough to fit a doll.

She put the finishing touches to the tiny cuffs then turned round to face him with an impish grin on her face. 'Oh, come on...' she said, her grey eyes bright with mischief. She held the little shirt in front of her eyes, put the iron over it once more, deftly smoothing out the few remaining creases from the round collar. Then she went across to her rocking chair where a tiny green waistcoat and a pair of orange breeches lay side by side on the cushion.

Instantly, he knew. 'You've got Sprīdītis out,' he said, looking round the room for the puppet. 'Where is he?'

'On my bed,' she replied happily. 'I thought it was high time he came out of that suitcase. But he was dirty.'

'I'm not surprised ... packed away for so long.'

Arnis went through to her bedroom where, sure

enough, the puppet was lying on the top of her patchwork bedspread. He gazed at the familiar face: an engaging little boy's face, round with high cheekbones, big blue eyes and a whimsical smile. But the eyes were so sad. As a small boy he'd never been able to understand how his father could have made such a face. His mother had tried to explain, telling him it was perfectly possible to have sad eyes and to smile at the same time, but he'd never been convinced.

Now, as he gazed at the wooden figure for the first time since leaving school, he became aware how beautifully made it was. He still couldn't fathom the strange face but his father had clearly been a master craftsman and had spared no effort in carving the dozen or so pieces of finely polished wood. He had lovingly crafted every last detail, from the finely carved fingers and toenails to the page boy hair cut. And the fine leather straps, which acted as the joints, remained intact even though the puppet was so old.

'Mum,' he called. She came and stood beside him with the tiny clothes in her hand. 'When did Dad make Sprīdītis?'

'Before the war.'

'How long before the war?'

'Quite some time. I don't remember exactly.'

'Before you were married?'

'Oh yes. Before I got married ... so before 1938.'

Arnis watched her face closely but her eyes told him nothing.

Then she snapped back to the moment. 'Come on,' she said. 'Help me put his clothes back on. I don't want the strings getting in a muddle again. It took me ages to sort them out last time.'

Carefully, he picked up the puppet and stood it in an

upright position. As he turned it towards his mother so she could put the shirt on, he noticed something else, something he had not seen before. A large letter K carved in the puppet's back. He smiled. Kārlis was his father's name.

'I never knew Dad had carved his initial on it.'

For a moment she looked startled. Then she saw the letter and smiled. 'Oh, yes, he always did that.'

'You mean, he made more than one?' he said, feeling slightly deflated because he'd always believed Sprīdītis was special.

'Oh, yes, lots of them. You remember the other characters in the story?'

He nodded. He knew the tale by heart. Sprīdītis had been his favourite childhood story and he could remember the characters well: the wicked stepmother, the giant, the king, the princess … he'd loved it so much that he'd got his mother to tell it to Michael but, much to his disappointment, Michael hadn't enjoyed it at all. He had thought Sprīdītis was a stupid boy. How could he go back home to his wicked stepmother and not marry a beautiful princess? None of the stories Michael had heard ended like that. The hero always got the princess and they lived happily ever after. Arnis's mother had explained to him that Sprīdītis had gone to seek his fortune in a faraway place but, eventually, he had learned that home was best.

'But why?' Michael had protested. 'His stepmother was horrible.'

'Yes, but Sprīdītis came home a hero. Wouldn't you have liked to be like that? And he did live happily after,' she had said emphatically.

But Michael was never convinced, Arnis recalled.

'Your father made all the characters into puppets,' she continued, explaining that one summer they'd had the idea to put on Sprīdītis as a puppet play at the open-air theatre in Kuldīga. 'But you were the star, weren't you?' she said, smiling fondly at Sprīdītis.

'What happened to the others?' he asked her.

'I've no idea.'

'Perhaps Dad took them to school,' Arnis suggested, although as soon as he'd said that he remembered the woman in London who had said she'd never seen his father's puppets at school.

Margarita gave him an odd look, then shrugged her shoulders. 'I really don't know.'

He helped her to finish dressing the puppet then she took hold of the wooden ring. 'We must hang him up. There's a big hook up there,' she declared, looking up at the ceiling above the window. 'Have you got time?'

Arnis nodded and went to the bathroom to fetch the stepladders.

'He does look rather grand,' she said when the puppet was safely in place.

Arnis leaned the stepladders against the wardrobe and went to stand beside her; to see it from her vantage point.

Margarita gave a huge sigh. 'Oh dear,' she said. 'There were times when I thought … after I put him away in the suitcase …' Her voice faltered. 'I said to myself I would never bring him out again unless we brought him home.'

He heard the tears in her voice and the muscles in his stomach tensed. Nothing made him more uncomfortable than seeing her upset, partly because he could never rid his mind of the guilt that it must be something to do with him. His self-concern arose less from an innate selfishness than from spending the first eighteen years of his life with his mother and no one else. And he still soaked up her emotions like a sponge. He put a protective arm round her and they gazed at the puppet as it hung in the window, framed by the frost-laden branches of the trees outside and the darkening amber sky.

She gave his hand a squeeze. 'Isn't it time you were off?' she said.

Arnis smiled. He did need to go but he sensed she wanted him out of the way, as if she wanted her own space to think.

'Oh and while I remember, can I have another bottle of my little white tablets?'

'Mum, I only brought you some last week.'

'Yes, but you know I like a spare bottle in my bag.'

He gave a worried nod, fearing what he'd suspected for a while that her angina was getting worse. But he knew she wouldn't increase the dose of her other tablets because they made her ankles swell.

He set off for the surgery feeling slightly unsettled. He was delighted to see Sprīdītis again but he was worried about his mother. The puppet had also made him think about his father and the note, and the entry in the records ledger. Not that they had ever been far from his mind during the past few weeks but, having been so busy, and meeting Anita, he hadn't done any more about it. Perhaps he would ask his mother when he got back that evening, he told himself. Almost immediately, he knew he probably wouldn't. He didn't want to make her anxious again.

Then, quite suddenly, he thought of someone else -

someone who might be able to help him. The old man they'd met in the café in Kuldīga. Why hadn't he thought of him before? He had told them he'd known his father. So, if his father had come back to Kuldīga, maybe the old man had seen him, or heard something about him.

CHAPTER 10

It was still on his mind when he arrived back at the surgery. So much so, he went to find Sigita. 'Can you get a number for me?' he asked. 'It's Siliņš. Fēlikss Siliņš. In Kuldīga.'

She picked up the telephone directory and he went through to the consulting room. While he was washing his hands, the phone rang. 'It's Mr Siliņš,' said Sigita.

'Well done,' he told her. Then she put him through to the old man.

'Hello, Mr Siliņš, my name is Arnis Rozenvalds. I don't know if you remember but we met in Kuldīga about a month ago. At the café. I was with my mother.'

'Your mother. Yes, I remember. Mrs Vilka. What can I do for you?' Siliņš sounded pleased to hear from him.

'Could I come and see you. I'd like to talk to you about my father.'

'Your father? Yes, of course. Come on Saturday,' he said. 'Bring your mother.'

'No, I won't do that, if you don't mind. She hasn't been too well recently.'

'I'm sorry to hear that. It would have been lovely to talk again. About the old times.'

'In the summer, perhaps. When the weather's better.'

As he replaced the handset, Sigita came through and asked if she could leave ten minutes early that evening.

'Markuss is coming to pick me up,' she said.

'Markuss?'

'Yes,' she said, blushing. 'He's on the same course as me. I took him to meet my mother last week. She thinks he's wonderful.'

When Markuss arrived to collect Sigita, Arnis could see why. Tall with dark blonde hair, wearing a smart black suit under his anorak, he looked like a young prince and had manners to match.

'Hello,' he said with a shy smile when Sigita introduced him. 'You don't mind Sigita going early?'

'No, not at all. You look as if you're off somewhere special.'

'Yes, we've got a visiting professor from Germany tonight. I have to look after him.'

*

Arnis finished off some paperwork and locked up. When he arrived home, he fumbled for his keys and then remembered he'd left them on the hall table after talking to a patient on the phone that morning. He knocked on the door. Within a few seconds he heard her footsteps on the parquet floor.

'Who is it?' she said in a nervous voice. She had always disliked anyone knocking at the door. He knew it reminded her of the night they had come to take his father away.

'It's me, Mum.'

Margarita opened the door and he saw the relief flood across her face. 'I'm sorry, I forgot my keys,' he said and followed her through to the living room where she was letting down the hems on the green curtains. He put some wood in the stove and sat down on the sofa. 'You were wrong about

Sigita,' he said.

'Oh, how do you make that out?'

'She's got a boyfriend. A very nice young man.' He looked round for the Alsatian. 'Where's Reksis?' he asked, wondering if Mrs Bilmane had taken him for a walk.

'In my room,' said his mother with a smile.

Puzzled, he went through to her bedroom where he found the Alsatian sitting under the window gazing up at the puppet. So hard was he concentrating that, apart from a brief thump of his tail, he completely ignored Arnis.

His mother followed him in. 'You'll get a stiff neck, Reksis,' she joked. Turning to Arnis, she added, 'He's fascinated by Sprīdītis.'

'He's probably jealous,' Arnis said. Reksis was very much a one-man dog and he was unlikely to appreciate any competition, even from a puppet ten feet above ground level.

'Ella called earlier,' Margarita announced quietly.

'How is she?' he replied without enthusiasm.

'She's coming to stay this weekend.'

'Stay? What? Here? How long for?' he said, filled with horror at the prospect.

'Just Friday and Saturday. Until Pēteris gets back from Tallinn. She'll go and stay with him on Sunday night.'

That raised a question in Arnis's mind. Why on earth was she coming when Pēteris...? He groaned inwardly. Get your brain in gear! he said to himself. Well, it had been a long day. Then, slowly, it began to dawn on him how he could take advantage of the situation. 'Mum, you don't mean this Saturday?'

'Yes, why?'

He didn't reply for a moment. He would have to play

this one carefully. 'Why don't I take the two of you out for lunch on Sunday?'

'That would be nice,' she agreed. 'We could go to Laiks. That new restaurant. Ella won't have been there.'

'OK, that's settled then. Oh, and if she calls again, tell her I'll meet her at the airport on Friday night.'

She looked at him suspiciously. 'What's got into you all of a sudden?'

'It'll look rude if I don't,' he said evenly. 'Especially as I've got to go out on Saturday.'

Giving him one of her I thought so looks, she said, 'Saturday? You never mentioned it.'

He told her he'd been invited to a medical society meeting in Kaunas, which was true, but he didn't add the fact he'd turned down the invitation and was going to Kuldīga instead.

'Well at least I'll have some good company,' she said.

That was exactly his own sentiment though he hadn't thought fate would intervene in such a timely manner. Had Ella not chosen to stay that weekend, he would have been concerned about leaving his mother for what would probably be a long day on her own, especially as she hadn't seemed so bright of late. But with Ella coming there was now no need to worry and he knew how much his mother would look forward to spending the day with her. Collecting Ella from the airport and taking them both out to lunch on Sunday was a small price to pay.

*

On Saturday morning he rose before his mother or Ella awoke and crept out of the flat with Reksis into a dawn that was colder than ever. Having been raised in Scotland, he was no stranger to cold. But there was cold and there was cold. Today it was at least fifteen degrees below and the wind from the east, which must have brought it down by another five degrees, cut through him like a scalpel. By the time he had dusted off the car and scraped the windows, his facial muscles felt as if they were in the first stages of rigor mortis and it took several squirts of de-icer before he teased the key into the lock.

He turned the ignition key and smiled, patting the dashboard as the engine purred into life. A thick mist obscured his view through the windscreen and enveloped both him and the dog as their breath turned into frozen air.

'Come on,' he muttered, clasping and unclasping the steering wheel, waiting for the welcome blast of warm air to start thawing his feet.

After a few more moments he eased off the handbrake and inched along the narrow street in the direction of the river. He was pleased to see they had cleared the main road and he headed off through the outskirts of the city, following the dual carriageway. He switched on the radio to catch the news headlines, then remembered he needed to check the oil.

As he drove into the filling station he began to think about Anita. It wasn't just that she reminded him of Penny. She was actually much brighter than Penny and, for the first time in his life, he realised he felt drawn to a woman not only physically and emotionally, but mentally as well. Penny had always said bright women intimidated him, that he would never have coped with someone like her cousin's wife who was an architect in Washington. Although he never said so, he agreed absolutely. He would have hated to be married to Virginia. She was bossy, talkative and boring with it. Much like Ella, but with brains, he thought wryly. In some unfathomable way Anita disturbed him too. He couldn't put his finger on it. But it scared him the way he connected with her.

He left the filling station and rapidly overtook a white bus on the open road. Glancing in his mirror, he caught sight of the destination blind. Kuldīga. Good. The road must be clear. Another couple of hours and he should be there.

The early morning sun floated like a pink sphere in the hazy frost amidst an unbroken width of pale blue sky. A landscape primordial in its simplicity, it was like going back to the beginning.

Half an hour later, he drew up at a T-junction. Leaning over the wheel he looked up and down the road. He frowned. This didn't seem right somehow. For one thing he couldn't remember seeing a saw mill so close to the highway. And the sun was straight ahead. That couldn't be right. He put his glasses on and unfolded the map to discover he'd taken a wrong turning a couple of miles back.

Tracing the main road with his finger he decided the quickest route was through Tukums, so he turned right. As he rounded the next bend the sight of a mill chimney with its vertically spiralling smoke brought a smile to his face. Force nought. How he'd enjoyed that as a boy, gauging the speed of the wind from the chimneys as he walked to school in the morning. Geography hadn't been his best subject but for some reason the Beaufort scale had stuck in his mind. Mr Mackie's diagrams had helped. They were a perfect model of simplicity with an ability to describe the complicated with a number. That had really appealed to him.

Arnis crossed an old stone bridge and came to the bus

station, bustling with people as bus stations always were. He smiled at the little old ladies standing in line, stamping their feet, muffled in layer upon layer, faces barely visible. How tough they were, with no thought of hypothermia.

He was soon back on the correct road and knew then he would still be in plenty of time to get to Siliņš's house before midday. The old man had said something about his granddaughter coming at five so he wanted to be sure they had enough time to talk before she arrived.

Then it struck him that he knew nothing about Siliņš. The old man had been very friendly that day in the café. He had spoken well of Arnis's father and was apparently delighted to see his mother, but Arnis was not naïve. He had no idea where Siliņš's political persuasions lay. Just because he had said his father was a good schoolteacher didn't mean he sympathised with his political stance. For all he knew the old man could have been a communist. Not that that would make any difference to his father now but he would have to tread carefully with him; work out whether he could trust what he said; weigh up his reactions.

Nothing in Latvia was ever quite what it seemed.

By the time he reached Kuldīga, he was feeling distinctly uneasy again. He motored over the now familiar bridge, passed the white church and stopped in the Town Square. He checked Siliņš's address, let Reksis out for a run round, then sauntered over to the row of wooden houses on the other side of the stream.

He singled one out and knocked on the door. Siliņš himself answered it. Wearing a pair of old grey trousers and a threadbare shirt, he looked older, more fragile than Arnis remembered.

The old man said nothing but turned round and tapped his way along the tiled floor, leading the way through a green door into a tiny room furnished only with a bed along one wall, a small table under the window, and a couple of brown armchairs. A log fire crackled in the grate and Siliņš banged on the back of one chair with the end of his stick, motioning Arnis to sit down.

'Tea?' he asked.

'No thanks,' Arnis replied 'Have you lived here all your life?' He wanted to get to know something about the old man before steering the conversation towards his father.

'Most of it. Except for a spell in Rīga. In forty-eight. I wanted to go to university.' He gave a harsh laugh and his face hardened. 'But with my past...' Arnis narrowed his eyes as the old man continued. 'The camp. Siberia. You couldn't go to university if you'd been there.'

He felt his heart miss a beat. 'Siberia? You were in Siberia?'

The old man looked surprised. 'Isn't that why you came? I thought you knew. I was there with your father.' Starting to stammer, the old man gazed into the fire. 'God, that place was a living hell. We had to work in the taiga ... cutting trees for railway sleepers.'

'Railway sleepers?'

'Yes, for a new railway line. It was horrible. In winter we had to start before it got light. There was never enough to eat ... a pound of bread if we were lucky. Thin soup made of rotten frozen potatoes. No meat. Bare boards to sleep on. No blankets. No heat in the huts.' The old man shivered demonstrably. 'In winter it dropped to fifty degrees below zero. Dozens of men died every day. We couldn't bury them because the ground was frozen so deep so their bodies got piled up in a corner of the camp.' He gazed into the fire and continued. 'By Christmas nearly all my friends were dead.'

Arnis was silent for a few moments, conscious he was undermining the old man's own story, but anxious to know about his father. 'My father? What happened to him?' he asked.

Siliņš shrugged. 'I don't know. He got so weak and thin he couldn't work. They let him go. Like me.'

Arnis felt his blood run cold. There was a part of him that had hoped Siliņš would say his father had died in the camp. 'What happened when you got back here?' he asked, wondering if the two of them had come back to Kuldīga together. 'Did you see him?'

Siliņš poked the fire with his stick, making sparks jump out on to the rug. It seemed an age before he replied. 'No. I never saw him after the camp.'

'You're sure?'

'I told you. No,' Siliņš said, beginning to show signs of irritation. 'Anyway you didn't go round looking for people. And they didn't look for you. Nobody wanted to know. They were scared if you'd been to the camp.' Then he raised his eyes from the burning embers. 'Besides, I came back after him.'

Sensing it would be counterproductive to press the old man any more at this stage, Arnis changed the subject. 'You remember that day when I was with my mother? You said my father taught you?'

'Yes.' The old man's face brightened. 'He was a wonderful teacher. History. I loved it. He made it come alive.'

That was exactly what the woman in London had said. Feeling a flicker of pride, he listened intently as Siliņš went on,

'He didn't stand a chance. Teaching history like that. Not that they needed a reason. Bloody Bolsheviks!' The old man started to riddle the fire furiously, nearly setting his stick alight.

'Were you and my father together in the truck?

'Yes, they took us to Rīga.'

Siliņš explained that thirty or forty of them had been squashed into a railway truck at Torņakalns. 'It was so full we had to take turns to lie down, and the toilet was a hole in the floor. They locked the doors with iron bars and surrounded the train with guards.'

'What happened then?'

'We were stuck in the station for days. No food and no water. A few people had food with them but no one thought to bring water. We didn't get any food until we got to Daugavpils,' Siliņš added. 'When we got there, some Latvians threw us some bread. Last decent bread we got.'

'Daugavpils. That's the route you took to Russia?'

'Yes.' The old man cleared his throat and gazed into the fire again. 'I was standing next to your father when we crossed the border. I'll never forget that. 'God bless Latvia!' your father shouted. Then we all started to sing.'

Feeling his heart well up with pride again, Arnis said quietly, 'Tell me more.'

Siliņš got up and fetched his pipe from the mantelpiece. 'They took us to Moscow. Some of the men were dragged off there. And I mean dragged off. They were barely alive. Then we heard them shouting people's names outside on the platform. Then more trains came. Estonians, Lithuanians, more Latvians. We were there for days. But that wasn't the worst of it.' Chewing on his pipe, the old man continued his story. 'We started to roll again. We knew we were going east. Sometimes we'd get stuck in sidings. We hadn't got a clue what was going on. It was so hot. We didn't all survive. Then they made us get out. Krasnoyarsk ... that was the name of the place.'

Arnis nodded. That corresponded with the record in the ledger in Rīga. He gazed at the old man's face. Devoid of emotion, Siliņš seemed disembodied, as if the whole thing had happened to someone else.

'What happened after you were released?' Arnis asked him, wanting to be sure the old man really hadn't seen his father again.

Siliņš didn't reply for a moment. 'Can you pass me a bit of that paper,' he said pointing to the newspaper on the table. He tore a piece off and rolled it in the palm of his hand, making a thin taper which he placed in the fire to light his pipe. He took a few puffs and scratched his beard. 'They gave me a few roubles and told me to go. I walked to Krasnoyarsk then I got a train to Moscow. Moscow was a mess. But I found a train to Rīga. Then Jelgava. I walked back from there. It took me the best part of a week.'

'Do you remember anything else about my father?' Arnis asked, still hoping to jog some long-forgotten memory in the old man's mind.

Siliņš thought for a moment, 'I'll have to fetch some wood.' He got up and shuffled out through the back door to the wooden veranda, letting a blast of icy cold air into the house.

He came back and placed a couple of logs on the fire. As he turned round, Arnis noticed his expression had changed, displaying a passion he hadn't seen so far.

'Maybe you know this, already ... I don't know if your

poor mother ever found out,' he said seeming uncertain as to whether he should go on.

'What do you mean?' said Arnis, feeling his scalp start to tingle.

'Does the name Edgars Kurmis mean anything to you?'

'No,' Arnis replied, his eyes narrowing.

Siliņš took another puff of his pipe. 'Maybe it would be better if you didn't know … but now I've started …' He stared out of the window where the snow was piling high on the window ledge, before turning to face Arnis again. 'Perhaps I was the only one who saw him.'

Arnis began to feel impatient with the old man. 'Saw him? Saw who?' he said, raising his voice.

'Kurmis. Edgars Kurmis,' Siliņš replied vehemently.

'Who is Kurmis?'

'He's the man who told the Cheka about your father. I was there. I saw it with my own eyes.'

'Go on,' Arnis said with a calmness in his voice that belied the churning in his stomach.

'They came here first, banging on the door in the middle of the night. They made me get dressed … ordered me into the back of the lorry.'

Arnis nodded. This was exactly as his mother had described it. 'But what about Kurmis?'

'I'd tell you if you didn't keep interrupting.' The old man's face was beginning to turn red with anger. 'They drove through the square, turned into Liepājas iela, then stopped on the corner. They started talking to someone outside the truck. I recognised the voice immediately. It was Edgars Kurmis. Do you know something? He was my brother's best friend.' Beginning to stammer again, Siliņš explained that Kurmis had passed a small box to the men in the truck. 'Then he gave them your father's name. 'Kārlis Vilks,' he said. 'He lives on Raina iela. Number 7.' I heard him.'

'Are you sure about this?'

'Sure?' The old man spluttered. 'Of course I'm sure. I told you. He was my brother's best friend. Your father's house was the next place we stopped.'

Arnis began to feel angry. 'Is Kurmis still in Kuldīga?'

'No. God knows what happened to him. Or his family. They probably went back to Russia.'

'Russia?' Arnis frowned. Kurmis was a very Latvian name.

'Yes. His parents came back from Russia after the First World War. They were refugees.'

Arnis nodded. A large number of people had fled from Kuldīga and the surrounding area during the First World War.

The old man took a few more puffs of his pipe before speaking again. 'I was so pleased to see your mother when you were with her in Kuldīga that day. Your father was worried about her. He'd sent her to hide in the attic, and told them she was visiting her sister. He was sure they'd go back and find her. But they didn't?'

'No. We left Kuldīga and went to Britain.'

'Your father would have been so thankful if he'd known that. He thought the world of your mother.' Then he stared at Arnis. 'So, he also had a son. He didn't say anything about your mother expecting a baby. Perhaps he didn't know?'

'Possibly. I wasn't born until the following February.' Not for the first time, Arnis felt upset that his father hadn't known anything about him.

'So, you never heard from him?' Siliņš said.

'No, we didn't. And you didn't hear or see anything of him when you came back to Kuldīga?' said Arnis wanting to be absolutely certain.

'No, I didn't. Nor Edgars Kurmis.' Siliņš gave a harsh laugh. 'I don't know what I would have done if I had seen him. I never forgave him after what I saw and heard from that truck,' he continued. 'He was a friend of the family. Yet, to my knowledge, he wasn't a member of the Komsomol or the District Communist Party. But after that, I did wonder whether his whole family wasn't Bolshevik. Then I heard his sister had been detained in the Cheka building in Kuldīga. Not that that means anything.'

Arnis nodded again. A victim and a perpetrator in one family was not unheard of.

Noticing the old man was now looking very tired, Arnis got up to leave. He fetched his coat and shook Siliņš' hand warmly.

'Thanks for telling your story. I really appreciate it. And if you do ever remember anything else …'

The old man nodded and Arnis left.

It was dark outside, but he needed a walk before driving back to Rīga. He went back to the car for Reksis and then headed back in the direction of the old man's house. He strolled along the street passing a row of wooden houses on either side, their roofs projecting in deep eaves beneath which logs were stacked for the winter. The smell of wood smoke percolated through the freezing air and light from the long low windows pooled onto the icy track.

In the distance a cockrel crowed, but otherwise the town was wrapped in a cloak of silence. At the end of the row of houses, there was a patch of waste ground, and then on the right a large brick building came into view. It seemed slightly out of place among the older wooden buildings and he stopped to look at it. In Britain it might have been a library or council offices, or perhaps a police station, but there were no lights on.

Staring at the entrance he noticed two arched doorways. Scarely daring to believe what he was thinking he called te dog and stepped forward, wishing that he had brought a torch. But as his eyes grew accustomed to the dark, he was able to see the archways more clearly. Over one, etched in the brick was the word boys, over the other girls. He felt a slight flutter in his stomach. Had this been his father's school? Was this where his father had taught? He went to the central door and turned the handle. Nothing.

Then he crouched down and peered through the keyhole. He could just make out a large hallway with a wide staircase on the right. The floor was covered in dust sheets and there were a couple of tins of paint at the bottom of the stairs. Otherwise it seemed to be empty. He walked round the building, hauling himself up at each window ledge to get a glimpse inside. Apart from a table tennis table in one room and a sink and cooker in another, he couldn't see anything. He went back to the street and glanced up and down hoping there might be someone he could ask. But it was deserted. Then, suddenly, Reksis barked and rushed off towards a narrow alleyway from where a young man, probably about Antons's age, appeared.

'Excuse me,' said Arnis.

The young man stopped.

'Is this… was this a school?'

'Yes, a long time ago' he replied casually.

'When?'

He shrugged. 'I don't know exactly. Not in my time. I went to the new school. You need to talk to the older people. They'll know.' With that he went off in the direction of the town.

Arnis stared at the building again before calling to Reksis then began to make his way back up the icy street. As he approached Siliņš's house, he noticed the lights were on in the front so he knocked on the door.

'You still here?' said the old man.

'The red brick building down the street...'

But Siliņš didn't let him finish. 'You found it then. I thought you might have been there last time. Yes, that was where your father taught.'

Arnis smiled. 'Thank you. You have been so helpful. I won't forget the help you've given me.' He wished he had been thoughtful enough to bring the old man a present, some vodka perhaps, but he hadn't even taken the trouble to notice whether there were any bottles in the house, so he couldn't be sure what Siliņš would like if he came again. He was angry with himself for that. The old man had told him a lot, and it hadn't been easy for him.

Deep in thought he drove back to Rīga. Visiting Siliņš had served to increase his certainty that his father had been released from the Siberian camp but he still couldn't be sure he'd made it back to Kuldīga. And there were people who claimed to have seen him in Australia.

But what about his mother? She'd often said what a lucky escape she'd had that night his father had been deported, and Siliņš had confirmed that. He wondered if she'd ever heard about Kurmis. Had anyone apart from Siliņš seen him that night? But she hadn't said anything - just that two men had come to the house and taken his father away in a truck.

Thinking of Kurmis made him furious. That man had ruined his mother's life; and his too. Had his father not been deported that night, they could have fled Kuldīga together. The boys at school wouldn't have called his father a criminal. His mother wouldn't have had to work so hard. Thoughts rattled round his brain like sweets in a jar.

Then, as his mind calmed slightly, he began to wonder whether his father would ever have left Latvia. More likely, when the Russians came back in 1945, he would have gone underground and joined the resistance. They would all have stayed in Kuldīga. How different life would have been. They might all have been sent to Siberia.

But none of that made it any clearer or better.

Only one thing was certain. If Arnis ever met Kurmis he would want to make him suffer the way his mother had suffered. What made it worse was that Kurmis was Latvian. Had be been Russian he could have coped with it better. But a Latvian informing on a fellow countryman, particularly in a town of this size... It was not surprising he was no longer in Kuldīga.

*

By the time Arnis approached the outskirts of Rīga, the next stage of his search had become clear: he would contact the Latvian community in Australia. He got back to the flat shortly after nine to find his mother had gone to bed. Ella had not.

'We had a lovely day,' she said. 'Your mother showed me Sprīdītis and talked about your father. I've never heard her talk about him so much before.

Arnis felt angry. Had his mother not been in bed he would have asked her why she never talked to him about his father. Instead he turned to Ella. 'What did she say?'

'Oh, it was mostly about the puppet. How your father carved it. Arnis. I think it's a lovely story.' She smiled wistfully. 'I envy you.'

'Envy?' he said, not feeling the most enviable person on the earth at that moment.

'Yes,' Ella continued. 'Your parents thought the world of each other. My father went off with another woman when I was five. My mother never loved him. She only married him because he said he was going to America. As you know, we didn't get there,' she said, referring to the fact that they had gone to Britain via Germany and stayed on in England because her father got a job there. 'You should be thankful. Your mother and father adored each other.'

CHAPTER 11

The next day was fairly quiet at the surgery and Arnis spent most of it thinking about Anita. By ten past five he was almost ready to leave when Sigita appeared in the consulting room.

'You can't go home yet,' she said. 'Mr Bērziņš is due at half past five.'

'Half past five! Sigita, I told you I didn't want any appointments after five.'

'Sorry,' she replied sheepishly. 'I thought you said that was tomorrow.'

'No, today.'

He gave a despairing sigh but then calmed down. Sigita didn't often get things wrong so there was no point in getting angry. It was just unfortunate she had made the mistake on the evening he was due to see Anita again. They had arranged to meet at half past six so that left him no time to go home and change.

'I could try phoning Mr Bērziņš,' Sigita suggested.

'Don't bother,' Arnis replied, cramming his newspaper into his briefcase.

Without another word, Sigita disappeared into the waiting room and he opened his desk drawer searching for the stapler to fasten together his meeting notes for the next day. He rummaged amongst the pile of prescription pads without success then he spotted it on the bookshelf in front of him.

Just at that moment, the doorbell rang.

Mr Bērziņš had arrived early and all he wanted was a repeat prescription. Relief! Arnis quickly scribbled the three items on the prescription pad and left Sigita to lock up.

He arrived home with ten minutes to spare. He had a quick shower, changed into his charcoal grey suit and red and black spotted tie, then he set out for the Laima clock.

He had seen Salome once before, many years ago with Penny, but he couldn't remember anything about it – opera was not really his scene and never had been. He wished he had made an effort to find out earlier in the day. If only he hadn't been in such a rush. He wondered if he might buy a programme before she arrived. At least then he could flip through the contents and appear a little more knowledgeable. But as he turned left into Kaļķu iela, he realised he would hardly have time to get to the opera house and back, never mind skim through the programme, so he carried on down the street towards the clock.

As he spotted the luminous face, he smiled to himself. How often his mother had spoken of the Laima clock when he was growing up.

'It was everyone's favourite meeting place,' she'd told him, explaining that she and her sister used to meet their aunt there, who would then drive them to Jūrmala for their summer holiday. 'Our holiday began at the Laima clock,' she would say. 'Benita and I used to bet each other ten santimi as to which of us would catch the first glimpse of it when we walked up from the station.'

When he had visited Rīga for the first time, it was the main thing he'd looked for but it didn't occur to him that, ten years later, he would also be meeting someone there.

He was surprised to see that Anita was already waiting. 'It's like World War Three in there,' she said, laughing and looking towards McDonalds, brushing a few flakes of snow off the lapels of her long navy blue coat. 'Some kid's birthday party. I only went in for a cup of coffee. It was manic.' Her emerald eyes reflected the light from the clock and he felt a tingle of expectancy coursing through his veins.

They walked across to the opera house, took their coats to the cloakroom and found their seats. It was already comfortably full when the orchestra began to tune up and Anita leaned forward. 'Just seeing if I can spot my cousin,' she said. 'He plays the cello.'

'Have you seen this before?' Arnis asked

'Salome? Yes. The last time I saw it was in London.'

'London?'

'Mmm, at Covent Garden. Have I got the name right?'

He nodded. 'That must have been expensive.'

She grinned and shook her head. 'Three pounds.'

'Three pounds! You must have had to stand for that.'

'Yes. And we had to queue for two hours to get the tickets. But it wasn't so difficult and it was well worth the wait. Still, I'm sure tonight will be just as good. This is supposed to be a superb production.'

Within seconds of the start, Anita was completely entranced. Sitting close to her again, smelling her perfume, and glancing at her from the corner of his eye on numerous occasions, his own thoughts were far from the orchestra or the music.

During the interval they went to the foyer and had a glass of wine and some canapés. When they got back to their seats, without thinking, he took her hand in his. She didn't resist and the softness of her skin, and the warmth, caused his heart to miss a few beats. As the lights dimmed he felt her leg pressing against his, just lightly but making firm contact that lasted through to the end of the final act.

They went to fetch their coats and made their way out of the concert hall. There had been another fall of snow and the branches were laden inches deep; the frozen canal was white without so much as a webbed footprint to disturb its icy perfection. The wind had dropped, leaving the air absolutely still and a myriad of stars patterned the dark blue sky. Even the trams were hushed, their quintessential rumble muffled by the snow on the sets as they ploughed their way along creating tiny fountains of whiteness.

As they walked, she chatted happily about the performance, apparently unconcerned that he had almost nothing to say about it. Maybe she sensed how little of it he had taken in. Perhaps she knew how much she had distracted him.

They stopped and gazed across the park and Arnis said, 'Do you fancy something to eat? You know that new place on the other side of Valdemāra. The food's good and you can have a conversation without having to shout.'

'Sounds good to me,' she replied. 'I only live round the corner from there. Let's go for it.'

They retraced their steps through the park and crossed Valdemāra. The icy cobbles gleamed under the streetlights and they continued walking until they reached the restaurant.

The steps led down to a large cellar divided across the centre by a brick fireplace. Arnis took her coat and they found a table opposite the log fire. Anita opened the menu and he stared at her as she sat with her hands under her knees studying it. She looked even lovelier tonight, her sylph-like figure shown off to best advantage in a straight black velvet skirt that finished just above her knees. She looked up for a second and teased a stray hair from her shoulder then her attention returned to the menu.

As she looked down, Arnis's interest was attracted to her breasts, firm and shapely, clinging to the underside of her fine black-ribbed jumper. He found he couldn't avert his eyes, not even when she looked up again, her face reflecting the glow of the candle. Responding with obvious pleasure, she gave a half smile and took a sip of water, resting her tongue momentarily on her bottom lip before looking down at the menu again.

'I'm going to go for the carp,' she said. 'And the spinach salad. You?'

'I think I'll settle for the steak,' he said, unable to concentrate on the detail of the menu.

After the waitress had taken their order, Anita leaned back in her chair and crossed her legs. 'It's nice to have a night off,' she commented.

'What are you working on at the moment?' he asked.

'An article on the new heart unit at the hospital. I spent most of the morning talking to one of the cardiologists ... Pauls Rubenis.'

'Rubenis!' Not Rubenis! Of all people. Only yesterday Arnis had argued again with the consultant because he was refusing to see one of his patients.

'You know him?' Anita asked.

'I certainly do.' If there was any anger in his voice it seemed to have passed over Anita's head.

'He seems to be doing good things at the hospital,' she

continued. 'They've started doing angiography. And he's got brand new Echo equipment. It was all very impressive. He's invited me to go back again when it's all done. Said it would give him an incentive to get it finished quickly,' she added with a grin.

'That's a good line. I'll have to remember that one.'

Annoyed that she seemed to have been so easily impressed by his bête noir he added icily, 'I hope you asked him where he gets the money from.'

'Donations from overseas.'

'That's what he told you?' Did she really believe that? He looked at her face and couldn't decide whether she did or not. But if she was that gullible, she wasn't the woman he'd thought she was. Only last week Mrs Dragunova had told him Rubenis was charging his patients extortionate sums of money for their treatment even though patients at the hospital should actually be getting most of their treatment free. The problem was most patients didn't know that. When unscrupulous people like Rubenis asked them for money they were too scared to question it so they paid up. Sometimes he felt as if he was the only person in Rīga to have any integrity at all.

'You obviously know something I don't,' Anita said with a grin.

Having no wish to see 'British Latvian GP says hospital system is corrupt' blasted across the front page of *Diena*, he said nothing except, 'You should write an article telling patients what they can get for free and what they have to pay for. Since the system changed, they really don't know.' He noticed her lips starting to twitch and he couldn't help but smile. She knew exactly what he was talking about. But he didn't pursue it as he noticed the waitress approaching their table. 'Here comes the food.'

His steak was delicious and he ate quickly, finishing before she was halfway through her carp. His mother had always discouraged him eating slowly and it was a habit he'd found impossible to break. But he wished he was more sophisticated, especially on an occasion like this. As he watched Anita savouring every mouthful of her carp, every leaf of spinach, he began to feel embarrassed.

But, if she noticed, she gave no hint of it. When she had finished she gave a long satisfied sigh and patted her stomach. 'That was excellent. I'd certainly come here again.'

'Would you like a dessert?' he asked.

'Yes, please' she replied with a smile. 'I wonder if they have Rupjmaizes Kārtojums. I love it but I'm too lazy to make it at home. What about you? Are you going to join me?'

'No, but I'll have an ice cream.' Much as he liked sweet things, he was not very keen on the dark bread and dried fruit mixture.

He signalled the waitress and poured the last of the wine. The desserts appeared almost immediately.

'Wonderful,' she said, as she savoured the dark moist bread, running her tongue round her lips. 'There's a lot of brandy in this one.' She rocked her chair back against the wall, then rested her left knee on the edge of the table, letting her skirt fall a couple of inches down her thigh as she carefully scraped round the edge of the bowl.

His eye rested on the hem of her skirt, longing to trace the edge of it with his index finger, and he began to be aware of his quickening pulse. As their eyes met he sensed a trace of a blush in her cheeks.

'Coffee?' he said with a half smile.

She looked at her watch and shook her head. 'No, it's getting late.'

Arnis took a deep breath and called the waiter. 'Lūdzu, rēkinu!'

He paid the bill and they left the restaurant, walking back in the direction of the old town, the snow falling gently, crunching underneath their feet. When they reached the second set of crossroads, she paused. 'This is where I live,' she said pointing along Alberta iela to one of the magnificent Art Nouveau buildings on the right. 'On the top floor.'

He took her hands in his and she shook the snow from her mane of auburn hair as she lifted her face. He kissed her, gently at first, relishing her full soft lips, probing the inside of her mouth with his tongue. His hands moved round her waist and he pulled her even closer. He moved his mouth to her ear, kissing the tip, nuzzling her hair against his cheek before moving back to her lips again.

After a few moments she pulled away, then, lowering her eyelids, she traced her finger round the edge of his lips. 'I've got an early start tomorrow,' she said.

He sighed and ran his fingers through her hair, pulling her close again, not wanting to let her go. 'When can I see you again,' he murmured.

'Sunday?'

'Sunday's fine,' he said.

Then he kissed her again. As he felt the tip of her tongue against his own he began to feel he would burst. When she eventually withdrew, he squeezed her hand before she walked away down the street. He walked slowly in the opposite direction, glancing backwards often. Only when he reached the other side of the park was he no longer aware of his heartbeat.

*

Over the next few days he tried to concentrate on his work and devoted such spare time as he had to seeing what he could find out about the Latvian community in Australia. He found the address for their association and wrote them a letter, telling them he had grounds for believing his father might have arrived in Australia as a refugee after the Second World War. He still had many doubts that his father had actually left Latvia but he had no intention of leaving any stone unturned. Whatever the Australian Latvians said, it might help him to get closer to the truth.

*

Sunday was a cold but beautiful day so he called Anita to suggest that they go for a walk on the beach. She agreed. Not knowing whether she liked dogs or not, he took Reksis out for a walk and then set off for her flat.

Ten minutes later he turned into a wide cobbled street. On the left hand side was a row of elegant houses. Theatrical facades in shades of pink, primrose yellow, pale green and coffee and cream. A mermaid above one entrance, a pair of owls above another, a bearded giant looking as if he'd mocked every passer-by for the last hundred years. A wrought iron balcony flanked by two angels, each bearing a long slender trumpet. Ornate pediments, oval windows, rich reliefs, a confusing interplay of gables, an occasional onion topped tower. Nowhere else in the city was Arnis quite so conscious of one-upmanship as each brilliant design effortlessly outdid the next. How it all worked together in one street was beyond his understanding. But it did and the fine decorative effects on

192

each building complemented each other beautifully.

He approached the house where Anita had her apartment. She was waiting outside leaning against one of the stone sphinxes that guarded the entrance. They drove off to Jūrmala where he parked in his usual spot and they made their way through the forest to the beach. The sand was covered with a light dusting of snow and tiny pale grey clouds chased each other across the duck-egg coloured sky. They ambled hand in hand towards Dubulti.

As they approached a large wooden house with pale green turrets, a young woman emerged from the pine trees. 'Anita,' she called, rushing across the sand dunes, her wavy blonde hair falling over her face.

'Renāte. Gosh, it's been ages,' said Anita. 'A friend of mine,' she said turning to Arnis. 'Let me introduce you.'

He groaned inwardly, hoping that Renate was not going to join them on their walk.

'So, you haven't got the stall any longer?' Renate said.

'No, thank goodness. Except in the summer.' Looking at Arnis, she explained, 'Renāte and I used to have stalls next to each other outside St Peter's on a Sunday. She sold CDs and I had jewellery.'

'Yes, and it's not something you miss in this weather,' said Renāte with a grin. 'How's Linda?'

'Linda. Oh, OK. She's over her morning sickness,' replied Anita.

'So we'll be able to call you granny any time soon? How does it feel to be old?'

'Hey, less of the old!'

Renāte laughed. 'I must go,' she said, giving Arnis a quick glance. 'But how about lunch next week?'

193

'Yes, that would be nice,' Anita responded. 'I'll give you a call.'

With that Renāte walked off in the opposite direction and Arnis heaved an inward sigh of relief.

'Renāte's an old schoolfriend of my daughter's,' explained Anita. 'I used to work with her mother when I was a lab technician.'

'You never told me you had a daughter,' he said.

'You didn't ask,' she replied.

'Does she live in Rīga?'

'No, in Berlin. Her husband's a psychologist.'

Arnis thought he detected a hint of disapproval in her voice.

'It sounds like you don't have much time for him.'

'You're right, I haven't. He's too much like Linda's father.'

He guessed she probably didn't want to talk about that part of her life so he said nothing. As they carried on walking, she put her hands in her coat pockets and stared out to sea. 'We split up ten years ago,' she said. 'He's married again now and the silly woman's welcome to him,' she added with more than a trace of rancour. Then she fell silent for a few moments before continuing in a more even tone. 'If we hadn't lived with my parents it might have been better. I don't know. My father never had any time for Ēriks. He said it was Ēriks who got him sent to prison.'

'Prison? Your father was in prison?'

'Yes, twice. On account of his writing. The police raided the flat and my father always reckoned it was Ēriks who split on him. Fortunately, my mother and uncle had been out the night before distributing most of what he'd written

194

and the police didn't look under the floorboards.'

'Which is where he hid it?'

'Yes, Daddy thought he'd got away with it but a few days later they came back and took him to prison. I thought it was a neighbour who'd told them, but my father was convinced it was Ēriks. To this day, I really don't know...'

'How long was your father in prison?'

'Six months, the first time. But when he came out, he carried on writing. Nothing would deter him. But we were always being watched. One day we had a new TV delivered, but we never switched it on because my father was sure it was bugged. Not that we missed watching television.' She gave a half smile. 'It was a joke. Brezhnev used to come on with a monologue of propaganada every evening. That's the time everyone used to walk their dogs.' They both laughed. 'It was a crazy system.' Then she continued. 'At school we had to mark the anniversary of the 1917 revolution every year. The teacher put a model of the *Aurora* in the classroom which we had to decorate with red ribbon. We had to remember the death of Stalin too - every single year. Sometimes I would say I had a bad stomach to get the day off school, but that was noticed, of course.'

Arnis nodded, and they were both silent for a few moments until Anita spoke again. 'I was telling you about my father. A year after he came out of prison, he was back in again. They picked him up one night when he was on his way home from work.'

'What was his job?'

'He assembled radios at the Vef factory. They were waiting for him when he got off the tram. That time he was in prison for two years. We got a letter once a month. That was all. My mother was allowed to visit but I wasn't.' She turned to look at him, her eyes full of tears. 'By the time he came out, he was so thin. His chest was in a terrible state. He died two years later...'

At a loss for words, he took hold of her hand and squeezed it tenderly.

'I'm sorry,' she said. 'I didn't mean to be miserable. At least he lived long enough to see Latvia independent again. But I have much to thank him for. I wouldn't be writing if it wasn't for him. He was always my best critic. Right from childhood ... when I wrote poetry.'

'So you write poetry too?'

'You sound surprised,' she said with a smile.

'Well...' She was right.

'Come on, out with it. Why are you surprised that I've written poetry?'

'I haven't known many poets but none of them were like you.'

'What's that supposed to mean?'

'I tend to think of poets as fragile characters. Perhaps with a tendency to be melancholic,' he added, trying to choose his words carefully. 'You're not like that at all,' he added quickly.

She held his gaze for a moment. 'Maybe you just don't know me well enough. Anyway, a lot of Latvians write poetry.'

He nodded. 'Like the Welsh.' This was not the first time he had observed the similarities between the two countries.

'Yes, I'd like to go to Wales. The Eisteddfod... am I pronouncing it right?' He nodded. 'It sounds as if it might

196

have something in common with our song festivals here. I met a Welsh journalist once at a meeting. He told me in Wales a great deal of oral tradition had been passed down through poetry and songs. It was interesting.'

'Yes, Welsh is a poetic language. Like Latvian, it lends itself to verse. How much poetry have you written?'

'A lot when I was in my teens. But I stopped soon after I left school. I haven't written any for years.'

'Why?' Admiring anyone who could write creatively, he thought it a pity that she should have given up something she was perhaps gifted at.

Anita laughed. 'Not you as well! My mother is always saying I should start again but I don't have the energy any more. It was easy when I was a cleaner at the children's hospital. I had nothing else to think about while I was pushing a mop around.' She gave him a wistful look. 'Do you know I couldn't get a place at university because of my father?'

'That doesn't exactly surprise me but he'd have been proud of you now,' Arnis said with a half smile.

'I hope so. You know, when I write something, it's almost as if he's still watching me … waiting to read it. That keeps me up half the night sometimes, I can tell you.' She laughed again. 'When I think of some of the articles I have had published, I'm sure he'd have made me re-write them.'

Arnis nodded. He'd often thought that his own father would have been the same when he was working for his exams. But it never happened. How he had missed having a father who would have been proud of him.

Anita continued, 'One thing I've done would have pleased him though.'

'What's that?'

'I've got his house back.'

'The one you're living in now? On Alberta iela?'

'Yes. He was born there ... but the Russians commandeered it. After Daddy died, I was determined to get it back. As if it was the only way I could make sense of everything that happened to him. When I did get it back, it was a wreck, and there's still a lot to do. As you'll see later,' she added with a grin.

Dusk was drawing in when they got back to the car. As they drove back to Rīga, Anita asked him about Penny. 'You never mention her,' she said. 'Did you love her?'

Taken aback at the directness of her question he did not reply immediately. 'Yes, I did, at first... then later on. When the boys were growing up...they were diffcult years.

'They usually are.'

'She wanted to go out to work.'

'She was lucky not to have to.'

'Perhaps.' He had to admit that was exactly what he had thought at the time. And he knew where Anita was coming from. Mothers had not stayed at home during the Soviet period. Everyone had had to work. Not that he could imagine Anita being happy to spend all her time on domestic tasks. She would have been bored, just the same as Penny had been; probably even more so.

'We ought to try that new restaurant near Centrs sometime.'

'Yes.' She looked at him. He could tell that she knew he was changing the subject. But he didn't like talking about his family. It wasn't just Penny. He'd never talked about his mother either, or the boys very much. It was a hangover from his school days when his mother had told him not to talk about his father. It had been compounded by the boys in his class who had accused his father of being a criminal, and the postman's son who had laughed at his mother for being frightened to open the door. He had got into the habit of not saying anything about his family. It was less painful. Though he felt a growing connectednness with Anita, he still could not bring himself to talk about his mother.

As they approached the city, he began to fear that he had destroyed the magic of the afternoon. But as he drew the car to a standstill outside her flat, she said 'Are you going to come in?'

He nodded and followed her up the steps with a sense of expectation. It was as if she was the woman he had been waiting for for a very long time. They entered a dark, green painted hallway with a disused lift in the middle and a spiral stairway encircling it. The black and white tiles on the floor echoed to the sound of their footsteps. When they reached the bottom of the stairs, he couldn't wait for a moment longer. He pulled her to him and kissed her. Her mouth opened willingly and he felt the responsive quiver of her tongue on his. He slid his hand under her coat and fondled her hip, her buttocks, then he lifted her skirt and found the smooth bare skin at the top of her leg. It was a long time since he'd been intimate with any woman and it was equally long since his heart had pumped so furiously. He stroked her thigh, ran his fingers round the top of her stocking and heard her sharp intake of breath. She wanted this as much as he did. He kissed her again and her mouth responded more urgently than ever until eventually she took hold of his hand and pulled him up the stairs.

Later, as they lay still entwined on the rug in front of

the fire, Arnis was pleasantly relieved there had been no trace of awkwardness between them. It had been so long since he'd made love he feared his own nervous anxiety might spoil everything yet it had all proved so effortless, as though he and Anita had made love together hundreds of times before. She had responded with a passion that delighted yet, at the same time, scared him. The same passion he had sensed within her the moment she had walked into the surgery. And now it was almost impossible to believe that was only two weeks ago.

*

Over the next couple of weeks they saw each other frequently – listening to more concerts, enjoying meals out, occasionally taking in a film. One night after she'd cooked them dinner at her flat, she got out some of her poetry. While she was clearing away the dishes, he sat on the sofa and began to read from the soft-backed red book.

'What do you think?' she said when she brought the coffee.

'Some of it's good. Very, very good.'

'What about 'Rīga in the Autumn'? What did you think of that?

'I don't think it's the best.' He looked at her uncertainly. 'I hope you're not offended.'

'Of course not. I wouldn't have shown them to you if I didn't want an honest opinion.'

'I love the one about the fisherman,' Arnis said enthusiastically.

She smiled. 'That was my father's favourite too. It was one of the first I wrote. He and I often used to go for walks together along the Lielupe.'

'Do I remind you of your father?' As soon as he'd asked the question, he felt embarrassed.

But she did not seem at all flustered. 'Yes, you do,' she replied. 'Not to look at. He was short and thin.' They both laughed. 'He was very generous, very kind...'

'But...'He could tell there was one.

She hesitated as if she wasn't sure whether to continue. 'He was a very private person. Even with his family. There were things he wouldn't talk about. Mother said the same. I don't think she minded.'

He swallowed. 'But you did.'

'I suppose he didn't want to burden us. Things were hard for him. But I wish he'd told me more. I could have understood. It's left me feeling I didn't really know him...'

'And you think I'm the same?'

'I don't know whether you have things you don't talk about. But you never talk about your family.'

'There's nothing to say.'

He wanted to change the subject, and fortunately Anita did it for him. 'My father was a serious person too.' Then, as if she'd seen the expression on his face, she added, 'Hey, that's not a criticism. I have no time for frivolous people.'

He smiled. 'You were talking about your poetry. The one about the fisherman. Did those walks along the Lielupe inspire it?'

'Yes.'

'You should write more.'

She hesitated for a moment. 'Actually, I am. I've just started again. These last few weeks...' She ran her hand through her hair and began to pour the coffee.

Arnis waited for her to continue but she began to talk

of the article she had to write for *Diena* by tomorrow morning.
'I haven't even started it yet,' she said.

'What's it about?'

'The flu epidemic forecast for the New Year. I already
know what I'm going to say so it won't take me more than a
couple of hours.'

He took her in his arms and gave her a lingering kiss.
'So, you're not throwing me out when I've finished my
coffee?'

'Absolutely not,' she said, beginning to unfasten his tie.

During the last few weeks before Christmas, Arnis felt his life
had really taken a turn for the better. He was enjoying being in
Latvia, rarely missing London. He relished the independence
he had at work, being able to use his skills and years of
experience in a new setting. Many things were still cheaper
than in London. As one of his British patients had said on more
than occasion, ten pounds went a long way in Rīga. The
concerts were even better than he had expected. And it was
wonderful having someone to share them with. Meeting Anita
made him realise how lonely he had been.

He found it difficult to accept her being away so much,
but he knew that she loved her work - and the travel which
was still so new for her. The last time they'd met she had
talked with great excitement of a conference coming up in
Chicago next year. Never having been to America before, she
was determined to go. No matter that it would mean sleeping
on a friend's floor for a week.

*

One night, they left the Dom after a concert and walked hand
in hand across the square. A cold wind blew angry gusts of

snowflakes against their cheeks. She had to be up early the next day to drive to Helsinki to report a cancer meeting so he did not suggest going back to her flat. 'What time will you be back on Thursday?' he asked her, planning where he could take her for dinner.

'It depends on which boat I get on. I haven't booked the return ferry to Tallinn. I might even stay on an extra night.'

She sounded so casual that he felt hurt. Why would she want to stay on in Helsinki? He hated the idea of her being away for longer than her work made it necessary. 'I'll have to come with you next time,' he said. He thought he could see a momentary flash of anger in her eyes, but she said nothing. He felt a stab of jealousy, wondering whether she had a lover. European medical conferences tended to draw the same group of people. Perhaps she had someone she met regularly. Perhaps that's why she was thinking of staying on in Helsinki.

'I'll call you when I get back,' she said with a firmness which told him she did not want him to call her. Then she gave him a quick kiss on the cheek and hurried away.

CHAPTER 12

Anita came back on the Friday night but said she couldn't see him until the Sunday because she had a huge report to write. They arranged to meet for lunch, and having had a busy week, Arnis decided to take it easy in the morning so he stayed in bed listening to the radio. His mother brought him a cup of coffee and as she went out into the hall, the telephone began to ring. 'It's Anita,' she called and brought the handset through to his bedroom. He took it off her and waited until she left the room.

'Hi. Are you OK?'

'Yes... I mean no,' she replied. 'Something's come up. I can't see you today.'

'What? Have you got some unexpected deadline to meet?'

'Er ... no, not exactly.'

'What then?'

'Sorry, Arnis, but I'm going to Germany.'

'Germany?' His heart sank. 'How long for? For work?'

'No, I'm going to stay with Linda.'

'Linda! Is there a problem with the baby?'

'No ... except it's due soon.'

'I thought you said it was due in January. We're not halfway through December yet.' He'd expected her to go nearer the time. In fact he'd been dreading it because he knew how much he was going to miss her. 'You mean you're going to stay in Berlin for two months?'

'I don't know. Maybe. It is my first grandchild,' she said in a small voice.

'But when will I see you?'

'I don't know, Arnis. I need to think … I need some space…'

'What does that mean? You don't want to see me?'

'I'm not sure … this is all going a bit too fast for me.

'We don't have to see each other so often, if that's what you want.' He hated the idea but if that was what it took…

'Arnis, it's not that.' She fell silent as if she was wondering whether to continue. 'My life isn't my own any more. You want to know where I am, what I'm doing, who I'm with.' She began to sound angry. 'Look I'll call you when I get to Berlin.'

'When are you going?'

She hesitated for a moment before she spoke. The answer was not what Arnis expected. 'I'm calling from the airport,' she said. 'I'm just about to board the plane. I'm so sorry, Arnis. Believe me.' With that, she switched off her mobile not even allowing him a chance to say goodbye.

He lay back in bed, feeling puzzled and hurt. He found it hard to take in what she'd said to him. Her departure had nothing to with her daughter's baby. Of that he was quite sure. She and Linda weren't that close. It had to be what she'd hinted: everything was happening too fast for her. Perhaps after ten years on her own she wasn't sure whether she wanted another relationship. She'd told him there had been no one serious since Ēriks. Perhaps she felt she'd got too involved too quickly. He thought of the night before she'd gone to

Helsinki. When he'd said he would go with her the next time. Perhaps it *was* anger he had seen in her eyes. Perhaps he had pushed her too hard.

*

When he woke the next day, he felt a sense of emptiness. He lay on his back, hearing the cries of the seagulls and the sound of scraping out in the street. At this time of year, it was like half the population was employed as yardmen with their huge flat shovels heaving the snow into massive piles on the pavement.

Hearing a quiet whimper he rolled over and felt a wet tongue on the back of his hand. Reksis put two paws on the edge of the bed and started to bury his head under the blanket, making rapid jerking movements until he separated the sheet from the mattress and crawled underneath.

Arnis rubbed his back, his sense of gloom deepening with the realisation that he would not be seeing Anita. He tried to imagine what she was doing, wondering what she was thinking, whether she was thinking of him. Suddenly it struck him that he had never woken up with her beside him, never seen her eyes opening, rubbing the sleep away. He could not picture her first thing in the morning. And that made him feel even emptier.

He closed his eyes and drifted back to sleep, waking up an hour later feeling gloomier than before. But this time it was more than Anita's departure: it was a dream, one of the worst he could remember. He'd dreamt about school, as he often did, but this was a different dream to the usual one where he was going into an exam he hadn't prepared for.

He frowned as he tried to recall the detail. It was

something to do with an essay. Yes, that was it. The whole class had been told to do an essay in which they had to describe what their fathers had done during the war. All the other boys started scribbling immediately but he sat in their midst chewing his pencil, wondering what to write. After penning two or three paragraphs about his father being a schoolteacher, he struck a line through it, knowing how the others would ridicule him for that. Their fathers had been in the army and that was the only place to be; soldiers fighting for their King and country.

So, instead, Arnis decided to write an account of his father as a member of the Latvian army fighting the Russians. He finished the essay, confident that he had embellished the story just enough to make it sound realistic yet convincing, and handed it in with a pride in his father's fictional achievements that could have equally been true had the Russians not sent him to Siberia.

A few days later the teacher returned to the classroom and handed the essays back. All except his. She read his out loud to the rest of the class – word by word, sentence by sentence. When she got to the end there was a stunned silence in the classroom. Then she ripped the sheets of paper out of his exercise book and tore them into hundreds of tiny pieces. All the other boys started to snigger behind their hands.

After the class ended, several of the boys were waiting for him in the corridor.

'Now we know why your father got sent to Siberia,' they shouted. 'Serves him right. What did you expect? Fighting the Russians. Our dads fought the Germans. The Russians were on our side. Who do you think you're kidding? Do you think we're all stupid…?'

They jeered him as he ran away down the corridor. As he turned the corner, the headmaster grabbed him by the scruff of the neck and marched him to a railway station where he pushed him into a brown railway truck with hundreds of others: aliens whose language he couldn't speak and who couldn't understand a word he said as he pleaded for compassion and mercy. He glanced at all of them in panic. There was nobody he recognised; they didn't even look like him. They were inhuman; characters from another planet.

With a terrific jolt, the truck set off, lifting off the rails into space. It crashed on a distant planet where it rattled across a bleak plain. They passed no living things: no farms, no animals, not even a single flower or a blade of grass. Then the truck ground to a shuddering halt and he was thrown out. The wind started to blow, a warm wind, which gradually grew hotter and hotter, until he was on fire; the flames beginning to lick at his trouser legs before they enveloped him. He turned round and saw the train disappearing into the far distance, leaving him utterly alone.

The vivid detail of the dream made his blood run cold and he buried his hand in the thick coat at his side, taking comfort from the dog's warmth. The radio came on and he ran his hand across his forehead; it was covered in sweat.

Dreams like that should never be remembered, he thought, and he got up in a hurry, got dressed and went through to the kitchen. He made his mother a cup of tea and took it to her bedroom, almost tripping over Reksis, who was sitting right beside him.

'Breakfast, Mother?'

'Breakfast,' she exclaimed. 'You know I don't eat breakfast in bed.'

It was true, she had never eaten breakfast in bed, not even on the rare occasions when she'd been ill. But it was so dark that morning that he thought it would be a treat. Besides, he wanted to do something to take his mind off the dream.

Being in no mood to argue with her, he went back to the kitchen, made himself a cup of coffee and cut two thick slices of bread. Thinking he ought to light the stove, he went through to the living room and cleaned out the grate. Allowing him to do that for her was one of the few concessions she made to her growing frailty. Knowing there would be trouble if he actually lit the wood, he piled a few pieces inside and left a box of matches at the side.

After swallowing his coffee, he put on his boots. 'I'll take Reksis to work with me,' he called out. 'Come on, lad.' Reksis rushed out and sat on the landing, thumping his tail, waiting for the familiar clunk of the lift. When they got down to the entrance hall, the woman from the upstairs flat came in, blasting them with an icy gust and a flurry of snow. Not that that bothered Reksis: he loved the snow.

Outside was almost a total white-out. Arnis stepped onto the pavement and strode along the narrow street towards the park. When he reached the main road the traffic was at a complete standstill and, such was the severity of the snowstorm, even the trams had stopped. Thankful he had left the car at the surgery the previous night, he ploughed through the park going over the dream in his mind. It seemed to encapsulate all his worst life experiences to date. But it was just a dream. He would never have produced a piece of work like that. By the time he was old enough to be writing essays, he had learned not to draw attention to his father's fate in Siberia, or to his own antipathy to the Russians. He knew how

209

foolish that was in a country that had recently emerged from a war with the Germans.

Nonetheless, the dream brought back bad memories of the taunting he had received at school because the other boys thought his father was a criminal. But having his essay torn to shreds in front of the class bore an uncanny resemblance to the story the woman in London had told him about his father tearing up the picture of Stalin in the classroom.

That brought Kurmis to mind again and Arnis felt the anger rising in his veins.

He reached the surgery at the same time as Sigita. Mrs Kļava was also there and he glared at Sigita who was doing her best not to laugh. She knew how Mrs Kļava riled him. The woman was little more than a nuisance at the best of times.

She had coeliac disease and he simply couldn't make her understand there was no medicine for it. She looked at him in disbelief when he told her to avoid bread. What was the point of advice like that when it was all she could afford to eat? No meal was complete without black bread and, although she liked beans and potatoes, she couldn't eat them all the time.

No doubt she was here again to ask for medication. Thanks to Western influence his patients now thought there was a pill for every ailment. It was unthinkable that there wasn't. The problem was exacerbated by the fact that in the old days they had usually been given one – whether it worked or not.

*

When the last patient left the consulting room, Sigita poked her head round the door. 'You won't forget Mrs Reinberga, will you?'

'Mrs Reinberga?'

'Yes, you remember. She's one of the new patients. I told you about her earlier. She can't get out in this weather. Her breathing is very bad and she wants a home visit.'

'Have we got a card for her?' Arnis asked.

'Yes, it's here. I've printed it out for you.'

He stared at the address on the card and tried to place it. 'It's one of the estates near the hospital,' Sigita said, looking up from the keyboard. 'Near the end of the trolley bus route.'

He nodded as he pictured the area in his mind, and called to Reksis.

As he was leaving, Sigita handed him a brown envelope. 'Sorry, I forgot to give you this.'

He stared at the postmark. Australia. He opened it immediately and read it quickly.

'Dear Dr Rozenvalds,

Thank you for your letter of November 29th regarding your father, Mr Kārlis Vilks. Unfortunately, we have not been able to trace him through our records either in Sydney or Melbourne. I also took the trouble to check with a few of our older members, both here and at the Latvian church, but they could not recall meeting anyone of that name. I am sorry to be of so little help to you, but it might be worth considering putting an announcement on the Latvian Radio programme. I am happy to do this for you if you wish, but will wait your further instructions.

Yours sincerely
Andrejs Germanis'

His first reaction was one of relief but he knew he couldn't jump to conclusions. The man had obviously gone to a lot of effort already, but Latvian Radio would certainly be worth a try. He glanced at his watch. It would be late evening in Sydney so that ruled out phoning Mr Germanis. Then he noticed an email address on the top of the letter so he dictated a reply to Sigita and asked her to send it.

When he left the surgery the snow had almost stopped. Colour was returning to their grey and white world and he motored up the street and on to the main boulevard. Christmas decorations were starting to appear and his heart lifted at the sight of the shop windows. Such illuminations would have been unthinkable ten years ago when people used to queue up for ages and think they had done well if they could go home with a single light bulb. It would soon be time to buy presents, but he quickly dispelled the idea because it reminded him that Anita would not be here to share Christmas with him.

He continued on over the river, passing a small park, then a sports stadium. Finally, he stopped at a set of traffic lights. Noticing the bus in front with its right indicator flashing, he guessed this was probably where he needed to be, so he followed suit and turned into a long straight street lined with old red brick warehouses which led to a large housing estate - one of those typical ghastly places erected in the seventies, badly designed, shoddily constructed, thrown up in a hurry and now dilapidated. Not that he was any stranger to places like this. Over the years he'd seen enough of them in London: collective properties peeling into a collective state of despised disrepair.

As the bus terminus came into view he drew up to the

kerb to check the address. Having no precise idea where it was, he looked round hoping to see someone he might ask for directions. And there he was. The old man shuffling along from the bus stop carried an accordion and Arnis recognised him as the chap he passed every day of the week outside the bank, squeezing his tortured repertoire from the battered instrument. He ran the window down.

'Do you know where Krievu iela is?' he asked the old man.

But the man merely grunted and shuffled on in the direction of the smoky bar on the corner.

Further along the street, Arnis spotted a group of elderly babushkas shutting up their vegetable stalls for the day. He drove up and leaned out of the window, having to shout to make himself heard above the rhythmic clicks and clacks as they worked. He wasn't sure he would get something sensible out of them but one of them shouted back, revealing a mouthful of fillings that glinted under the light of the street lamp. 'First block on the right.'

A few minutes later he pulled up into a courtyard, one of the bleakest he had ever seen. Grabbing his bag from the passenger seat, he made his way over the frozen ground to the main door. A black cat was scrabbling in a pile of rubbish bags in the hallway and a strong smell of rancid fat drifted down to meet him as he climbed up a stairway painted in a depressing bottle green. Reaching the third floor, he peered round in the fading light for number ten and pressed the buzzer.

An elderly willowy-looking man came to the door and let him into a dark vestibule packed with boots and overcoats. 'Come in, come in,' he said, a crinkly smile doing little to enhance a pair of sad brown eyes.

Arnis followed him through to the living room which, although warm and cosy, had, like most of these places, clearly seen better days. A low orange sofa was placed against one wall, its Rexine cracks concealed under a gold-coloured curtain. At right angles to the window was a teak-veneered glass-fronted display case. Three matching blue and white china cups and saucers were set on an exquisitely embroidered tablecloth.

Smiling, Arnis thought back to the home visits he'd made in his early days to places just like this where the table had always been beautifully set in readiness for the doctor's visit. Somehow, it almost felt like a homecoming but the intervening years placed it in a sort of time-warp. But fifty years of communism had not destroyed the yearning for beauty or human pride.

'The doctor's here, dear,' the old man called out then he smiled again. 'She's through here,' he said. With a shaky hand, he beckoned Arnis into a smaller room where an elderly woman with snow-white hair and a bright blue quilted jacket sat up in bed. She quickly extinguished her cigarette and held out a knobbly hand in greeting.

'What can I do for you?' he asked her.

'It's my breathing, doctor. The inhalers don't seem to be working any more.' The old man went out of the room and she nodded her head towards him. 'He worries when I'm like this,' she whispered, 'And he does so hate doing the cooking! But I feel so breathless.'

Arnis sounded her chest and was not surprised to find she had an infection. He wrote a prescription for some antibiotics and a short course of steroids. The old man reappeared with two cups of coffee and a tray of pastries then

214

he went back into the living room to watch the television.

The old lady seemed to want to chat so, having a bit of time before his next appointment, he settled once more on the edge of her bed.

She started to talk about her family, pointing to a photograph at the side of her bed. 'This was my son ...Viktors,' she said with a mixture of pride and sadness.

'What happened to him?' Arnis asked gently.

'Chernobyl,' the old lady replied, staring at the photograph. 'He was sent to clean up.'

Arnis gave a sympathetic nod, well aware of the numbers of Latvians who'd been ordered to clean up after the tragedy.

'Not a day goes by when I don't think of him. See, look,' she added picking up the photograph. 'He was such a good boy.' Her eyes filled with tears. 'No one could help him. No one,' she said plaintively, taking a tissue from the box on her bedside table. 'It was too late by the time we got him to the doctor. His tumour was the size of a tennis ball.'

Taking the photograph from her, he stared at the smiling face framed with longish thick brown hair and a fringe swept to one side. Almost immediately, he was drawn to the boy's deep-set eyes. They looked intelligent and thoughtful, the eyes of a poet or a musician. But more than that, they looked familiar. He knew he'd seen those eyes before. He couldn't mistake them. They were Anita's. He swallowed hard and felt his cheeks begin to turn pink.

He was not mistaken. Mrs Reinberga reached behind the curtain and produced another photograph from the windowsill. 'And this is my daughter,' she said.

Arnis gasped involuntarily. Though he'd recognised

the eyes, it was still a shock. At a loss for words, he said the first thing that came into his head. 'She's a very pretty girl.'

'Yes,' Mrs Reinberga replied. 'Very pretty. That's half her trouble.' She looked at him, obviously noting his quizzical expression. 'Men. They're her downfall. She attracts them like a magnet. But she never keeps them.'

He felt the hairs standing out on the back of his neck but he remained silent, waiting for her to continue.

'She always ends up running away and she's done the same thing again recently. I'm sure of it. I don't see her that often but I do know the signs. She was so happy when she came a few weeks ago. She was obviously seeing someone she was very fond of then ... right out of the blue ... she calls me one morning to tell me she's going away. Just like the last time. The thing is...' - Mrs Reinberga paused and gazed at the photograph of her son - '... she's scared of getting too close to anyone since Viktors died. She adored her little brother.' She paused again, tears returning to her eyes as she fondled the photograph of her dead son. 'I'm so sorry, Doctor, I don't know why I'm telling you all this.'

An awkward silence fell between them.

Arnis fractured it. 'You have a beautiful daughter, Mrs Reinberga.' He took one last look at the photograph of Anita and handed it back to her mother. He swallowed his coffee and left feeling more embarrassed than at any time he could remember.

As he drove back to Rīga, he could hardly believe what had happened. Though he knew Anita had a mother, he'd had no idea of her name or where she'd lived, or indeed that she'd got married again. Anita had never mentioned a new husband. Perhaps she didn't like him. Quite possible, given

216

how much she'd loved her father.

As his equanimity began to return, the encounter struck him as so odd that he began to laugh. Rīga certainly is a small place, he thought.

CHAPTER 13

When he arrived back at the surgery, Sigita handed him a piece of paper. The message was brief and to the point:

'Will do. It'll be announced on the radio tomorrow. I'll let you know if I hear anything.

Andrejs Germanis'

Inwardly hoping he would not hear any more, he went into his consulting room and took the photograph of his father out of his wallet. He stared at the familiar face, feeling he was as far from finding out what had happened to him as he had been a year ago. His next plan was to go back to Kuldīga to see if he could find anyone else who had known him. There must be other members of the Vilks family around. His father's father had been the owner of the cloth mill and, although Arnis didn't know how big the family was, he knew they must have been influential. Surely someone would know something.

*

Arnis decided that he must phone Antons during the evening. He knew he had devoted too much of his time recently to his own affairs, and the search for his father, and he felt guilty when he realised Antons must have finished his first ambulance course and would now be working as a paramedic's assistant.

He also wanted to hear if Antons had heard anything from his brother, Henrijs.

Since Penny's death, Henrijs only contacted Antons, and then only infrequently. Arnis sighed, regretting he hadn't spent more time with them both when they were younger. Henrijs had often pointed out the only time he could get his father's attention was when he brought home his end of term school report.

'I want a father, not another schoolmaster,' he'd yelled one day.

That had hurt a lot, especially when, a few moments later, Henrijs wheeled his brand new bike through the house to go for a ride in the park.

As a boy, Arnis never had a bike of his own. If he wanted to ride a bike, he had to borrow Michael's. So when he had a family of his own, he swore that neither of his sons would go short of anything. But it infuriated him when they - Henrijs, in particular - took everything for granted. Though he accepted they would one day grow up and realise how hard it was to pay a mortgage and buy nice things for their children, he had been determined that they wouldn't have to start from nothing. He always intended to help both his sons get established in whatever they wanted to do. So it came as something of a shock when Henrijs left university and said he wanted no help from his father.

The wonderful aroma of frying bacon and warm dough welcomed him when he opened the front door. He recognised it instantly as pīrāgi and knew his mother must be feeling better. She hadn't cooked that for several weeks. He went straight into the kitchen and found her, hands covered in flour, happily rolling out the dough. A pan of cabbage was boiling on the cooker.

'Hello, love,' she said with a twinkle in her eye, pointing to the big brown mixing bowl on the kitchen table. 'I've left some for you.'

'Wonderful!' He seized the bowl, and rolled the scraps of dough between the tips of his fingers before he popped them into his mouth.

'Did you have a good day?' Margarita asked.

'So-so. Much as usual,' he replied, not wanting to mention his visit to Mrs Reinberga. He still felt embarrassed about Anita, and he didn't want to admit what had happened that afternoon. He changed the subject completely. 'Did you once say Dad had a sister?' he asked as he savoured the raw dough.

'A sister?'

'Yes.'

Margarita said nothing and he turned to look at her. By then she had her back to him stirring a pan of soup.

'Mum...?'

'What made you think of that?' she queried.

'Nothing particularly. I was just thinking, that's all.'

'Yes,' she said. 'He did.'

'What was she called?'

'You've never asked me before,' she replied. 'What's brought this on all of a sudden?'

'Nothing. It's just that ... well I was thinking today how little I knew about Dad's family.'

'There's not much to know,' she said quickly. 'They were a funny lot.'

'You didn't like them much, did you?' This wasn't the first time he'd had that impression.

220

She shrugged. 'His mother was a bit of a snob. I wasn't good enough. Oh, and while I remember, Antons phoned about half an hour ago. He said he hadn't heard from you.'

'Yes, and I haven't heard from him either.'

'Now, now. Why don't you give him a call while I'm getting this ready.'

Arnis scraped out the rest of the dough realising his mother had cleverly managed to change the subject again.

But why? No matter how much she'd disliked her husband's family, he felt he had every right to know about them, and his concern for her feelings in the matter was beginning to evaporate. He was losing patience with her silence, her unwillingness to tell him anything. To make matters worse, Ella had said his mother talked to her about his father on the day he'd gone to Kuldīga. But what had she said? And why didn't she talk to him? He felt as if he had to grovel for every single piece of information.

Determined to find out more, he tried again. 'What was Dad's sister called?'

'Anna.'

Anna Vilka. That was a start. 'Was she married?'

'Not when I knew her. Come on, love. This is ready. If you're not going to ring Antons …'

He watched her pour two bowls of creamy vegetable soup and smiled as she floated a large knob of butter on each. As a child he had always loved to swirl it round with his spoon, creating golden islands, watching the fat coalesce until the surface of the soup glistened, waiting for the creamy coloured liquid to cool sufficiently for him to eat it. Unlike his mother, who always ate hers immediately, he couldn't take very hot food.

As he followed her through to the living room he noticed that the table was laid with the best china, a privilege usually reserved for Sundays. 'Gosh. Are we having a party?'

'I thought we'd have a treat tonight as it's nearly Christmas. Come on, open this,' she said passing him a bottle of Chardonnay from the sideboard.

It was a wonderful meal. She was a good cook and pīrāgi was his favourite dish but tonight she had excelled herself. The pastry was lighter than ever, every mouthful sliding down the back of his throat; the soup a perfect blend of tastes without too much potato.

'That was good, Mum,' he said, helping himself to another pīrāgi.

As he was about to drink the last of his wine, she said suddenly, 'Let's have a toast.'

'A toast?'

'Yes. To Latvia. To the future. I know I'm always grumbling about it, but ...'

He laughed. For one who so rarely complained about anything in England, she had found the changes in Latvia very hard to take. Many were the times he had come home in the evening to hear her grumble about the service in the shops, people pushing in front of her in the queue at the post office, the poor quality of the clothes for sale.

Her new winter coat had annoyed her most of all. 'So badly made,' she'd said sadly, showing him the seams, which to him looked perfectly good. But nobody could match the skills of the tailor in Kuldīga who had made every coat she'd had before the war.

'But I'm so glad we came back,' she continued as they both raised their glasses. 'To Latvia.'

'To Latvia,' he echoed. 'And to Dad.'

'Yes,' she said with a smile. 'To your father.'

They clinked their glasses and a wistful look came over her face. 'You know...' She hesitated for a moment before adding something that took him completely by surprise. 'Your father loved you very much.'

He stared hard at her, fearing what he had begun to suspect for a while – that her mind was beginning to wander. How could his father have loved him? Having been deported eight months before he was born, he hadn't known anything about him, let alone seen him. He swallowed hard, worried she was losing her memory. She had always been so sharp and, to make matters worse, he knew it would be well nigh impossible to get her to admit she needed help. That would be an admission of defeat and she would never wear that.

Over the past few months she had got into the habit of denying every sign of infirmity, blaming her swollen ankles on her medication, which she thought was completely unnecessary and didn't take properly. Her growing deafness she would put down to a slight cold, and as for walking out in the street with a stick or even taking his arm, that was only for other poor old souls and she clearly had no plans to become one of them.

'I wish your dad could have seen you grow up,' she continued. 'He would have been so proud of you. All the things you've achieved ...'

'Mum...' Quite suddenly he had an overwhelming desire to tell her what he had found out about his father but the words stuck in his throat.

Seeming to sense his anguish, she reached across the table and put her hand on his. 'We've had some good times, haven't we? You and I?'

He nodded in reply, scarcely able to swallow the growing lump in his throat.

'Especially after we got to Oban,' she continued. 'Do you remember the journey over there? It was so beautiful. I really began to believe things were getting better.' Then she laughed. 'Except for those ham sandwiches we bought at the station. I remember thinking about the pastries we got at the railway stations here. The way they melted in your mouth. But those Scottish sandwiches. They were so dry. Funny, the things that come back to you. Like the fields. Do you remember? I couldn't get over how empty they were.'

He nodded again. In their early days in Britain, she had often remarked about the fields. She couldn't understand how so much land could be put to so little use apart from leisure.

'We've been here over six months,' she continued, 'and the time has gone so quickly.' She leant back in her chair, pre-occupied with her own thoughts. After a few moments, she gave a deep sigh. 'I'd love to go to Kuldīga again.'

'Kuldīga?'

'Yes.'

'When?'

She leaned forward again to take hold of his hand. 'I know. Why don't we go for Christmas? I'd love you to see it. The sound of the bells on the horse-drawn sledges, the Christmas trees in the town hall, the shops bustling with people, a pig's head for Christmas dinner, barley sausage, the sound of the accordion, the moon shining on the frozen waterfall. I can see it now...' Her eyes shone, and he felt a tear welling in his eye.

'Oh dear,' she added, looking away from him. 'It was a

wonderful life.' Then, in a small voice, 'It's all gone now.'

'Apart from Sprīdītis,' he said, hoping to bring a smile to her face.

'Yes, Sprīdītis. And you. I didn't lose you.' She squeezed his hand then thought for a moment before continuing, 'You remember that woman who came to the guest house?'

He nodded, knowing exactly what she was going to say next. Neither of them had ever forgotten the small tubby woman with the dark green mackintosh and ginger hair. Margarita had got quite friendly with her and had told her a bit about Latvia and why they'd had to leave.

The woman had listened intently, then responded immediately by saying she understood exactly what it was like to lose everything. 'I lost my cat recently,' she'd said. 'That's why I'm here. My sister said I should have a break. To help me to get over it.'

Margarita had struggled to stop herself being rude to the woman, and she had never forgotten it.

'Oh dear, this won't do ... feeling sorry for ourselves,' she said, standing up and collecting the plates. 'Let's watch a Fawlty Towers video after we've cleared up.'

They washed the dishes and put a couple more logs in the stove then she settled herself in her wicker rocking chair by the corner window. Much as he wanted to learn more about his father's family, he was afraid she might begin to ramble again and, besides, he couldn't resist the idea of watching The Rat. It was a few years since he'd seen it and they were both in need of a good laugh. He switched on the video and opened the box of Bendicks Mint Creams Ella had brought with her last time.

His mother got on with some sewing while she watched. As the video came to an end, she quickly put the final stitches in the cushion cover. 'There,' she said. 'That's the last one finished. I think I'll turn in now.'

While she got ready for bed he went to make some tea. As he was about to take it through to her, she called out, 'Can you bring my book?'

He went to her rocking chair, picked up her paperback, and went to check the stove. He gave the dying embers a quick stoke, switched out the light, and went to look out on to the square. The snow was falling once more and the huge soft flakes reflected in the glow from the lights on the Christmas tree. He gazed at it for a few moments then went to his mother's bedroom where she was waiting expectantly, her hands clasped together on the top of her duvet.

Her eyes gleamed as she seized the book from his hands, opening it up at the last chapter. 'I must finish this before I go to sleep,' she said.

'What is it?' he asked. The book was covered in an embroidered sleeve she'd made many years ago.

'The Secret Garden,' she said with a wide smile. 'This is the best bit, right at the end where the father comes home and finds that his son has got better.'

Not knowing the story himself, he listened while she explained how she had read it for the first time in the 1930s after it had been translated into Latvian. 'Everything I knew about England I learnt from reading this. Very accurate it was too. Big draughty houses, tweed skirts, stern housekeepers. Little did I know ...' She shook herself and shivered. 'When I read it the first time, I wanted to be the little girl ... playing in that big rambling garden with all the pretty flowers and the

226

birds singing.' She was silent for a moment. 'But this time …
this time, it's the little boy. I can't wait till he runs to meet his
father. His father hasn't seen him walk for a long time. His
mother died, you see, and his father never got over it. But he
was so afraid of losing his little boy as well that he over-
protected him and the boy spent all his time in bed. Until his
cousin came to live at the house. That was the little girl. She
unlocked the gate of the Secret Garden where nobody had
been since the little boy's mother died. Towards the end of the
book she takes him there too, and that's where he learns to
walk again. It's a lovely story.'

He smiled, pleased to hear her sounding so happy.
'Good night, Mum,' he said, giving her a long hug. 'Sleep
well.'

Before going to bed himself, he went to tidy the
kitchen. Then, as he was about to get undressed, he looked
round for Reksis. The Alsatian usually followed him
everywhere and he wondered if he had got locked in the
bathroom. He checked but there was no sign of him. Noticing
his mother's door was ajar, he poked his head into her room
and saw Reksis lying at the side of her bed.

'Come on, lad,' he said in a low voice. 'You know she
doesn't like you in here at night.'

But the Alsatian stayed still, his head resting firmly
between his huge black paws. 'Come on,' Arnis insisted.
'What's the matter?'

But Reksis still refused to move. Puzzled, Arnis bent
down and rubbed the dog's shoulders but it made no attempt
to get up. He decided to leave him be. Expecting he would
soon follow, he left the door open and went to bed. Almost
immediately, he fell into a deep dreamless sleep.

*

Was it minutes later? Or hours? Arnis had no idea but he was woken suddenly by Reksis who was burrowing his nose under his arm, at the same time scraping vigorously at the sheets with his paws.

'Reksis,' he said as he tried to get his brain back in gear. 'What is it, boy?'

The dog began to whine - quietly at first from the depth of his throat, then more persistently.

'Quiet, Reksis!' Arnis said, trying to subdue the Alsatian so he could hear if there was anyone about. This served only to make Reksis more frenetic as the whines turned to low barks. He nudged Arnis's face repeatedly with his snout but Arnis pushed him away. Eventually, the dog gave up and trotted off to the door where he stood for a few moments fixing Arnis with a stare before finally disappearing into the hall.

Quietly confident there were no sounds of an intrusion, and too exhausted to bother getting up, Arnis lay on his back and listened again. But there was no sound to be heard so he assumed the young couple in the flat below must have disturbed the dog. Now that the sleep had cleared from his eyelids, he glanced at the luminous face of the clock. It was three twenty-two. He frowned. Ivars and Agate weren't usually this late.

Unable to keep his eyes open any longer, he rolled onto his side and again fell into a deep sleep.

When morning came the radio alarm failed to wake him so the news was half over before he finally came to with a start and hurriedly jumped out of bed. Still more asleep than awake, he went through to the kitchen and made a pot of tea. His brain was still muddled from a confusing and disturbed sleep so he was slow to notice that Reksis who, first thing in the morning, was always waiting for his breakfast, was not waiting today. Frowning, he picked up the tea tray and carried it through to his mother's room where, as usual, he put it down on her dressing table before going to draw back the curtains.

A faint brush stroke of crimson tinged the ochre backdrop of the early morning sky. 'What was it they said in England, Mum? Red sky in the morning, shepherd's warning?' He returned to the dressing table to pour the tea. Then he glanced over his shoulder and saw she was laying partly on her side, still wearing her glasses, looking straight at him but not saying anything. Replacing the teapot on the tray, he walked quickly to her bedside and lifted her hand. It was warm and he squeezed her fingers gently between his own then drew them slowly up to his cheek before he kissed the back of her hand.

Her other arm was laying across the pillow, her hand still holding The Secret Garden. His first thought was that he hoped she had read it right to the end. Not wanting to take it from her, he left it exactly where it was with her thumb on the last page. He sat beside her on the edge of her bed. She looked so peaceful he didn't want to move her. Not just yet.

Reksis came to his side and sat at his feet, staring up with doleful eyes. He lifted a paw and placed it gently on Arnis's knee. Arnis bent slightly and caressed his ear still squeezing his mother's fingers in his other hand.

They both stayed like that for a timeless period. At that moment, time was meaningless save that an era had just come to an end. She was the bravest person Arnis had ever known. Eventually he let go of her hand and bent over to roll her gently on to her back. He folded her hands across her tummy and placed The Secret Garden between her fingers. Then he removed her glasses and gently closed her eyes. As he bent to kiss her forehead, his tears began to fall.

'Rest in peace, mother,' he whispered. 'And thank you … for everything.'

CHAPTER 14

The long silence was punctuated only by the unmistakeable sounds of stifled sobs.

'Antons, are you okay?'

The silence continued for a few seconds more then Antons replied. 'Dad … I can't handle it. I'll call you back later.'

The line immediately went dead and Arnis replaced the handset. He understood. It had been the same for him for the last hour; an hour that seemed like an eternity with an incessant need to try and swallow the lump in his throat; opening his eyes wide to dispel the tears; forcing them to concentrate on any inanimate object that might help to take his mind away from the reality.

He rose from his seat and walked towards her bedroom. The door was still open and Reksis was standing guard at the bedside, one paw resting on the cover, whimpering softly. Even for the dog, life was not the same; routine had changed. Today there was no tail wagging, no scurrying around the kitchen excitedly waiting for a bowl of biscuits to be placed on the floor. His appetite had gone.

The telephone rang again and Arnis rushed to grab the handset. The slight echo indicated another international call.

'Antons, is that you?' Arnis said.

Another delay – a silence that made things worse and

brought the lump back to block the airways.

Then a voice. 'Dad ... it's Henrijs. I just heard from Antons. It's a great shock.'

'For us all.' Tears again welled in Arnis's eyes and he couldn't say more.

Then Henrijs spoke again. 'Dad, I'm really struggling to find the right words to say ...'

Arnis interrupted. 'I understand ... don't worry. I'm just pleased you called.'

There was a brief pause before Henrijs replied. 'I'm devastated by the news,' he said. 'Gran was a great person. We will all miss her.'

Arnis couldn't answer. At a time when a family needed parental leadership, the sorrow had stopped the words flowing.

As if recognising this, Henrijs said, 'I'm not looking for sympathy but I feel terribly guilty about not seeing Gran for so long. There were things I should have told her. I should have made the effort to come over and see her.'

'Don't blame yourself, Henrijs. Your job keeps you busy and she understood that. She often talked about you. She loved you very much.'

Arnis heard a sob. 'And I loved her. If only I could have told her that before she went ...'

'We all wish we had said things that needed to be said before it was too late, but we can't turn the clock back.' Arnis reflected on the things he should have told her; things that now hung in his conscience, destined to remain there.

'Look, Dad,' Henrijs continued, 'I know we haven't always seen eye to eye but I do know your loss is even greater than mine, and I am thinking about you.' He paused for a few seconds before he resumed. 'I don't want to make the same mistake twice so I have to say … I do love you, Dad, and I do appreciate all the things you tried to do for me. I'm a stubborn bastard at times … and I regret it.'

A distinct sob echoed down the line then it went dead.

*

Antons came over on the first available flight and Arnis met him at the airport. Tears welled in their eyes as they embraced unashamedly in the arrivals halls and no words were necessary. Eventually, they broke apart and Arnis picked up Antons's rucksack. As they headed towards the exit, Arnis heard a voice calling 'Dad!' and turned to look.

He dropped Antons's bag and walked towards his other son. Henrijs threw his arms round his father and pressed his face to his shoulder, muffled choking sounds coming from his throat.

Arnis hugged him tightly. 'Don't try to say anything, son. We can talk later when we're ready.'

Antons joined them and all three hugged in a way they had not done since Penny had died.

*

The funeral took place three days before Christmas at the white Lutheran church in Kuldīga, the church where his mother had been married sixty four years previously. In addition to Arnis and his two sons, only five other people attended: Sigita, Bruno, Ella and also Vieda, another friend of his mother's both of whom had both flown over specially, and Ella's son, Pēteris. Arnis had wanted Fēlikss Siliņš to come, but when he'd called a few days previously, his daughter had answered the phone and said he was in hospital.

The service was in Latvian, of which Henrijs and Antons could understand very little, but enough to take in what was happening. Though there were few of them, they managed to sing Margarita's three favourite hymns in good voice: Be Thou My Vision, O Jesus I have promised and The Lord is My Shepherd.

At the end of the second hymn, Arnis pulled a piece of paper out of his jacket pocket and stood up to face the congregation. After everyone had sat down he cleared his throat.

'Thank you all for coming today' he said. 'I know my mother wouldn't have wanted you to make the journey, but I am deeply grateful that you have. She was a wonderful person and I shall miss her very much. Known to me as Mum, to Antons and Henrijs as Gran and to her friends as Margarita, she was a lady of great courage and kindness, and she had a wonderful sense of humour. She was born in 1912 and only recently I learned that one of her earliest memories was at the end of the First World War when her grandfather brought home a large salmon he had caught in the river just a few hundred yards down the road from where I am standing. The early years of her life are somewhat shadowy. She was brought up on a farm on the edge of the town and was educated here in Kuldīga. When she spoke to me of those years there was always a smile on her face, and I knew they were the happiest of her life. After leaving school she worked in the bakery and helped on the farm until she got married in 1938 to Karlis Vilks, a teacher at the local school. Three years later her married life was brought to a cruel end when my father was deported to Siberia. By then she was expecting me, though my father never knew. In 1945, she took the bravest step of her life and took me to Britain which is where we lived until six months ago. She worked very hard throughout her life but she always made time for me, especially when it came to exams. Had it not been for her encouragement, I suspect I would have achieved very little. She had mixed feelings about being back in Latvia, because it is now so different from the country she remembered. But only the night before she died, she told me she was glad we had come back. She was a very brave lady and a person of great religious faith, which I know carried her throughout her long life. She brought me up to trust in God and never to be afraid to do the right thing. She loved her family and I am so grateful to have grown up in that love, as I know Henrijs and Antons are too. She will leave an enormous hole in our lives, but I hope we can carry on in a way that would make her proud of us.'

Arnis folded up his piece of paper and went back to the pew. He felt an enormous sense of peace, and though he had found it difficult to speak, he was glad he had done so. He had let the minister in London speak at Penny's funeral and he had regretted it ever since.

After the service, they all had lunch in a restaurant by the river, but before setting off back to Rīga, Arnis wanted to show his sons a little of Kuldīga. Together they went on to the bridge and gazed at the waterfall. In the bright grey light of the northern winter, the river looked liked like glass, a tethered horse grazed on the opposite bank and a hooded crow called from the top of the wrought iron lamp.

From the bridge they went to the red-bricked school which Arnis was delighted to see in daylight. It was still locked and empty, but he was able to tell Henrijs and Antons that this was where their grandfather had been a teacher. Next they walked to the market place so that Arnis could show them where his mother had had a stall, then they headed for the main street.

The shops were decorated for Christmas, but none of them wanted to look. Only three months previously Arnis had walked this way with this mother. It made him think of what she'd said the night she died about wanting to come back to Kuldīga for Christmas and he began to fight a lump in his throat. As he pulled a handkerchief out of his pocket, he noticed the name on the blue and white street sign. Raiņa iela. He was surprised he hadn't spotted it on previous visits. He motioned his sons to follow him and they walked along until Arnis found number seven.

'This is where my mother and father lived,' he said.

And where I was conceived, he thought.

It was a pale blue, two-storey house with a window either side of the ornately carved front door, which had a beautiful handle crafted in the shape of a fish. There was a fan light above the door and on the first floor, three more windows. The shutters were closed on every window so it was impossible to see in. Not that Arnis wanted to. He was curious to see it but he felt no sense of homecoming or of belonging.

'Do you know who lives here now, Dad?' asked Henrijs. He did not know that this was the first time his father had seen the house.

'No,' replied Arnis. He did not care.

As he stared at the front door, he began to think of what Fēlikss Siliņš had told him. Of his father being taken away in the truck by the Russians; of that traitor Kurmis. His mother hiding in the attic. Terrified, not knowing whether it was safe to come down in case one of them had remained in the house to take her prisoner too. Anger fused through his veins. Had he been able to find Kurmis at that moment he would not have trusted himself.

Without another word they walked back towards the church where the car was parked. Bruno's car was still there. 'They're probably still in the restaurant,' said Henrijs. 'You wait here Dad and we'll go and look.'

Arnis thought of Fēlikss Siliņš and wondered whether he was out of hospital. 'OK. There's someone I'd like to see before we go back. I won't be long. I'll meet you here in fifteen minutes.'

He went round to Siliņš's house and was pleased to see wood smoke circling above the chimney. The old man answered the door, looking much weaker than when Arnis had last seen him. 'Come in,' he said. 'I'm so sorry about your mother. She was a fine lady.'

'She was indeed,' replied Arnis.

'I wanted to come to the funeral, but my daughter didn't think it was a good idea in this weather.'

'Quite right,' said Arnis. 'How are you?

'My lungs aren't so good. I got a chest infection.'

'How long have you been home?'

'Since last night.'

'You must look after yourself. Have you got a good doctor?'

The old man shrugged. 'My daughter thinks I ought to see a specialist.'

'I might be able to help you,' said Arnis.

'Oh?'

'Yes, I'm a doctor. I know a good pulmonologist in Rīga.'

Siliņš looked anxious. 'How much will that cost?'

'Don't worry. I'll take care of that,' he replied. He felt it was the least he could do for a man who had helped him so much.

They continued to chat for a few more minutes then Arnis got up to go. 'I'll get in touch with the specialist and let you know when she can see you.'

The old man stood up and picked up his stick from the back of his chair.

'Don't worry,' said Arnis. 'I'll see myself out.'

'By the way,' Siliņš called after him, 'I forgot to tell you something.'

Arnis turned on his heel. 'What was that?'

Siliņš shuffled towards him. 'I was in Rīga a few weeks ago.'

'And?' Arnis enquired.

'And I saw Edgars Kurmis.'

Arnis's feet were rooted to the spot and his heart skipped a beat. 'You saw Kurmis?'

'I did indeed. Judging by the look on your face, I was as amazed as you are. But I'll tell you this. Had I been twenty years younger, I would have got hold of him and throttled the life from his body.'

It was a thought that had crossed Arnis's mind many times since Siliņš had first told him about the traitorous Kurmis. 'So what happened?' he asked.

'Nothing,' Siliņš replied, spreading his hands in despair. 'If we had fought, we would have been two old men trying to settle a score and we would both have looked very foolish.'

Arnis looked at his watch, feeling torn between

wanting to spend more time with Siliņš and knowing that Henrijs had to catch the evening flight to Brussels. So he said good-bye to the old man and hurried back to the town square. The others were already waiting. Henrijs and Antons joined him and they drove straight to Rīga airport. There were only thirty five minutes before the flight was due to leave, so they dropped Henrijs off and went back home. Antons stayed on with his father for another week.

*

On the evening before Antons was due to return to London, they chose to stay in and watch television. It had been an exhausting and traumatic two weeks and neither of them felt like going out.

During an advertisement break, Antons turned to his father and said, 'Fancy another beer, Dad?'

'Yes, why not? There's plenty in the fridge.'

Antons disappeared to the kitchen and returned seconds later with two bottles of Aldaris. He gave one to Arnis and then sat cross-legged next to Reksis in front of the china stove. The Alsatian rolled over on his back and waved his paws excitedly in the air as Antons rubbed his tummy. Then, out of the blue, Antons said, 'Did you ever find any more information about Granddad?'

Arnis put his hands behind his head and stared at the ceiling. 'Yes, I have. Quite a lot, in fact.'

Antons listened in silence as his father told him the whole story, starting with the photograph, the visit to Kuldīga, the note in the bottle, the entry in the ledger at the records office, the old man Siliņš, Kurmis, the camp in Siberia, his suspicions that his father had gone to Australia: everything.

He finished by explaining what he had heard from Australia and about the radio appeal that might yet bring further news.

As soon as Arnis finished the story he felt a huge surge of relief but it evaporated within seconds - replaced by an aching sense of guilt as he began to wish he'd told his mother. He remembered the night she died, how cross he'd felt when she seemed reluctant to talk about his father's family. But perhaps he had sometimes galloped ahead of her, leaving her at the point where they had discovered the note. Soon after that time he had begun to take seriously the suggestion that his father really had abandoned the search and gone to Australia.

He'd often wondered if she probably thought the same so he had never mentioned his visit to the records office or to Siliņš and he had justified his silence on the basis of not wanting to make her feel any worse. By the time he got into correspondence with the Latvian organisation in Australia, saying nothing about it to his mother had become a habit. He had convinced himself that was how she wanted it. Her reluctance to discuss matters seemed to confirm it.

And yet there was Sprīdītis, the puppet she'd kept for over sixty years. And Ella, who had confirmed what he'd always known: how much his mother had loved his father. Those thoughts confounded all other logic and Arnis felt dreadful. She must have died thinking her husband had abandoned them and he could so easily have put her out of her misery. He could have told her everything he'd told Antons. Instead he had said nothing and perhaps made it worse for her. He could hear her telling him how proud his father would have been of him. But he certainly wasn't feeling proud of himself.

*

Arnis surged into the New Year with fresh determination and immersed himself in his work. During the first few days, his mind and his body went into overdrive. Never had he been so tireless, so efficient. Not once did he get behind with his appointments and every letter was answered the day it appeared.

'I can't keep up with you,' Sigita said. 'You're going to be ill if you carry on like this.'

But he dare not slow down because he was scared he might come to a standstill and not get going again. Wallowing in misery had never been an option for his mother and he had no intention of allowing himself to do that. She had always been determined, uncompromising, and self-reliant; the same qualities that drove her to escape the terror of the Russians and survive the long sea journey to Britain. She had never given in, and neither would he. His future was down to him now; and only him.

But it didn't last.

He couldn't get his mother out of his mind. She came back to him nightly by way of the same dream in which she drove a horse and cart at a fast gallop across a wide-open plain with him running after her. No matter how fast he ran, he never caught up with her, and he always woke from the dream feeling utterly alone. As a boy, he had mostly been a loner and he never tired of his own company but, with his mother gone, he felt desperately alone.

As the days went by he began to regret that his mother had not met Anita. Would she have liked her? Perhaps she would have helped him to understand why he'd connected

241

with Anita so quickly - and more fully why Anita had gone.

Reksis was his only distraction from the sense of complete isolation. The Alsatian never left his side, sleeping on his bed and going with him to the surgery. But the dog must have been suffering similar feelings of loneliness because Arnis couldn't leave him anywhere, even for a few seconds, without he started to yelp and howl. And Reksis constantly reminded him of the night of his mother's death and made him feel guilty. Guilty because he had ignored the dog in the early hours of the morning his mother had died. He had never made so much fuss before, certainly not in the middle of the night. He must have known.

Perhaps his mother had called out. Perhaps she'd sent Reksis to get him. Perhaps she'd been in pain. His dog had known, but he hadn't, and he tortured himself thinking he could have done something if only he had taken notice of Reksis. He was a doctor and that made it so much worse.

The enormity of what had happened began to sink in. As he searched within himself for the resources to carry on, he realised just how much he had relied on his mother. A fog began to cloud his brain and minor details became unimportant. He did everything he had to do but his energy and motivation had gone. At the end of each day he could barely remember the patients he'd seen, whether he'd had any lunch, or where he'd left the car.

He might have carried on like that for months had Antons not phoned one evening. 'Hello, Dad, how's things?'

'So, so.'

'Dad, I've been thinking about Granddad and what you said.'

There was a silence and Arnis waited for him to

continue. 'I want to go to Siberia.'

'Siberia?'

'Yes, I want to see where Granddad was. We can take the train from Moscow.'

'We?'

'Yes. I want you to come too.'

'But I thought you were going to Cuba next summer?'

'Summer? I was thinking of going to Siberia before that. I'm planning on February.'

'February? But you're going skiing.'

'I was, but I've changed my mind.'

'Antons, it's the middle of winter. Why don't we wait a bit?'

'Dad, I've made my mind up. Are you coming or not?'

Arnis sighed. 'Why such a hurry? I'll have to find someone to run the practice. And then there's the visa. It'll take me most of the next month to get that.'

'Stop exaggerating. It's not that bad.'

'That's what you think. You should see the queues at the embassy.'

But his son was not about to be put off. 'Dad, we can meet in Moscow. It will only take us three days to get to Krasnoyarsk so you needn't be away for too long.'

'You really have done your homework haven't you?' Arnis said.

Antons's enthusiasm was infectious and, as he talked on, Arnis began to warm to the prospect of the trip. Besides, the idea of going to Siberia had occurred to him in the past; even before he'd come to live in Rīga. He could make the same journey his father had made, see Siberia for himself, perhaps even find the place where his father had been. With Siliņš's help, they might even establish the precise location of the camp.

'You're up for this then?' Antons said.

'Yes, OK, but I need time to think about it. I'll call you back tomorrow.'

Arnis put the phone down.

*

The following morning he felt even more enthusiastic than he had before. His old energy returned and, within a couple of days, he had made arrangements for Sigita to look after Reksis and for a young doctor to look after his patients. She had recently finished her GP training and was delighted to get some experience in a small practice.

Arnis submitted his application for a visa at the Russian embassy then, later that same day, he telephoned Siliņš. 'How are things with you?' he asked after introductions.

'Not so good today,' Siliņš replied in a hoarse whisper. 'My throat's bad. You doctors are hopeless. All I get is a packet of pills and a lecture about smoking. I wouldn't mind, but I see my doctor smoking on the clinic doorstep every morning.'

'Have you seen the pulmonologist yet?'

'Dr Punka?'

'Yes.'

'I've got an appointment later this month. Thank you Arnis. I really appreciate your help. He gave a slight cough. 'Anyway, you haven't called to hear my troubles. What can I do for you?'

'The camp where you and my father were detained in Siberia? Can you remember it's name?'

'Why on earth do you want to know that?' Siliņš queried.

'My son and I are going.'

'To Siberia? Are you out of your mind? It was a living hell that place. Wild horses wouldn't drag me back there.'

But Arnis was not going to be put off. 'What was it called?' he insisted. 'Can you remember?'

'God, how could I ever forget? It was called Kraslov.'

'Kraslov. How far was it from Krasnoynarsk?'

'Distance-wise, I don't know. All I can tell you is … when they let me go … it took me two days to walk back to Krasnoyarsk, if that's any help,' he replied with a harsh laugh.

'Which direction?'

'It was to the north east of Krasnoyarsk. Let me think. It took a couple of hours in the truck. The road was awful. It must have been fifty or sixty kilometres, I suppose.'

'Anything else you can remember about the camp?'

'No … except it was near a railway line. I told you. We made sleepers.'

'Anything else?'

'No, that's it.'

Arnis knew that was all he was likely to get. 'Well, thanks for that. I really appreciate it. And I hope your throat soon gets better.'

*

The prospect of finally doing something positive to find out more about his father brought new determination. Over the next few days he settled back into his natural routine, feeling far less lethargic than before though he was inclined to occasionally break off from what he was doing and stare blankly out of the surgery window.

He spent few waking hours at home, preferring to eat out, returning to the flat just to sleep; unable to face any of the rooms his mother had spent most of her time in. They were a constant reminder of her.

When he went into the living room the first thing he saw was his mother's wicker rocking chair, still standing in the corner window. She had loved that window with its view of the Dom Square and the huge church. Even more, she had loved to watch the comings and goings in the street below. She always knew which waitresses were on duty at the café on the corner; how many people had been to the concerts, and whether it was the fat woman with the pink headscarf or the thinner woman with the blue headscarf who had swept the cobbles that morning.

After the red-bricked claustrophobia of South London, she relished the light of this lovely airy room, the occasional whiff of the sea breeze, and the sight of the seagulls, their wings tipped pale pink in the wintry afternoon sun. But now her chair remained empty though, for several days after her death, there were occasions when he could have sworn he'd seen it rocking very gently back and forth.

He had never regretted bringing her back, even though she had been saddened about some of the mess the Russians left behind in Latvia. She had settled in Britain but the homesickness never left her. The day her foot touched the tarmac at Rīga airport, a huge smile lit up her face and the tears had glistened in her eyes. That was a moment Arnis could never forget.

Her happiness had later been dimmed by anger and distress at what the communists had done to her country but she'd grown to realise she could avoid the grey Soviet uniform with its new cheap capitalist cloak of Marlborough and Coca Cola - even the sound of Russian being spoken - by staying in the old town. And that she did.

Before the autumn days finally turned to winter, she enjoyed pottering around the streets, delighted as old buildings were returned to their former medieval glory. She looked out for new shops or restaurants where they could have lunch on Saturdays - her treat, she always insisted. But she would never cross the park to the other side of the town if she could avoid it, preferring the old cobbled streets where the cars didn't screech round the corners, where she could amble about in peace, where she could close her mind to the reality that so much had changed.

About the only thing she ever missed from her flat in London was the silver birch Penny had bought her when they had been for a day out with the boys to the south coast.
Trees were almost sacred to her. When they lived in Scotland there was nothing she loved more than to walk in the forest. But no tree was more sacred than the birch with its beautiful silvery trunk.

Arnis stared at the wicker rocking chair and, without thinking, he did something he had never done before. He sat in it. Just for a few moments. Wondering if he would ever get rid of it.

Her room remained untouched, left exactly as it was on the night she died. Sooner or later, he would have to go through her things. A prospect he didn't relish.

He prepared a snack and then decided to have a quick look around her room to get an idea of how much there was to do. As he passed her dressing table he noticed a small green and white ceramic pot where he was pretty certain she kept her jewellery. Thinking he needed to put it in a safer place, he removed the lid to find not her watch and brooches but a small plastic bag filled with fine soil. He couldn't imagine why she'd brought that back to Rīga. It was soil he had scooped up from the park on his first visit to Latvia nearly ten years previously. She'd asked him to bring it and, although she'd kept it on her mantelpiece in London, he hadn't realised how she still treasured it.

Next he opened the wardrobe. She had always made most of her clothes and he found blouses, dresses and skirts she'd worn when he was small. She never threw anything away. At the back of her wardrobe, he found something he hadn't seen for a very long time. Carefully wrapped in a clear plastic bag was her national costume - a long gathered skirt in green and gold striped twill with a short bodice which she wore over a white linen tunic-shaped blouse with a stand-up collar decorated with blue cross stitch. There were also two shoulder cloaks - a white one edged with a bright yellow and red embroidered trim, topped by a planer dark blue one that had tassels hanging from the lower edge. He could remember her making it after they'd moved to Oban. Unsure what to do with it, he put it back in her wardrobe, and made neat piles of everything else.

Finally he had a quick look in her dressing table drawers where he was not surprised to find several unopened packets of tablets. She'd never had much patience with any medication, saying it made her feel worse than her angina, which in any case she could control better herself by walking very slowly and taking her time. Arguing with her was pointless, it always ended up with him surrendering, less out of sympathy for her, more because of her indefatigable will. Right about most things, she'd always said when the end came it would come suddenly, and as guilty as he'd felt about ignoring Reksis on the night she died, he was glad she'd been spared the agony of a long drawn-out illness.

As he walked back to the hall, he gazed at the urn he had collected from the undertaker the previous day. In the past, she had said he could bury her ashes under the birch tree in the back garden in London. But she had left no instructions after they came back to Latvia probably assuming she didn't need to say anything. She didn't; there was only one place they could go.

*

Arnis put Reksis in the car and set out once more for Kuldīga, taking the southerly route round the edge of the town until he reached the familiar avenue of leafless birch trees, with the pines straight ahead. Soon he came to the tell-tale mound – all that remained of the farm that had once been her childhood home. Apart from a fine dusting of snow, everything looked just the same as the last time he had seen it. He switched off the engine and gazed across the huge hedgeless field.

Everything was so bleak and suddenly he wasn't sure. Perhaps it was just the effect of the wintry scene that deterred him for a moment but then he knew this was exactly what she would have wanted. With Reksis at his side, he walked over to the frozen mound and climbed the two or three feet that took him to the summit.

He stared at the tiny bag of ashes; such a small token of a life that had lasted for so many years, but at least they would end their journey at the same place the journey had begun.

Gently, he tipped out the contents, scattering them across the mound, watching every grain as it fell into the snow. A sudden gust of wind snatched the lightest remnants and carried them beyond the mound until they too finally sank to the ground.

Arnis bent down to pick up the urn and walked back to the car. This time alone. When he turned, he saw Reksis lying quietly on top of the mound, unmoving except for his fur blowing in the light breeze. Arnis didn't have the heart to call him so he placed the urn in the boot, leant against the bonnet, and let him be.

As he gazed at the silent landscape he began to see not a bleak wintry scene, a huge expanse of emptiness, but a small farmhouse on a spring day. There was a lilac bush next to the front porch and wood smoke drifted lazily from the chimney. Apple and cherry blossom carpeted the ground. Couples danced in the farm yard to the accompaniment of a fiddle and an accordion. The air was filled with the sound of laughter and happy voices. The smell of newly mown hay filled the nostrils. In the distance, he saw a black horse pulling a plough. A young girl, with a long white pinafore tied round her waist, was carrying a basket full of wild strawberries. Her smiling grey eyes shone out from a healthy tanned face, her wavy hair was bleached by the sun. She walked towards him. When she was only a few yards away she waved and smiled. She called out his name.

Arnis blinked his tear-filled eyes. When he opened them again, she was gone.

CHAPTER 15

In some ways, Arnis wished Antons hadn't been so keen to make the journey so soon. Right now, he felt he needed more space. Although it was a trip he knew he had to make, he would sooner have put it off until the summer. But this was the first time in years that Antons had asked him to go anywhere with him and he had no intention of adding to the list of things he wished he'd done with his youngest son.

As the day drew closer, his enthusiasm started to increase but he was also a little apprehensive, as much about spending the next fortnight with Antons as he was about finding the camp where his father had been incarcerated.

How would the two of them get on together within the confines of a two-berth compartment on the train? They hadn't spent so much time in each other's company since the last family holiday and that was the summer before Antons did his A-levels.

During the few days Antons had been over for his grandmother's funeral there had been plenty to do, but thrown together for day after day with nothing to occupy them but the unchanging scenery? Yet Antons didn't seem to find the prospect too daunting and when the time came for Arnis to fly to Moscow his anxiety had begun to evaporate.

It was a glorious day, icy cold but with a clear blue sky. Snow blew like spindrift from the Dom tower. As he made his way to the car with Reksis, a sound like splintering glass indicated the roof men were busy knocking icicles off the eaves. Further down the street, some of their colleagues heaved snow onto the pavement showering unsuspecting passers by in artificial snowstorms.

Arnis drove round to the surgery to deposit the dog with Sigita and check that his locum had turned up before heading off to the airport. When he arrived he took Reksis straight up the stairs. The young doctor was already there but there was no sign of Sigita. He frowned. It was ten to nine. She was normally here at quarter to.

'Don't worry,' said Elizabete, with a smile. 'I'm sure she's on her way. You go. You can leave the dog with me,' she added looking at Reksis.

Arnis was unsure about this because Reksis knew Sigita, but a complete stranger? That might cause problems. And if the patients started to come in…

His dilemma was solved when he heard Sigita's soft footsteps on the stairs.

'I am sorry,' she said, as she came through the door. 'I ran all the way along Dzirnavu iela. It's a good job they've cleared the pavements.' She began to undo her coat. 'Wait while I get my breath back,' she added.

She regained her composure as she changed into her shoes then she went to switch the computer on. 'I'll make some coffee,' she said giving Arnis a sideways glance that indicated she had something to tell him in private. 'Can you give me a hand?'

He followed her on to the landing and into the tiny galley kitchen which looked out on to a small weed-filled courtyard surrounded by disused single-storey buildings. She filled the kettle and lit the gas.

'OK, what's so important that you can't make coffee on your own?' Arnis asked, smiling knowingly.

'I've just seen Anita,' she said in a low voice. 'That's why I was late.'

That took Arnis by surprise. 'Anita? Did you speak to her?'

'I did. She told me her mother isn't well. She was taken into hospital in a hurry. Did you know?

'No, I didn't,' he admitted. He hadn't heard a word from Mrs Reinberga since the day he visited her.

'Apparently she's coming out today,' Sigita continued.

'Where did you see Anita?'

'On the corner of Alberta iela. Near her house.'

'Was she on her way to the hospital? Did she say?'

'No. I mean yes. She said she was walking to the office.'

The office. That probably meant Reuters. Had she been going to *Diena*, she would have taken her car. He swallowed hard. 'How long ago was this?'

Sigita shrugged. 'Ten minutes perhaps. Like I told you, I ran all the way here.'

Ten minutes. Anita would be nearing the park by now.

He didn't hesitate a moment longer. He felt in his pocket for his car keys. 'I have to go,' he said. 'Please give my apologies to Elizabete.'

'And to Reksis?' Sigita shouted as he rushed down the stairs.

He drove towards Brīvības iela hoping, by some miracle, that there wouldn't be a queue of traffic. But as the bright blue onion-topped domes of the Russian church came

253

into view, he could see it was worse than usual so he carried straight on to Barona iela where he took a right turn, heading towards Aspazijas. Five minutes later he approached the opera house and spotted a parking place. He threw the car into the slot and rushed along in the direction of the Hotel de Rome. As he reached McDonalds he looked at his his watch. Twenty minutes had passed since Sigita saw Anita. He checked the entrance to the park but there was no sign of her coming up the path. Surely she couldn't have passed this way already. He stared towards the Freedom Monument, then back to the park and then he spotted her, walking up from the canal.

His heart missed a beat and he took several paces in the opposite direction. When he reached the corner of the next street, he turned round again. Sure enough, she was crossing the road behind a tram and he walked towards her, studying her face, longing to see her broad grin; longing to feel her lips on his cheek.

Anita noticed him just as she was about to go into Reuters and she didn't seem at all pleased to see him. 'Hello,' she said. Her voice was curt but polite, making him feel as if he was nothing more than a business colleague.

He reached out to touch her elbow but she quickly withdrew it. To him, it felt like a stab wound. For a few moments neither of them spoke but someone had to. He said the first words that came into his head. 'How's Linda?'

'She was OK when I last called. She's had the baby. A boy. He was born a week early.' She began to look upset.

'Is everything OK?'

'OK?' She gave him an anxious look, then shook herself. 'With the baby, you mean? Sure, everything's fine. He weighed four kilos.'

Arnis narrowed his eyes. 'And you?'

'I'm fine too,' she said hurriedly, glancing at her watch. 'Look, I'm sorry but I've got a meeting,' she said.

She started to walk towards the door and Arnis grabbed her hand. 'What's wrong? Tell me,' he said plaintively. But she made no reply and shot him a look of such anguish that he felt puzzled and scared at the same time. Not knowing what to say next, he squeezed her hand but she jerked it free and wiped a tear from the corner of her eye.

As Arnis rummaged in his pocket for a handkerchief, his airline tickets fell out on to the pavement.

'Are you going somewhere?' she asked.

He could sense the hope in her voice. 'Yes, Siberia,' he replied.

Now it was her turn to be surprised. 'Siberia?'

'Yes ... with my son. We're going to Krasnoyarsk to see where my father was.'

'Your father?' Her eyes narrowed and she gave him an odd look.

'Yes, you remember me telling you about him?' Though he hadn't told her much about his family, he was sure he had told her his father had been deported to Siberia and he felt somewhat hurt by the thought she could have forgotten.

'Yes ... I mean, no. Sorry, I don't remember,' she said, looking more and more flustered. 'Anyway, I really must go.'

Continuing to search her face, he was mystified by the expression in her eyes. He frowned, thinking her reaction might be similar to that of Siliņš – amazement that anyone would want to go willingly to Siberia. 'Look, can we talk when I get back? Arnis asked.

She looked uncertain. 'I don't know,' she replied. 'I might be back in Germany ...'

Now it was Arnis's turn to be uncertain. 'You're going back?'

She took a step towards the door without answering his question. Then she turned and took hold of his hand. Not with any warmth, more as a compassionate gesture. One that seemed to say 'Goodbye' for the last time. She kissed him softly on the cheek. 'I'm so sorry,' she said.

That was it. There was no further explanation. She went into the building and closed the door behind her. For a few moments, he stared at the door then he cast his eyes upwards at the dark brown façade. To no avail.

He retraced his steps to the car and drove to the airport feeling as if he had a huge open wound inside him. Why had she behaved like that? Why didn't she want to see him? What had he done wrong? He began to think about the day he'd seen her mother. Had he annoyed the old lady in some way? Had she said something to her daughter? If he had, he didn't have any idea what that might be. He thought she had warmed to him as much as he had warmed to her.

*

Arnis was still filled with puzzlement fifteen minutes later when he reached the airport. He parked the car and sat for a while, cursing himself for not having tried harder and for letting her go without an argument. The fact was, she might not be there when he got back. She had actually said something about going back to Germany. But what if she was planning to live there permanently? She had said once before that she wouldn't mind working there and she spoke fluent

German. As a freelance journalist, she would probably have no difficulty getting work.

The troubling thoughts in his brain swirled round like the snowflakes outside, and the idea of never seeing her again was too awful to contemplate. He tried to calm his mind and think rationally. How long would her meeting last? An hour? Could he catch her on her way out? If so, he'd have to miss his plane but it was worth a try. Anything was better than missing the last chance to see her before she went off. He could easily get a later flight.

Without another thought, he started the engine again and selected first gear. Only when he reached for the handbrake did he give any thought to Antons. He wouldn't be too thrilled about waiting at Moscow airport for another few hours, but he could text him. He stopped the engine again and jumped out of the car. Leaving his bag in the boot, he rushed into the airport building and quickly located the Aeroflot desk.

'I'm booked on the next flight to Moscow but what time is the following flight?' he asked the girl.

'Four fifteen,' she replied automatically.

His heart lifted. 'Can I change my booking?' he asked, handing her his ticket.

She looked slightly annoyed. 'There will be a charge.'

Arnis drummed his fingers on the desk as she did whatever she had to do. Eventually, she said, 'Sorry, I'm afraid the flight's already full.'

Full. He groaned aloud.

He thought quickly. They weren't due to go to Siberia until Monday so he got her to check the flights for the following day.

Her answer was the same. 'All the flights are full.'

Looking at her in disbelief, he did something he had never done before. He produced a twenty lati note and held it in front of her eyes.

Her patience snapped. 'Look, there's nothing,' she said, turning the screen to face him. 'You can come back tomorrow to see if there's a cancellation but with Latvia playing Russia I very much doubt there will be. I've already got people on stand-by.'

He had completely forgotten the international ice hockey match. For a moment he thought about cancelling the trip altogether. Then he thought about the effort Antons had put into planning the expedition; and the research he'd done into the camp. No doubt he would still go to Siberia on his own but, much as Arnis wanted to find Anita, he knew he couldn't let Antons down. Was Anita really worth the risk of souring his relationship with his son again? He had to admit she was not. With a heavy heart, he went back to the car and fetched his bag.

*

He bought a cup of coffee in the departures lounge and stared at the tarmac through the plate glass windows. He could have sworn he saw a picture of Anita etched on the surface. He shook himself. How could he persuade her to see him again? What could he do that would show how much she meant to him? What did she like?

At that precise moment, he heard his flight being called and decided it would have to wait until he reached Moscow. Then he had a better idea. He reached for his mobile and dialled a number. The seconds seemed to pass very slowly then a voice answered.

'Sigita, I need a favour,' he pleaded.

Sigita laughed. 'I thought you were on your way to Moscow. Come on, then. What do you need?'

'Could you go to the stall at the bottom of Brīvības and choose a really nice bunch of flowers? It doesn't matter what it costs. I want the very best. Do you think you can scrape enough money together? I'll pay you as soon as I get back.'

'OK, I'll see what I can do,' she said. 'Would you like me to deliver them as well?'

'Could you? I'd be really grateful if you could.'

'How grateful?' Sigita said, then she added, 'I'm only joking. Where do you want me to take them?'

'Two Alberta iela, flat five,' he replied.

There was a short silence after which she said, 'Ah, they're for Anita, are they?'

'They are.'

'Then I can't take them to that address. She doesn't live there any more.'

'Doesn't …? But you said you'd seen her near there this morning.'

'I did, but she's no longer there. She let her flat to my aunt … that's the aunt who split up with my uncle. I told you. Remember?'

Arnis wasn't sure that he did remember but then he had a habit of letting chit-chat bypass him. Often deliberately. But if Anita had let her flat, perhaps his worst fears were confirmed. She was leaving Rīga. His heart sank.

Sigita started to giggle. 'It's a good job somebody's got a handle on things round here,' she said teasingly 'Anita's staying with a friend called Laura. And I know her.'

Anyone Sigita didn't know in Rīga was obviously not

worth knowing. He told her so frequently.

Sigita continued, 'Laura works at the Radi un Draugi so I can easily find out where she lives. Don't worry, I will make sure Anita gets the flowers,' she said, obviously enjoying the moment.

For a second, Arnis almost changed his mind. What was the point of sending flowers if Anita really was leaving Rīga? But her image again came to his mind, and the memory of the last time they'd made love...

'Thanks,' he said to Sigita. 'Thanks a lot. I won't forget this.'

'No, nor will I,' she said, laughing.

'I'll leave it with you then,' he said to end the conversation.

'Wait a minute,' Sigita said. 'You've forgotten something. What are you going to put on the card?'

'Card?'

'Oh come on, you must have sent flowers before.'

'I'm not very good with words but I'm sure you'll think of something,' he added, beginning to feel embarrassed.

Sigita was scandalised. 'Are you crazy? She'll freak if she finds out you've sent your receptionist to buy flowers for you and write the message. I would anyway. If Markuss did that I'd kill him. She doesn't know you're on your way to Moscow. Have you no idea? Think of something really romantic,' she said, clearly relishing the fun.

'OK. Put something like ... Wait. Let me think...' His neck started to redden.

'Yes?' she said, obviously enjoying making him squirm.

'Put... Dear Anita.' He gave a deep breath.

'Is that it?'

'No, hang on.' Phrase after corny phrase floated through his mind. 'I've waited all my life to meet someone like you. I'm not going to let you go now.' And others. But they all sounded pathetic.

He swallowed hard. 'Put... I love you.' There was a silence at the other end of the phone. 'Have you got that?'

'Yes, don't worry at all,' Sigita replied, her tone suddenly serious. 'Consider it done. I'll go straight away.'

He switched off his phone and his stomach felt as if it was tied in knots. After finding his seat on the aircraft he got out his trans-Siberian handbook and tried to dismiss Anita from his mind but his inner turmoil became worse as he tried to think whether he'd done the right thing or not. If only he could have found out why she was so upset. But not knowing for sure, he had no idea what her reaction would be. Maybe he'd made it worse by sending her flowers.

Half an hour later the drinks came round. 'Tomato juice,' he said to the girl.

'Vodka and tonic,' said the young chap sitting next to him. 'I've had a bad morning,' he said, turning to Arnis with a grin. 'I nearly didn't make the plane. My editor was in a foul mood.'

'Who do you work for?' Arnis was happy to let the young man talk.

'*The Baltic Times*. Not for much longer though. I'm going back to Canada in the summer.'

'Sounds like you're looking forward to it.'

'Yes. Yes I am. The politics in this country does my head in.'

Arnis had to smile. With more than thirty political

parties jostling for power, the Latvian political scene was certainly complicated.

'What do you think about the citizenship issue?' the young man continued.

'It's been ratified by Parliament,' Arnis replied evenly.

'About time too,' said the young man. 'It's ridiculous when you've lived here for fifty years and you can't get citizenship, just because you can't speak Latvian.'

Arnis said nothing. He did not entirely agree and in normal circumstances he would have been interested to engage in a debate, but he couldn't get Anita out of his mind. He let the young man continue, which he did at great length, and in a similar vein. 'Russian ought to be allowed as an official language alongside Latvian. After all, there are more Russians in Rīga than Latvians. And even Latvians have to speak Russian if they want to communicate with people from Estonia and Lithuania.'

'No, they don't,' Arnis said sharply. The young man's last comment made him cross. 'Not the young people. A lot of them are as fluent in English as you and I.' He knew that the journalist could not argue with that. But he was clearly an opinionated young man - typical of so many foreign correspondents whose unthinking reaction was to side with an ethnic minority.

Sipping his tomato juice, he stared out of the window, and he felt a sense of relief when the 'fasten seat belt' signs came on again. Ten minutes later, the wheels touched down in Moscow and again he began to think of Anita, wondering whether Sigita had managed to deliver the flowers. He tried to imagine Anita's face when she saw them; when she read the words on the card. That worried him and he began to wish he hadn't said what he said. He hunched down in his seat, suddenly imagining everyone was staring at him, and waited till most of the other passengers had disembarked.

The queue through immigration did nothing to help matters and only when he saw Antons on the other side of the barrier did he begin to feel in a more positive frame of mind.

'Hi, Dad. Bang on time. Glad I didn't have to hang around. This is such a gloomy place,' he said.

Antons was in fine spirits and he chatted incessantly about the things he wanted to see in Moscow. 'I was wondering how many concerts we could fit in between now and Monday,' he concluded as they boarded the Moscow bus. By the time they reached the city centre, the snow was falling heavily making it extremely treacherous underfoot.

They checked into their hotel and then went for a walk. Antons's enthusiasm was infectious and Arnis felt quite exhilarated as he took in the grandeur of a city he'd never really wanted to visit. They filed into Lenin's mausoleum and ate a grilled chicken lunch in GUM. In the afternoon, they went to see the Kremlin and Arnis agreed to Antons's suggestion that they should buy tickets for the Bolshoi, even though he had no interest in ballet.

They managed to get seats for that evening and had a snack of red berry pancakes and cream at a restaurant next to the Conservatory before they made their way to the theatre to watch the Nutcracker.

During the interval, a petite middle-aged woman in the row behind, leaned forward and said. 'Where are you from?'

'Rīga,' replied Arnis as he turned around.

She smiled. 'Ah, Latvia. My great grandfather was Lithuanian. I try and get back to Vilnius for the song festival

263

occasionally but it's not so easy these days.' There was a sad reminiscent look in her eyes then she smiled again. 'So what brings you to Moscow?'

'We're going to Siberia,' Antons replied.

She nodded, as though she understood but said no more until the curtain dropped at the end of the performance. 'See that,' she whispered with an impish grin that reminded Arnis of his mother. 'I'll bet you don't have one like that in Rīga
any more.'

Arnis followed her eyes and saw the large golden embroidery on the face of the curtain. She was absolutely correct: there were no hammer and sickle signs left in Rīga.

Arnis gave the lady a wry smile.

CHAPTER 16

The next day they arrived at Yaroslav station to find the platform was seething with people. With their vast array of bags they looked like a herd of pack mules laying in for a long siege, and as the dark green coaches reversed into the platform a feverish expectation set up. They pushed their way onto the train to find their compartment. Furnished with brown floral curtains and a brown and white striped carpet, it had a bunk on each side and a sink under the window. As the train eased its way out of the station, Arnis began to feel as if he was dreaming, and neither the hiss of the samovar nor the faint sound of a balalaika was enough to make it feel real.

The Moscow suburbs dissolved into the grey dusk and Antons, whose thoughts had inevitably turned to food, went off to investigate. He came back a few moments later with a long face. 'I shouldn't bother going down there. There's nothing apart from cabbage soup and meat balls,' he moaned.

'What did you expect? A Big Mac?' said Arnis

Antons rooted in his backpack for a block of chocolate. 'In my dreams,' he replied. 'But hey, it's not all bad news. The guy at the end of the corridor is a scuba diver ... from Liverpool.'

'That's the last I shall see of you then for the next three days,' said Arnis wryly.

Reacting almost as though his father's words were a

personal blessing, Antons disappeared down the corridor. He had taken up scuba diving the previous summer and had rapidly developed an enormous passion for it.

Arnis stared out of the window trying to orientate himself. He spread a map across his bunk and traced the route to Krasnoyarsk with his forefinger; the same journey his father had been forced to make nearly sixty years earlier but without the luxury of a blue-uniformed attendant to bring glasses of steaming tea. Although it was not particularly hot in the compartment he began to sweat and turned off the heating, wondering how he might have coped if he'd had to lay on a hard plank floor, fighting the other occupants for a small space to rest. An aching body. Wondering when the journey would end. The train wheels creaked and groaned, snatching at his questions, but returning no answers: I really don't know, I really don't know, I really don't know...

Suddenly not wanting to be alone with his thoughts, he decided to try the restaurant car. Despite what Antons said, the meatballs were actually quite good and the egg salad with sour cream was better still. He ordered a glass of beer as a huge man with a flame-coloured beard started to play an accordion. Two women stood up to dance and he was gradually mesmerised by the rhythm.

Thoughts of the crowded deportation truck began to dissipate only to be replaced by Anita, of the last conversation they'd had. Wanting to force her from his mind, he immediately ordered another glass of beer and his eye was drawn to a man sitting at a table on the opposite side of the dining car. The man smiled and introduced himself. 'Hello, I'm Ernst,' he said. 'I'm on my way to see my son in Irkutsk,' he added. 'He's running a bear sanctuary there.'

The next hour passed pleasantly enough as Arnis talked to the man who, it turned out, was a computer programmer from Munich. It was past ten o'clock when Arnis made his way back to the compartment where he found Antons writing his journal.

'Hi, Dad,' he said without looking up from his pad of paper. 'Where have you been? I see you're being your usual sociable self.'

Ignoring the remark, Arnis sat down and peered out into the inky blackness. Apart from the flickering lights of a few scattered communities, it seemed like a very bleak and lonely landscape. Feeling his eyelids start to close, he lay back on his bunk and was asleep almost instantly.

*

He awoke before the sun was up, filled with a sense of gloom and emptiness. Suspecting it was due to a bad dream, he dressed quickly. Antons was still asleep so he went out into the corridor and sauntered up and down for a while, hoping his mood would lift. Outside, the unchanging scenery swept by, barren apart from a sprinkling of isolated huts and electric pylons. The snow-glazed desolation mirrored his own sense of emptiness and he was glad when the train pulled into a station for a short stop.

As he climbed down the steps the sight of a few traders cheered him a little. Clad in woolly hats, quilted coats and fur boots, not to mention a thick layer of feisty determination, they were all ready to squabble should any traveller dare to buy pirozhki, blini, a few buns or a piece of roast chicken from one but not the other.

A few moments later, Antons appeared with another

guy, presumably his new scuba diver friend. They both did twenty press-ups on the platform and then jogged off in the freezing air. The same pattern was repeated at every station halt. By the time they reached Ekaterinburg, Arnis was getting used to the routine. Leaving the two youngsters to their gymnastics, he strolled along the platform and went into the station hall. Like all the other stations they had passed through, this one was also thronged with beggars, drunks and lines of people waiting for tickets.

After a quick look round he went to a newspaper stand, hoping to buy a postcard to send to Sigita. He couldn't see any and was about to leave the stall when he suddenly remembered something Siliņš had said. Ekaterinburg was the name of the station where his father had bought a newspaper.

He pictured his father standing where he was now, newspaper in hand, surrounded by travelling companions trying to get a glimpse of the headlines, anxious for news they had been deprived of for more than a month. Perhaps they were cautiously optimistic as they read that the German army had attacked the Soviet Union. Hoping it was the beginning of the end; that Russia would lose the war; that they would soon be able to return to an independent Latvia. Perhaps it was the first time they'd been let off the train since leaving Rīga. Perhaps someone had mentioned that this town was the place where the Romanovs were murdered.

Arnis scanned the row of newspapers and picked up a copy of the local one before he went back to his compartment.

*

The train rolled eastwards, its motion so quiet and slow that sleep was easier that night. The next morning, the scenery

268

looked exactly the same as it did the previous day giving the impression they had barely moved. At the next station, Antons rushed off to replenish their supplies of beer and victuals, mainly chocolate, while Arnis sauntered up and down the platform chatting to Ernst.

When he got back to the compartment, Antons was busy unpacking the food he'd bought and a whiff of hot chicken quickly dispelled any notion he had of visiting the restaurant car. The chicken dinner soon disappeared, along with a fresh pineapple they had bought in Perm the day before. A glass of vodka topped off the meal and then Arnis started to clear up the debris. That was when he realised Antons had cut the pineapple slices on the Ekaterinburg newspaper. He was cross with his son, and was on the point of saying so when the attendant came in with a tray of tea. After that, nothing was said. There was no point anyway. The paper was damp and sticky but he couldn't bear to let it go. He folded it up and placed it under his bunk.

*

With less than twenty-four hours to go before they would reach Krasnoyarsk, Arnis was feeling increasingly apprehensive. He began going over the things Siliņš had told him about the camp. He tried to picture it; long low wooden huts, barbed wire fence, isolated from the rest of the world in a desolate wilderness, the like of which had been the backdrop for most of the journey so far. But would there be anything left when they got there? They knew that it had been closed down in the fifties, but had it been destroyed?

As if in answer to his unspoken thoughts, Antons produced a sheaf of internet print-outs from his backpack. 'I came across a group of people in Krasnoyarsk who have set up an association in memory of the people who perished in the camps,' he said. 'I got in touch with them.'

'And?'

'I got all the information about the camp. And how to get there.'

'You make it sound so easy,' Arnis said. 'I suppose you did all that on the internet.'

'Trouble with you, Dad, is you're medieval. You won't learn to use new technology,' replied Antons, smirking.

Arnis laughed. It was true, though he was using email more these days. And he had to acknowledge that the internet had proved useful in this case.

*

On the final day of their journey, a small clutch of smokestacks came into view and they immediately looked at one another. A few moments later, the train came to a stop and Arnis felt almost reluctant to leave its now familiar comfort. A freezing wind blew as they made their way over the bridge and a constant barrage of piercing shrieks rained down like a fusillade from the loud hailers announcing the next departure. They weren't at all like the cultured voices over the tannoys at London's Victoria station and for the first time in months Arnis felt a trace of nostalgia for Britain. It was less than a year ago but it seemed so much longer.

As they searched for a taxi, an army vehicle pulled up on the forecourt and a squad of soldiers jumped out. Arnis stared at the young, sallow-skinned lads and suddenly felt an overpowering sense of hatred for them; his mind finding it difficult to separate them from the soldiers who would have marched his father through this same station yard more than half a century ago. He watched angrily as they stamped on to the platform. Only when the last of them had disappeared did he look round for Antons who, by then, was on the other side of the station forecourt standing next to a yellow Lada.

They both climbed in and the taxi set off for the town. The centre wasn't quite as grim as the outskirts suggested and the pall of smokestacks and squalid slums soon gave way to long straight avenues lined by honey-coloured apartment blocks. The onion-topped domes of a distant church blazed bronze under the wintry midday sun.

The driver spoke a few Russian words; enough for Arnis to understand that he wanted to know where they were from.

Arnis told him.

'Rīga!' the driver's face paled and his huge blue eyes watered. 'I came from Latvia. From Cēsis,' he said. 'I was deported here in forty-nine … eight years after my father.'

Arnis felt his stomach turn. He knew some Latvians had stayed on in Siberia but he hadn't expected to meet one. He listened in silence, trying to understand the rest of his story.

'My father died in the camp,' he continued. After that, they couldn't understand him.

Arnis gazed at the driver thinking how easily this could have been him. Had his mother and father been deported together, he would have been born here. He'd been lucky, though that didn't ease his guilt. He knew his life had been easy by comparison to this man's.

'Do you think he speaks Latvian?' Antons whispered from the back seat. If the driver heard him, there was no

271

flicker of recognition.

When Arnis asked him the same question in Russian, he looked sheepish and shook his head. 'No. I've forgotten it.'

'Have you been back to Latvia?' Arnis asked, quite sure the man would not really have forgotten his Latvian.

'No,' he replied. 'What have I got to go back for? All my family is dead.'

He drove on and they sat in silence until they reached the hotel. As he opened the car door, Arnis felt a tap on his shoulder and turned round to Antons who lowered his voice and spoke in English. 'Dad, do you think he might take us tomorrow?'

Arnis thought for a moment. It was too good an opportunity to miss. 'Do you know where Kraslov is?' he asked him.

The driver shrugged.

'My father was there,' Arnis explained. 'We want to see it.'

'There's nothing to see,' the driver said off-handedly.

'Nevertheless, will you take us?'

The man's face registered momentary fear then he saw the dollars in Arnis's hand. 'Yes. OK. Nine o'clock. Here.'

Arnis gave the man twenty dollars and he drove off.

Antons's expression was one of incredulity.

'What's the matter with you?' Arnis asked.

'Are you crazy? You gave that man twenty dollars. That's probably more than a month's wages here. I wouldn't mind, but it wasn't as far as Westminster Abbey to Buckingham Palace.'

Arnis didn't feel any need to defend himself and led the way up the steps into the hotel foyer. A slim blonde girl was sitting behind a high semi-circular teak-veneered desk. Surrounded by cigarette smoke and two plastic pot plants, she ignored them and carried on reading her book. Arnis was in no mood for a surly receptionist and slammed his passport down in front of her.

She ignored the gesture and continued reading to the bottom of the page, then she looked at his passport and ran her pen down the list of names. 'Room 106,' she said, taking a key from the row of hooks behind her.

Alarm bells rang in Arnis's head. Room 106 would be on the first floor. If there was a disco later on, as there usually was in these sorts of hotels, that would mean a sleepless night, or at least, a mostly sleepless night, and he didn't relish the thought of incessant throbbing music until the early hours. 'Can we have a room on a higher floor?' he asked.

'We're full,' she said unsympathetically.

Arnis gazed at the rows of keys but she didn't flinch and resumed reading.

Trying to keep a straight face, Antons whispered in English, 'Go for it, Dad.'

Not desperate to provide Antons with any more entertainment, he scowled at the girl. 'Look. I want a room on the top floor.'

She ignored him completely and Antons couldn't control himself any longer. He went outside and burst into laughter.

That was the last straw. 'I am not having room 106,' Arnis said loudly and forcibly.

Antons came back in just as she slammed another key down in front of his father. 'OK. You can have room 406.'

'Thanks,' Arnis said. 'That's better.'

It wasn't.

Room 406 smelled of smoke, the cheap pink floral wallpaper was peeling at the edges, and a picture of Lenin hung above the dressing table. Not totally unexpected but the bedside lights didn't work and only one of the four bulbs in the central light fitting actually lit. Worse, there was no hot water and the brown-painted radiator under the window was stone cold.

Antons started to laugh again.

'OK, you think it's so funny,' said Arnis chucking him the key, 'so it's your turn now. Don't come back until you've got us a room fit to sleep in.'

Antons returned less than five minutes later with the key for room 306, as it turned out, pretty much a replica of 406 but with hot water and a working radiator.

'You're losing your touch, Dad,' he said with a grin. 'She'll do anything for me.'

They both showered and changed, which put Arnis in a slightly better frame of mind. Now all they needed was food. They headed back downstairs.

The dining room was deserted apart from one couple in the far corner. As they ate a quite decent meal of steak and fries, Arnis realised just how many other empty rooms there probably were.

*

The temperature had fallen dramatically overnight. Wearing the warmest clothes they could muster to combat the intense cold, they waited outside for the taxi driver. Right on time, a horn peeped and the yellow Lada drew up in front of them.

They got in and the driver smiled. 'I'm Vilis,' he said.

Five minutes later they crested a huge bridge over a wide river and Vilis gesticulated downstream. 'My father. Norilsk,' he said.

Arnis nodded and stared down at the opaque grey water which was obviously too polluted to freeze over, even in midwinter. He knew Norilsk lay far to the north of here, well beyond the Arctic Circle. That must be where Vilis's father had been sent and there was little wonder he had died. He glanced at Vilis, wondering what he was thinking.

As the suburbs slipped away, the view opened up and Vilis began to talk a little. With a few common words of Russian between them, they managed to communicate in a fashion. Vilis seemed to be particularly interested in Rīga and Arnis was able to assure him it was a much better place after the Russians left, despite the damage they left behind.

Vilis said little after that, obviously turning things over in his mind. Eventually, he produced a tape from the glove box and put it in the cassette player. Arnis immediately recognised the Beatles music and as Yellow Submarine started to play he thought of Penny, of the coffee bar in Forest Hill where he used to meet her. That was where he'd first heard the song. How much simpler life had been then.

Straight ahead, the horizon was blotted with chimneystacks and slagheaps, the surface evidence of countless coal mines, some worked out and derelict, others where the wheel was still turning. It was a dismal landscape. He wondered if his father had travelled this way from Krasnoyarsk. If so, what had he been thinking about? What had his ambitions been? Had he dreamed of returning to Latvia one day to become the headmaster of the school in Kuldīga? Had he wanted to a family? What had been important to him? The more Arnis thought about it, the sadder he felt. He didn't know any of the answers and probably never would.

*

A little while later they turned off the main road and drove to the edge of a small town. Vilis switched off the music and said, 'Another five minutes.'

They continued along the main street driving over potholes smoothed by thick black ice. A few babushkas were clearing snow from the steps but otherwise the town seemed deserted. They cleared the town limits and crested a slight rise, from there dropping down towards a small coniferous forest. Apart from a line of electric pylons, the countryside was empty.

Arnis looked at Vilis as he started to slow down. Was this it? Was this where the camp had been? It was just an ordinary rural spot - bleak but still ordinary with nothing to show there had ever been a camp there. Vilis speeded up again and they drove into the forest. A long five minutes, Arnis thought to himself.

Moments later, the trees thinned out and Vilis slowed down to cross a disused railway track. Arnis glanced ahead and then he knew they were almost there. This was what they'd come to see. In direct line of sight were two rotting watchtowers and a broken barbed wire fence.

Vilis stopped the car and Arnis and Antons got out. The stillness was extraordinary and they stood in total silence for some while before they walked towards the barbed wire perimeter fence. Arnis began to wish that Vilis had been right; that there really was nothing to see. He stared at the silent watchtowers, the barbed wire, the disused railway track, willing them to disappear. Why couldn't they have destroyed it? Or left a memorial stone. Anything would have been better than this. The watchtower, looking as if it had just been deserted, made him think of the guards who had manned it. Had they relished their savage duties? Or had they turned a blind eye when someone strayed near to the perimeter fence?

Antons had already climbed over the barbed wire fence and Arnis joined him at the base of the watchtower. Then they walked together towards a ruined hut. The remains of a door hung like a skeleton from an iron frame. Antons pushed it aside and they went into the rotting building.

They stood there in silence until their eyes got used to the darkness then they could see there was nothing inside. Had they not known what it was, it could just as easily have been a disused farm hut. But it had at one time held men; his own father perhaps. What must that have been like for him? His freedom taken away. Longing to take a breath of air no longer enclosed by barbed wire or littered with the harsh shouts of soldiers. Staring along the railway track he was being forced to build, but having no possibility to use it. Bed bugs, lice, the constant threat of dysentery, hunger, blistered feet, aching shoulders. A sense of self-preservation the only thing left, preventing him from insanity. Had he tried to escape?

Antons was obviously thinking similar thoughts. 'Granddad must have been strong to cope with this. Imagine what it must have been like in these freezing conditions. Coming here night after night, tired, hungry, deprived of freedom, deprived of life. I don't think I could have survived that.'

'Me neither,' Arnis muttered. 'That generation was made of sterner stuff.' Suddenly, he thought of his anger at the threat of losing his independence as a GP back in London. Momentarily he felt a sense of shame, which was quickly overtaken by the realisation of the depth with which his father must have hated this place. Not just the physical deprivation, perhaps not even the fear of losing his judgement in the long agonising ordeal of interrogation, but the loss of his homeland and all that he had worked for. He thought of the note, of the record of his father's release and many other things. As the minutes passed, he felt he no longer cared where his father had gone after he was released. Anywhere must have been better than this.

They each said a silent prayer then they went outside.

There was nothing more to see and nothing more to do. They had learned nothing that would tell them what happened after Arnis's father got away from this dreadful place, and there was nothing to show he had ever been there – no memorial to the men who had suffered for the cause of defending the rights of their own country. Arnis regretted not bringing a plaque with his name on; or a cross. He could have easily had something made in Rīga before he left.

He turned to Antons with a tear in his eye. As if reading his thoughts, Antons said in a quiet voice, 'Why don't we write a letter to Granddad. We can leave it inside the hut.'

Arnis looked at him as though he was seeing him for the first time. It was as if Antons was a different person, not the lad he'd known for twenty-six years. A stranger, and yet not a stranger. He smiled as Antons began to root in his jacket pocket for some paper.

Finding nothing appropriate, he said, 'We'll have to go

back to the car and get something. Besides, a pen probably won't work in these temperatures.'

Vilis was waiting patiently, keeping himself warm with the heat from the engine. They climbed in out of the chill and then Arnis got out his pen and thought for a few moments.

'What do you think I should write?' he asked, turning to Antons.

Antons shrugged. 'Tell him we came here looking for him ...'

And so Arnis began to write:

'Dear Dad,

We came here to remember you and to see this awful place where you were held for so many years, removed from the family who loved you. Although we never knew you, I want you to know we never stopped thinking about you. As a child I longed for you to be with us. I missed you during my schooling. It would have been so much easier with you to help me. I missed you when I went to university, when I qualified as a doctor, when I got married, when Henrijs and Antons were born. I hope you would have been proud of me, and of your two grandsons. Because I am proud to have had you for a father.

With all our love

Arnis and Antons.'

He passed the note to Antons. 'What do you think?'

Antons nodded his approval and together they walked back to the hut and pushed the note over a nail on the inside of the door. They gazed at it in silence for a few moments, then Antons said. 'That's all we can do, Dad.'

They closed the door behind them and walked away.

CHAPTER 17

Arnis made sure he arrived early on his first day back at the surgery, expecting there would be a great deal of catching up to do. In fact, there was hardly any. The locum and Sigita had kept the practice running very efficiently.

Sigita explained that they hadn't actually been too busy but most of the patients had asked for him. That made him smile.

He went through to his consulting room and signed some letters. As he heard the first patients entering the waiting room, he felt very glad to be back home.

Sigita showed in the first patient and dropped a printed note on his desk. He glanced at it briefly then he read it again when surgery was over.

'Dear Arnis

I put your message out on Latvia Radio but I'm sorry to say that there hasn't been any response. No one in Australia seems to have heard of your father. But if I can be of any further help, please let me know.

Andrejs Germanis'

In some ways, the news brought relief. It didn't help answer any questions but it seemed to eliminate a possibility that, after all, had mostly been based on speculative hearsay. The words of the old man in Kuldīga came into his mind. 'He was a man of very high integrity,' Siliņš had said. 'Your father loved Latvia and always said he would die for it. That's what kept him alive in the camp. Towards the end, he was like the rest of us ... weak and sick ... but he never lost his will to defend his country.'

Arnis smiled to himself, more certain than ever that his father had died as a partisan fighting the Russians in the forest. All that remained was to find out for sure. If he made another trip to Kuldīga he might be able to trace his father's family. Someone should know them. And Siliņš might also have some information about them.

But there was something he had overlooked completely and it was so obvious, he kicked himself for not having thought of it before. Why had he never thought to check the telephone directory for the name of Vilks?

As he walked across to the bookshelves to fetch the directory, Sigita came in carrying a small white envelope. He took it from her and recognised the handwriting immediately. He teased a small card from the envelope and read it.

5.02.2003

'Dear Arnis,

By the time you read this, I will be in England. I think it is best if we don't see each other again. We had some good times that I shall always remember. Thank you for those. But I don't love you. I could never love you. I'm so very sorry. I think I'm too independent to commit myself to anyone. I love my freedom too much.

Please don't take this too hard. In time a new door will open. Think ahead. Life can take unexpected turns and we need to be prepared. I hope that eventually you may see our

281

meeting as fate without which other things could not have happened. Everything happens for a reason. Take good care of yourself. Be strong.

Thanks for everything,
Anita'

England! That was not what he was expecting. So she hadn't even chosen to be close to her daughter and her new grandchild. With a heavy heart, he read the card again. His eyes lingered over every word. Independence. Freedom. Things he related to very well. Yet things he knew he would have been prepared to give up to be with Anita. For the hundredth time, he wished he hadn't pushed her about going to a conference. He was sure that's where things had gone wrong between them. He'd been too possessive. She had said as much on the telephone the day she'd gone to Germany. He should have known better. Penny had once accused him of treating her like a possession.

He read the last few lines of the letter again again and began to feel quite confused. *'I hope you might see our meeting as fate without which other things could not have happened.'* What did she mean by that? Then anger began to rise in his chest as it dawned on him that she was only trying to make herself feel better. All this mystical stuff about fate. She sounded exactly like his mother. As for going to England, that was almost the worst of it. How long had she been planning it? Had she already been offered the job when he last saw her? Had she said she might be back in Germany just to make him think she was going to see her grandson again, letting him hope that she would come back to Rīga? Maybe she wanted to let him down gently. Or was it that she didn't want to tell him to his face?

He began to feel more and more angry.

Sigita reappeared with another drink and some pastries and he forced himself to smile. 'I did take the flowers,' she said, giving him a look that said she knew.

He took a mouthful of pastry but it tasted like sawdust. He had a few sips of coffee and then put his head in his hands, feeling an acute sense of loneliness, worse than at any time since his mother had died.

Suddenly, he felt a nudge against his leg. He had completely forgotten Reksis, lying quietly, as he always did, on his grey blanket in the corner. But Reksis sensed his misery.

'I've blown it, lad,' Arnis said, rubbing the dog's head and fondling his ears. 'I've lost her. She isn't coming back.' He gave a deep sigh. 'Oh dear, this won't do, as Mum would have said. We mustn't feel sorry for ourselves. Anyway, you don't leave me, do you? You're always here, aren't you?'

Reksis licked his hand and thumped his tail on the floor.

*

The twenty-sixth of February was Arnis's sixty-first birthday and he woke with a sense of expectancy. But he was sure it had nothing to do with the anniversary as his mother had never made much of birthdays and, as the number got higher, they became something he wanted to forget. So he didn't understand why he felt so chirpy on this particular day.

For the previous few days, he had taken no pleasure in anything. Everything had been a huge effort: dealing with patients, taking Reksis for a walk, getting up in the morning. Especially getting up in the morning.

On his way out to work, he checked the post box and

found four cards - one from Antons, one from Ella and one from Vieda. The fourth took him by surprise: Henrijs had not sent him a birthday card for many years.

He arrived at the surgery feeling more buoyant than ever. Not even the sight of Mrs Dragunova dampened his spirits. In any case the waiting room was already full, so he would have a good excuse to limit her to five minutes at the very most.

The evening surgery was even busier than the morning one. By the time the last patient left, he was really looking forward to putting his feet up at home with a can of beer and a video. After he tidied up, he heard Sigita talking to someone in the waiting room. He opened the door. A man and a woman were standing with their backs to him staring intently at his practising certificate, chatting to Sigita. The woman was dressed in a maroon mack and a black beret, the man in a shabby grey overcoat and a blue cap. As the woman turned, he stared at her in shocked recognition.

It was Anita's mother.

He was so taken aback that he did not hear Sigita's words. 'Did you know Mr and Mrs Reinbergs also come from Kuldīga?' she said.

Mrs Reinberga's eyes narrowed and she stared intently at him, making him feel positively uncomfortable. Intuitively he felt their visit must have something to do with Anita but Sigita had a look of childish excitement on her face and was obviously determined to speak first.

The old man made as if to say something, but Sigita was too anxious to rush out her news. 'It seems they knew your mother,' she said. 'They weren't sure, even when they saw the name on your certificate but when I told them her name was Margarita, and that you were born in Kuldīga, that your mother had taken you to England, that you had become a doctor, and that you came back to Latvia with her last year…'

Her words came out in a torrent, and Arnis hardly had time to digest that they were from Kuldīga when the old man spoke in a shaky voice. 'Your mother really is here? In Rīga?' His face lit up and he sounded as if he couldn't believe it.

'Sadly, no, she's not,' Arnis replied in a more matter-of-fact tone than he felt. 'She died just before Christmas. Actually it was the night after I visited you, Mrs Reinberga.'

On hearing those words, a look of anguish swept across his face. It was as if the ground had disappeared from beneath him and his tremor, which hadn't been so obvious up to that moment, became very conspicuous.

'You'd better sit down,' Arnis told him. 'Sigita, can you get a drink, please?'

The old man lowered himself slowly into a chair and gratefully accepted the glass of water Sigita had fetched. His hand was shaking as he put it to his lips.

'Did you know my mother well?' Arnis asked.

He looked up into Arnis's face and replied quietly, 'We were good friends for a long time.'

'So you knew my father also? Kārlis Vilks?'

The old man's face changed in an instant, his eyes glazed and his anguish was replaced by a sterner expression. 'Kārlis Vilks,' he repeated. 'Yes, I knew Kārlis Vilks.'

'Do you know what happened to him? He was deported to Siberia, but I don't know what happened to him after that. I think he was released, but I haven't been able to find out any more. I think he might have come back to Kuldīga. Did you ever see him again?' He felt excited as if the old man might be able to tell him something.

The old man hesitated before he replied. 'No, I never saw him again.'

'You were in the camp, too?'

'No.'

Arnis cast his eyes to the floor, his hopes snuffed out. Then he thought of something else. 'Perhaps you knew my father's family,' he said hopefully. 'Mother told me he had a sister called Anna but I never managed to trace her. Perhaps he had other brothers or sisters ... perhaps they had children who are still living in Latvia. Can you help me?'

The old man rose shakily to his feet. 'Sorry, doctor, I cannot!' he answered with a strange conviction in his voice.

Mrs Reinberga joined in the conversation for the first time. 'Perhaps now is the time to tell Doctor Rozenvalds what he needs to know,' she said.

The old man glared at her. 'No, I will not.' Then he headed towards the door. Just as he reached it, he turned and glared at Arnis. 'I had no time for Vilks. In fact, I hated the man.'

His eyes were now blazing. 'Vilks always thought he could get his own way and usually did. He thought his family's money could buy him anything he wanted. He walked all over people and thought nothing of it. That's why I despised him so much.'

Arnis was now quivering with rising anger. Everyone else had spoken so highly of his father, how dare this man criticise him?

But the old man had not finished. He shook his finger at Arnis and said, 'When the Russians took him away, he got everything he deserved.'

At that point, Arnis lost it. He pushed past the old man and snatched the door open. 'Please leave my surgery and do not return,' he said angrily. 'You are no longer welcome here.'

CHAPTER 18

Arnis woke with a start in the early hours of the morning. The events of the previous evening made sleep difficult and the old man's vicious comments were swirling around in his brain. He swung his legs out and sat on the edge of the bed, trying to make sense of it all. Reksis sat at his side, thumping his tail on the floor, uncomprehending compassion in his eyes. But Arnis was far away, his hands pressed against his cheeks, gently rocking to and fro.

The old man had to be mistaken, he tried to convince himself. Everyone else who had known his father had praised his qualities as a teacher and his courage as a man who would not tolerate the Russian occupation of Latvia, never flinching from an opportunity to deride the Soviet Union and all that it stood for. Though his mother had not talked about him very much, there had been no hint from her that he was not the Latvian freedom fighter that Arnis believed him to be. She had obviously held his memory very dear. Carrying the puppet he had made on the boat across the North Sea; treasuring it all her life. So why did the old man feel so differently about him?

Why had the two of them come to the surgery? He felt a prick of conscience that said they had probably come because they needed medical care. When the old man had slandered his father, Arnis had asked them to leave, giving them no chance to talk about any symptoms of illness. But his sense of guilt quickly evaporated as the words about his father hit him like a hammer. 'I had no time for Vilks. In fact, I hated him.' Why?

And why had they been so interested in his practising certificate? They knew his name was Rozenvalds because it was on the prescription he'd left after he visited Mrs Reinberga. Though Rozenvalds was not a common surname in Latvia, it seemed strange that they would identify him as the man who had a mother they happened to know who came from Kuldīga.

Undoubtedly, Latvia was a small country. The longer he lived there the more he realised it. There were occasional stories in the newspapers of returning ex-patriots unexpectedly meeting people they hadn't heard of in sixty years. People they didn't know were still alive. It had happened to his mother the day they met Fēlikss Siliņš in Kuldīga. Now he seemed to have met two more people who had known his mother and father. If they really had come from Kuldīga, it was not surprising they knew them. They were probably about the same age. A bit younger perhaps. But it was the way they had linked him with his mother that didn't make any sense. No sense at all.

He lay back on his bed, willing the day to begin; longing to get to work, longing to have to think about something else. By the time the clock struck seven he was exhausted, but he rose quickly and put the espresso machine on. As he drank his coffee he thought of something Anita had said in her letter. Unable to recall the precise words, he went to his bedroom and picked up the envelope from the top of his chest of drawers.

He unfolded the note and spotted what he was looking

for 'I hope you might see our meeting as fate without which other things wouldn't have happened.'

Had the old man said something to her about Vilks? Did she know Vilks was his father? Did she think that their meeting was fate because it would help him to get to the truth about Vilks? Was that why she had looked at him so strangely on the day he had told her he was going to Siberia? Perhaps by then she'd known something about his father. Vilks had been in the camp. Of that there was no doubt. Siliņš had been with him. But perhaps she knew something else?

He looked at the clock. Five to eight. He did not need not to be at the surgery for over an hour. He gave Reksis his breakfast and took him for a walk. As he strolled along the river bank, the freezing wind began to clear his brain sufficiently to make him realise there was one thing he could do that might answer his questions. He reached into his pocket for his phone and dialled Anita's mobile number. There was no reply, but it was only half past six in England. Unable to resist the thought of hearing her soft voice, he waited for her recorded message, but instead there was an impersonal one saying that the number was not recognised. He then called her two old office numbers in Rīga, but he was not surprised when they said they could not give him her new contact details. They offered to call her and though he was sure she would not phone him, he left a message anyway.

He switched off his phone and set off in the direction of the surgery, intending to ask Sigita if she could find out from her aunt, who was now living in Anita's flat, whether she had her forewarding address.

But when he arrived at the surgery, Sigita seemed anxious. Casting thoughts of Anita's whereabous from his mind, he asked her what was wrong. He was sure it had something to do with the old couple.

But it hadn't. 'A woman called Paula has just phoned from the bank. Can you call her back? Immediately,' said Sigita.

He was not in the mood for this. They were dealing with his mother's bank account. How much more information could they want about her? He was sure he'd given them all the details they'd asked for. He sighed and picked up the phone on Sigita's desk. 'Hello, Arnis Rozenvalds here. Is that Paula?'

'Yes,' she replied. 'Thanks for calling back. But I'm afraid there is a problem.'

'Problem?'

'Yes, with your papers.'

'Papers? What do you mean? Anger began to rise inside him. He was certain they were being deliberately awkward.

But she refused to answer his question. 'I think you'd better to come in. I can't explain on the phone.'

He slammed the handset back in its place and looked at Sigita. 'What time is the last appointment this morning?'

'Twelve thirty,' she replied as if to say don't snap at me like that.

The phone rang. 'You get that,' he said crossly.

'It's Mr Siliņš,' she said putting her hand over the mouthpiece.

'I'll take it next door,' he said, wondering whether the old man had some more information about his father, or perhaps about Kurmis.

But that wasn't the reason for his call. 'You know the

pulmonologist you referred me to?'

'Dr Punka,' replied Arnis.

'Yes. She wants to see me again on Friday.' He sounded hesitant. 'The thing is...I was wondering whether I could come and stay with you. It would just be for one night. My daughter is working and she can't bring me to Rīga. I'm happy to travel on the bus, but the appointment is at four o'clock, so I shall miss the last bus back.'

'Of course you can,' said Arnis.

'You're sure it won't be any trouble?'

'No. I usually finish surgery about seven. Give me a call when you're ready and I'll make sure I'm home.'

He put the phone down and turned to Sigita. 'Could you do something for me?' he asked her.

'What is it?'

'Could you ask your aunt if Anita left any contact details?'

'Yes, I will,' she replied a smile appearing in her eyes.

*

At ten to one Arnis followed the last patient out and went straight round to the bank. Expecting to have to wait, he was pleasantly surprised when Paula appeared almost immediately. 'Come through,' she said. He followed her into a small office where she motioned him to sit down. On the top of her large white desk was the brown envelope he'd brought in before going to Siberia. She undid the flap and pulled out the two pieces of identification she'd asked for: his mother's birth certificate and his own. She looked at them carefully, then at him as if she was trying to weigh up what his reaction would be to what she was going to say. Then she picked up the smaller of the two certificates. 'This one,' she said. 'It's not an official certificate.'

'Not an official certificate!' What on earth did she mean? It was the only one he'd ever had.

'No. It's a fake.'

'But, it can't be... Give it to me.'

'I'm afraid it is. Look, it's very different from you mother's.

First, she showed him his own birth certificate. All the details were clear. 'Arnis Rozenvalds. Date of birth February 26 1942; Mother's name: Margarita Vilka; father's name: Kārlis Vilks.' Then he looked at his mother's. 'Margarita Rozenvalda with the date and place of her birth. The copperplate handwriting also gave the full names of both her parents and her father's occupation – farmer.

He held the certificates side by side. It was the first time he'd looked at them both together. He had handled his own on a couple of previous occasions: on his marriage and for a passport application. But he hadn't seen his mother's until he got it out of her tin trunk to give to the Registrar before the funeral. After picking it up from there, he'd taken it straight round to the bank with his own in a separate envelope, and he hadn't compared them.

It was obvious what the woman meant. They were both printed on creamy-coloured parchment, both carried the Kuldīga stamp, and both were the same size. But that was where the similarities ended. His mother's was attractively ornate yet his own looked cheap by comparison.

'Mine was issued during the war,' he said lamely, not wanting to believe there was a problem.

But her answer was very definite. 'Latvian birth

certificates have never looked like that. The war made no difference. I should know, I've seen plenty of them in this job. This may look like a birth certificate but I can assure you it's not.'

'What do you want me to do?'

'We can't release your mother's money until you produce a proper birth certificate.' He could tell she was doing her best to be polite. She gave him a sympathetic smile and continued, 'You can easily get another one.'

'Where? Here in Rīga?'

'No. You'll have to go to Kuldīga. The town hall has all the official records.'

'Thank you,' he said, feeling his left cheek beginning to flicker. He went straight back to the surgery where he found Sigita busy updating the records on the computer. She looked up at him, her face ready to break into a smile, but when she saw his expression, she stopped. 'What's the matter?' What's happened?'

'Nothing, it's OK.' Immediately he felt as if a cock ought to crow. Remembering what Anita had said to him: that he didn't share his problems.

But his recognition of his own denial was cast aside as he wondered whether Sigita had managed to get Anita's contact details. 'Did you call your aunt?' he asked her.

'Yes,' she replied. 'Anita didn't leave any phone number.'

'Did your aunt know where she'd gone?'

'England. Other than that, no.'

'Didn't she know where Anita was working?'

'No, she knows nothing.'

He looked at Sigita and was sure she was telling the

294

truth.

For a moment, he couldn't believe Anita had said so little. Until he realised that she, more than him, knew just how fast gossip spread round Rīga. It was clear she did not want her whereabouts known.

Without saying another word, Sigita got up, poured two cups of coffee.

Arnis pulled a chair up to her desk, his thoughts returning to what had happened at the bank. He did not want to discuss it, but the concern in Sigita's clear blue eyes made him feel that, at the very least, he owed her an explanation of his anger the previous evening. He began by telling her about his father, what he knew about him, why the old man's comments had been such a shock, why he wanted to get in touch with Anita. Then he told her about his birth certificate. 'It seems that I'm not the person you think I am,' he concluded with a flippancy which belied the way he felt.

Sigita was not taken in either. She reached out and gave his hand a quick squeeze. 'There's probably some perfectly simple explanation,' she said soothingly. 'Perhaps your mother lost your original birth certificate. It wouldn't have been surprising given the journey she had to make. Perhaps she got a duplicate.'

Arnis wanted to believe her, but couldn't. He knew his mother too well. 'She didn't lose her own birth certificate. She'd have kept them both together.'

'But it was war time. People do strange things...'

'No, Sigita,' he said firmly.

'But if she didn't lose the original, why have you now got a fake?'

He could tell she wished she hadn't said that. But it

was a question that needed an answer.

'I don't know,' he replied 'As you say, there has to be some explanation. But I'm blessed if I can think what it is.'

He could see she was beginning to feel anxious for him.

'You're upset because of that old man last night. Vilifying your father like that. He was horrible. Now this. You look exhausted. Why don't you go home and get some rest? I can deal with the patients. If there's anything urgent I can send them to the hospital.'

He looked at her gratefully. Perhaps she was right. On this occasion, he did not feel strong enough to immerse himself in his patients, which is what he usually did when he was upset and worried.

'Have you got the car?' she asked.

It took him a moment to remember. 'No,' he replied. 'I'll call a taxi.'

'No, I'd rather walk.' He was sure a car ride would make him feel sick. As he got up to go, he checked the appointment book for the following day. There were only six appointments. Sigita looked at him. He could tell she knew what he was intending to do.

'I'll cancel them. Don't worry.'

Then he asked her to get the number for the town hall in Kuldīga. He picked up the handset and asked for the records office. 'Can I make an appointment?' he asked.

The woman at the other end of the phone sounded surprised. 'You can come when you like. You don't need an appointment. I'm here all the time. Except for weekends.'

'Tomorrow?'

'Yes. What do you want to know?

'I want to check my birth record. Is that possible?'

'We've got all the records from the eighteen hundreds right up to the present day,' she replied.

'That's fine. I'll come about eleven.'

Arnis went home and tried to sleep, but he could not get his birth certificate out of his mind. He got up and made himself a snack of black bread and hummus. As he ate, he remembered the words of the guide in the Occupation Museum.

'Latvia is a country where the past is more uncertain than the future.'

At the time, he'd thought her words described Latvia very well. Now they struck a very much more personal note. He began to mull over things he hadn't thought about for a long time. As a young boy, he'd thought it odd that his mother never celebrated their birthdays – neither his nor hers. She had made a point of celebrating their name's days instead because these were more important to Latvians, she'd said. His school fellows had made it obvious that they thought it a very strange custom, compounding their view that he was different; a foreigner from a land they hadn't heard of; a land they believed was full of bears and igloos because their parents told them so; a country that had disappeared from the world map; a country that no longer existed except in the imagination of its fiercely independent people.

Then there was that strange thing she'd said the night she died - that his father had loved him. She had looked at him with her clear grey eyes and said his father loved him. But had she being trying to tell him something else? Or was she struggling to shield him from something that she didn't want him to know?

*

Early the following morning, he left the flat with Reksis leading the way, dragging his lead along the cobbles as they went to fetch the car. A strong fresh wind ruffled the Alsatian's thick fur as he stopped for a sniff outside the camera shop, delighting at the return of familiar smells now the last of the snow had gone. The past few days had made all the difference, bringing with them an unseasonable warmth. Not that Arnis particularly noticed the weather. He had only one thought on his mind, and that was to get to Kuldīga as quickly as he could.

A couple of hours later he reached the edge of the town and parked in exactly the same spot as the last time. Checking his watch, he realised it was already five past eleven, so he hurried towards the town hall, up the steps and through the huge dark brown door which opened into a large hallway. The woman at the desk sent him up to the first floor where he entered a light, airy room with a tall arched window. In the middle, a slim woman with short straight dark hair was waiting for him at a highly-polished wooden table.

'Sit down,' she ordered, opening the thick black register in front of her and turning it to face him. Then she went through to an adjacent room to talk to someone else.

With trembling fingers he found the year 1942 and started to turn the pages, flipping quickly through the month of February until he came to the twenty-sixth. The names Vilks and Rozenvalds were not there. Wanting to be absolutely sure, he looked at the few days either side of the twenty-sixth. Still the names did not appear.

His heart was beginning to thump as he ran through

January before moving on to March, giving the entries just a cursory glance. Though he was sure he couldn't have been born after March, he carried on looking through April and into May. He was just about to turn back to the the entries for the previous year when he spotted his name.

'Name of child: Arnis. Date of birth: May 26th 1942.'

Arnis stared blankly at the information, stunned as if he had been hit by a hammer. Surely there had to be some mistake. The record showed that he had been born eleven months after his father's deporation in June 1941. He continued down the page of the ledger.

'Time of birth: 8:15 am.
Place of birth: Kuldīga.
Man/woman: Man.
Family name: Rozenvalds.
Name of Mother: Margarita Rozenvalda
Occupation of mother: Farmer
Mother's Nationality: Latvian
Mother's Religion: Lutheran.
Name of Father: …'

Again he stopped. He was astonished. There was no further information. All his mother's details were filled in but his father's were completely blank. He shook his head in disbelief. What on earth had she done? He took his notebook out of his pocket and began to copy down the details. At that moment, the dark haired woman came back into the room.

'I can make you a photocopy of that,' she said.

Arnis stopped scribbling. 'Thanks. That would be a great help.'

'You have proof of identity?' she asked officiously.

In years to come he would remember that remark; even see the funny side of it. But right now it wasn't at all funny and he felt extremely angry. He rooted through his jacket pocket and pulled out both his passports. He put the British one back and handed her the Latvian one.

She scrutinised it carefully, peering at his photograph, then at him. Not looking as though she was entirely convinced, she nevertheless snapped it closed and passed it back to him. A few moments later she returned with the copy, which he folded carefully into his passport and put back in his pocket.

She shut the ledger and picked it up, ready to leave the room again.

He opened the door, hurried down the stairs and back to the car, his mind in turmoil. What on earth had his mother done? Why had she lied to him?

He let Reksis out of the car and they walked along the narrow street towards the river. There was a hint of spring in the air and he wanted to clear his head. As he approached the bridge, the black wrought iron lamp came into view: the place where he had stood with his mother on that first visit. He stood underneath it and his eye followed the gracious curve of the waterfall. The sun danced on the water and he caught a glimpse of a rainbow in the spray rising above it. He continued to stare at the light mist but the rainbow disappeared and was replaced by a heron which vanished just as quickly, flapping its huge wings as it soared up towards the milky blue sky.

Reksis appeared by his side with a stick in his mouth. Arnis took it from him and was about to throw it along the road when his eye was drawn to a pair of initials etched into the top of the bridge.

E M 1935

He remembered his mother strolling along the bridge that day, he remembered the rapt attention with which she gazed at the stonework in the same position he now stood under the wrought iron lamp. Before he had thought nothing of it but was this what she'd been studying so closely? He remembered the smile on her face, then later the atmosphere in the car as they'd driven out of the town, the way she'd snapped at him as if she wanted to be left alone with her thoughts. Looking again at the initials, he began to wonder. The date matched her time in Kuldīga and M could have been for Margarita. But, if so, who was E?

CHAPTER 19

Darkness had already fallen when Arnis arrived back in Rīga and the two-hour drive had done nothing to calm his addled brain. He parked the car and went up to his apartment. The phone was ringing. He decided to leave it but as soon as the answerphone activated, he heard the voice of Fēlikss Siliņš. 'Hello, Arnis. I'm just leaving the hospital.'

Arnis groaned. This was the evening Siliņš was coming to stay. He had completely forgotten. Much as he liked the old man, he could have done without a visitor tonight. He picked up the phone, covering up his feelings in a polite tone. 'Hello. I'll meet you in the Dom square. There's a photographic shop next to my apartment. About twenty minutes?'

'Yes, fine,' said Siliņš. 'I know where you mean.'

By the time Arnis got downstairs, the old man was already there. He took him up to the flat and showed him into the spare bedroom. As soon as he was settled in, Arnis took Reksis out for a walk and went straight round to the off licence.

'A bottle of whisky,' he said to the girl behind the counter. '… a large one.'

He knew drink never solved anyone's problems but tonight what he wanted more than anything else was the welcoming numbness that might take his mind off the day's

302

unexpected revelations.

As the girl wrapped the bottle, he began to wish he'd never seen the sepia-tinted photograph of Kārlis Vilks. It had started a trail of emotions that ended in complete confusion. Was Vilks his real father? Had the authorities made a mistake over his birth date? Had his mother deliberately tried to deceive him? If she had been honest with him, she could have saved him all this anguish. But none of that explained the significance of the tea service she and Vilks had buried at the farm. Or the puppet. Those two items had been her most treasured possessions and the K on Sprīdītis's back was his father's initial. She said that herself. Which again seemed to prove that Kārlis Vilks was his natural father. There must be some rational explanation.

Arnis paid the girl for the whisky and then thinking how rude he had been to leave Siliņš on his own, he bought a box of chocolates as well and headed back to the flat. When he reached the square, the air was quite still. The moon hung like an orb above the Dom; the massive bell tower bathed in its pale yellow glow. Lights shone from the long arched windows and a steady flow of concert-goers poured towards the entrance. He remembered he should have been going in with them as he already had a ticket for the performance but, much as he loved to hear Bach played on the huge cathedral organ, it was now the last thing he wanted to do. The idea of sitting amidst rows of people, some of whom might recognise him, was more than he could handle. The only company he needed was his own … and the bottle of whisky. He made his way back to the flat.

As he opened the door he was confronted by Mrs Bilmane, a tenant from one of the ground floor flats. Reksis rushed up to her and she bent down to stroke him.

'You don't get so many walks now, do you?' she said to the Alsatian. Looking up at Arnis, she added, 'He must miss your mother as much as you do. I know I miss her. We used to have some lovely chats about the old days.' Then, almost as an afterthought that just had to be said. 'Your mother thought the world of you, you know.'

Arnis wished she hadn't said it because it only added to his confusion. He knew she loved him. Of that, there had never been any doubt. But there were doubts about other important matters. And they had still to be resolved. He nodded his head to acknowledge Mrs Bilmane's statement and stepped into the lift, leaving Reksis to rush up the stairs. When he entered the hallway of his flat, the answering machine was flashing but he ignored it and went straight through to the living room where he dumped the bottle of whisky on the coffee table before he went to fetch a tumbler from the kitchen.

Hunger gnawed at his stomach but he couldn't be bothered to prepare food and returned to the living room. As soon as he filled his glass, he sat on the sofa, put his feet up and closed his eyes. Within seconds he opened them again as he remembered he had a guest. A guest who was nowhere to be seen. He put the glass back on the coffee table and walked over to the door of the spare room. He put his ear to the door and listened but could hear nothing. 'Mr Siliņš,' he whispered.

There was no reply and he raised his voice slightly. 'Mr Siliņš.'

Again there was no reply. Arnis raised his hand to knock on the door but changed his mind. The old man must have had a long day, he told himself, and returned to the living room.

As he reached for his glass, his eye was drawn to the photograph of his mother he had placed on top of the television the day after she died. It was always his favourite and her eyes still smiled at him from the neat silver frame. This was now as close as he could get to her, or she to him. At a time when he longed to be able to talk to her, to ask her questions, all he had was a photograph. So she could never tell him why she had said his birthday was in February when the official records showed May; or why Kārlis Vilks's name was missing from his birth record. Yet she was probably the only person who knew the facts, and her reasons for disguising them - if that is what she had done.

Things he'd found out during the last six months suggested Vilks was already in Siberia weeks before he was conceived but for sixty-one years he'd believed he was the son of a school teacher - the man on the top deck of the boat, the man who'd torn up the picture of Stalin in the classroom; the man whose political convictions had brought about his deportation to Siberia.

Arnis drained his glass and refilled it. His head was beginning to thump but he had things he wanted to put out of his mind and the whisky was beginning to do that. Or was it? Was it just stopping him from making a sensible diagnosis and reaching a proper conclusion? He decided he no longer cared and took a long swig from the tumbler.

As his head started to spin slightly, only one fact remained clear. His mother had been married to Kārlis Vilks, that much he knew for certain, and Kurmis, through his treachery, had deprived her of a longer marriage. She, and himself, had been subjected to years of poverty and hardship thanks to the efforts of a traitor.

His mind began to race and he realised there was no point in going to bed so he downed the rest of his glass and poured another. Moments later, the doorbell rang and he glanced at his watch, wondering who would be calling at eight-thirty in the evening. He staggered to his feet and tried to steady himself as his head reeled. Then he walked slowly to the door and opened it.

'We're sorry to disturb you so late in the evening, Dr Rozenvalds, and at your home, but we had to see you.'

Arnis blinked his bleary eyes lest the vision was a nightmare. When he opened them again the vision was still there. Two of them. He stared at them, anger beginning to tense his body, struggling to find the words to say to them. 'I told you I never wanted to see you again. Either of you.'

'But you must,' Mrs Reinberga said. 'We have to tell you the truth.'

Arnis stared straight past her and glared angrily at the old man. 'So you don't think you've already done enough harm slagging off my father? You want to rub salt in the wounds? Is that it, you sadist?'

The old man looked nervous and troubled as though he didn't really want to be there. He started to turn away but Mrs Reinberga grabbed his arm and held it firmly. 'Tell him,' she ordered.

He was still reluctant to speak and remained silent for a few more seconds as she glared at him. 'Perhaps it's best left alone,' he said eventually.

She was not having any of it. She tugged his arm sharply and repeated her order. 'Tell him!'

'Look,' the old man said hesitantly. 'You...' He stopped and swallowed hard. 'You ... may be my son.'

Any remaining traces of whisky vapours in Arnis's brain cleared immediately and he wondered if his ears had deceived him. 'Son?' he questioned incredulously.

'Yes,' said the old man more definitely. 'I am your father.'

This time, Arnis decided he'd had enough. The old man must be insane but he wasn't planning to take any more of it. He lost his temper and shouted, 'You have the gall to come to my surgery giving me all that vilifying bile, then you turn up on my doorstep claiming to be my father. How dare you?'

The man was taken aback by the verbal assault but he recovered quickly. 'If you are Margarita Rozenvalda's son then you are also my son,' he insisted, fixing Arnis with such an intense stare that he felt totally bewildered.

For only the second time in his life, the first having been when he turned on the school bully in Oban, Arnis rushed forward and pushed the old man back across the landing, pinning him backwards over the balustrade with an arm across his throat. The woman tried to drag him off but he pushed her to one side and pressed the man further back until the pain and terror showed in his face.

'You are not my father,' he shouted angrily.

The old woman again grabbed his arm and tried to pull him away. 'Don't do anything stupid,' she said. 'I can guess what happened.' There was pleading in her voice but, at the same time, there was also a deep-seated anger. Arnis glanced sideways at her as she continued. 'It was your mother, wasn't it? She told you Vilks was your father.'

Her comments did not help Arnis's demeanour. 'So you're going to berate my mother now, are you? I will not listen to any more of your stupid ranting,' he shouted, again turning his attention to the old man.

At that moment, he realised they were no longer alone. Fēlikss Siliņš had emerged from behind, dressed in his pyjamas.

'Don't do anything stupid,' he said quietly. 'You have too much to lose.'

Arnis turned his head to look at Mr Siliņš. 'Do what?' he asked, relaxing the pressure on Reinbergs's throat slightly.

'Kill him,' Siliņš replied calmly.

For a while they all stood in suspended animation then Siliņš levered Arnis's hand away from his adversary's throat with a strength in his grip that belied his frail build. The old man moved quickly way from the banister and tucked his body partly behind Mrs Reinberga's, gently touching his throat as he swallowed to lubricate it.

Arnis was now more confused than ever. 'Kill him?' He was extremely angry with the old man but he had not the slightest intention of killing him. 'Why would I want to kill him? he asked Siliņš.

Now it was Siliņš's turn to look confused. 'You know who this is, don't you?'

'You've lost me,' Arnis said.

'It's the man I told you about,' said Siliņš sounding angry.

Arnis narrowed his eyes. 'You mean the man who... No,' he said to Siliņš. 'It can't be.' His eyes turned towards the old man. 'This is ...?'

Siliņš completed the question with the answer. 'Edgars Kurmis.'

'Kurmis!

The old man said nothing.

'I thought…' He was sure he'd heard Sigita say the man was called Reinbergs.

'Whatever you thought, I can assure you this is Kurmis,' said Siliņš. There's no doubt about it.'

Again the anger rose within Arnis and he advanced on Kurmis. 'You traitorous dog!' he shouted.

Mrs Reinberga stepped in front of Kurmis to protect him.

'Stop it! What is wrong with you?' she screamed at Arnis.

'I see your game now,' Arnis said, ignoring her question and staring angrily at Kurmis. 'You're both trying to cover his treachery by pretending he is my father. Well, you won't get away with it. I'll see you both in hell! Kārlis Vilks was my father.'

'How could Vilks be your father?' she screamed. 'He was deported in June and you weren't born until the following May.' A look of disgust swept across her face. 'I suppose your mother lied about that too.

'Lied! My mother did not lie…' As the words formed on his lips he felt uncertain.

'You were born on the twenty-sixth of May, 1942 and I saw you when you were a few days old.'

'Enough, Anna!' said the old man, easing out from behind her. 'This is a terrible shock for Arnis and you're not making things any easier.'

'But Margarita lied to him,' said the old lady sharply. 'He deserves to know the truth.' She turned to Arnis again. 'Vilks wasn't your father.'

Arnis only half heard what she was saying; his ears

and brain had honed in on her name – Anna. 'You're Anna Vilka … Kārlis Vilks's sister?'

Her face froze. 'Vilks's sister!' she exclaimed. 'How dare you? Vilks only had one sister and her name was Frida.'

Arnis glanced quickly at Fēlikss Siliņš – Frida was the name he had remembered from his days of confinement with Vilks and his expression now confirmed it.

By now a small crowd had gathered on the staircase, curious to investigate the commotion. Siliņš took the initiative. 'I think this is not the place to talk,' he said quietly, and ushered them towards the apartment door. 'We need to calm down and discuss things rationally.'

Inside, he spotted the glass and whisky bottle on the coffee table and went through to the kitchen where he quickly found three more glasses. 'I think this may help,' he said when he returned. Sitting on the sofa, he filled all four glasses and handed them round.

Kurmis still looked uneasy. It was clear he could understand why Arnis was angry to find out his father was not the same person he had always considered to be his father but he didn't yet seem to understand the renewed anger when his true identity was revealed. 'Why did you think Anna was Vilks's sister,' he asked.

'Because my mother told me my father's sister was called Anna,' Arnis replied tersely, still feeling no obligation to feel closer to the man who claimed he was his father.

'Then I think that proves your mother did tell you the truth about some things,' Kurmis said. 'Now I must try to explain why she covered up other facts.'

Arnis still had no reason to trust the man but he knew he should at least listen to his explanation before he produced his trump card.

Kurmis continued. 'Your father's sister was indeed called Anna,' he said. 'Anna Reinberga is *my* sister.'

'Your sister! But I thought … So you are not husband and wife?'

The old man looked astonished. 'No, we aren't.'

So Anita…' He could not get his head around this.'

'Anita is your cousin,' said the old man. 'I am her uncle and Anna is her mother.'

The old lady looked momentarily horrified. 'Oh, no…You didn't think Anita was your sister, did you?' she said.

'No, I didn't,' replied Arnis quickly. 'Anita told me her father was dead. So I knew … this man… was not her father. I assumed he was your husband. I thought you had married again.' It had never occurred to him that the old man might be Mrs Reinberga's brother.

'You must believe us,' the old lady said plaintively. 'Edgars is your father. I am your aunt.'

Arnis looked at both of them, not knowing what to believe. He couldn't get his head around the revelations and his insides felt empty. Then Anita's letter came to his mind. Was this why she'd said their meeting was fate without which other things could not have happened? Was this why she'd broken off their relationship so suddenly? Had her mother told her she was having a relationship with her cousin?

'I always wondered what had happened to you and your mother,' Kurmis continued. 'And when you left the prescription for Anna she spotted your name straight away. We talked about it. Anna thought you looked the right age. She got very excited. She was all for ringing you up the next

311

day. But it all seemed too much of a coincidence to me. Then when your receptionist told us your mother's name and that you were born in Kuldīga...'

'Go on.' Arnis was trying hard to remain calm but increasingly conscious of the muscle flickering in his cheek.

'The thing that surprised me was ... well, that Margarita had told you that Vilks was your father. No wonder you were so angry.'

'And I still am. But perhaps not for the reason you think,' said Arnis raising his voice, feeling his face turn red.

Kurmis looked bewildered. 'What do you mean?'

Arnis couldn't wait any longer to confront Kurmis with the information he'd learned from Siliņš. 'Someone saw you on the street the night Kārlis Vilks was deported ...'

Kurmis's face filled with panic. Arnis had played his ace and the effect convinced him the allegations were substantiated.

'Who saw me?' Kurmis asked.

Fēlikss Siliņš stayed quiet and Arnis saw no reason to draw him into the conflict unless it became absolutely necessary. 'Never mind who,' he said. 'You got Kārlis Vilks deported by telling the Russians about him,' he said, feeling increasingly angry but resisting the temptation to get up and shake Kurmis. 'And you expected me to be pleased when you told me I was your son? I certainly wouldn't be proud to call you my father. You worked for the Russians.'

'I never worked for the Russians!' The statement burst from his lips with enormous venom.

'But you don't deny you were on the street that night ... that you informed on Vilks,' Arnis pressed.

'No I don't,' Kurmis replied in a quiet voice.

312

The calmness of his confession took Arnis by surprise, so much so that he failed to notice the expression of anguish on Anna's face until she spoke. 'I never knew that, Edgars,' she shrieked. 'I know you hated Vilks but I would never have believed you'd get your revenge that way.'

Kurmis glanced guiltily at her. 'Calm down, Anna. Let me finish.' He turned back to Arnis. 'Vilks got my sister pregnant.'

Arnis narrowed his eyes and turned to Anna. 'You mean …?'

'No, no, not Anna,' Kurmis explained quickly. 'We had another sister … Ilze. She fell for Vilks in a big way. But he was a smooth talker and he was rich.' Kurmis gave a harsh laugh. 'All the girls fell for him … not just Ilze. But Vilks made her pregnant and then disowned her when she told him. After that, he wouldn't have anything to do with her and she daren't tell our father. She was so ashamed she didn't even wait for the baby to be born. She left Kuldīga and we never saw her again. To this day we don't know what happened to her.' He rubbed his hands together angrily. 'I never forgave Vilks for that.'

Arnis could understand that kind of anger but Kurmis had had plenty of time to make up a plausible story, one that might make Arnis feel sorry for him. 'Why should I believe you?' he asked.

'I can't make you but please believe me when I say I never worked for the Russians. Anna will vouch for that, won't you?' he said, turning to his sister.

Anna had turned quite pale and ignored his plea. 'Edgars, you did a terrible thing.'

'But I did not work for the Russians. You know that,

Anna. Why would I have worked for them? You know how I wanted Latvia to be independent again.' Turning to Arnis, he continued, 'After the Russians were driven out in forty-one, I joined the Latvian division of the German army. I fought on the Russian front. But I soon realised that was a waste of time because the Germans wouldn't guarantee an independent Latvia when the war was over. So I left the army and came back to Kuldīga. That was the first time I saw you,' he added. 'You were nearly eighteen months old.'

Arnis still wasn't convinced. 'If what you say is true you must have started seeing my mother within weeks of Vilks being deported.' Memories of his mother flooded back and he was sure she wouldn't have started a relationship with another man so soon after her husband had been taken away.

Kurmis must have read his thoughts. 'I know what you're thinking but you're wrong. Let me tell you why. Your mother never loved Vilks ... she married him because that's what her father wanted. Vilks was the local mill owner's son and old Rozenvalds was an ambitious man. He wanted her to marry into money. That's why I never got a look in. I wasn't good enough for her father.'

Arnis was having some difficulty reconciling Kurmis's story. Then, suddenly, it dawned on him. In his mind's eye he saw the initials E and M on the bridge at Kuldīga – Edgars and Margarita. And the date - 1935. Did that mean they had been seeing each other before she married Vilks?

Kurmis's next words answered his question. 'Your mother and I had known each other for a long time. We met when we were sixteen. She came to my dad's workshop with her father and I fell in love with her the minute I saw her ... her chocolate brown curls and grey eyes. She was so pretty.

The following week she came in with her mother. They were having a new door made for the farm and they wanted to check when it would be ready. After that she started coming every week.'

He paused and there was a look in his eyes that spoke of happy days and beautiful memories. Then he continued, 'For a long time I thought she came just to check on the door and had no interest in me at all. When I finally plucked up the courage to ask her out, I was amazed when she said yes. We went to Liepāja for the day. By bus. It was a beautiful spring day and we had a picnic by the sea. In the afternoon, we went to the theatre ...'

Arnis was so engrossed by Kurmis's story that he listened in stunned silence to the rest.

'So why didn't you marry my mother?' he asked when Kurmis finished.

'I told you. I wasn't good enough. I did ask her father for her hand but he told me no apprentice was going to marry his daughter. By the time I finished my apprenticeship and got my diploma she was already married to Vilks. We still met secretly from time to time but she wouldn't leave him. She wouldn't hurt her own father or go against his wishes no matter how much she suffered. It was only when Vilks had gone that she told me she never loved him.'

'And then you had an affair?' Arnis asked.

Kurmis looked down at the floor and nodded his head.

'Yet you didn't see my mother until I was eighteen months old. How was that?' Arnis wanted to hear the whole story in the hope that a full picture would help him to make up his mind.

'When I left the Latvian army I joined the Forest

Brothers. We fought the Russians in the woods.'

Arnis felt a tingle in his spine. At one time he'd been convinced his father was a partisan and had died in the forest. And he'd had that dream where he'd written the essay describing how his father had fought the Russians. Had that been a premonition?

'How long were you with the Forest Brothers?'

'Until 1951.'

'So you never saw my mother after that first visit to Kuldīga?'

'No. It was far too dangerous. I lived in the woods and by the time I did get back to Kuldīga, she'd gone. I wasn't surprised. As Vilks's wife, her days in Latvia were numbered.'

'But if you hadn't shopped him to the Russians ...'

Kurmis stopped him in mid-sentence. 'You have to understand that Vilks would still have been deported even if I had said nothing.'

'But saying something may have put my mother at more risk than necessary,' Arnis suggested accusingly. His anger with Kurmis had not diminished.

Kurmis looked slightly uncomfortable. 'Your mother always knew she was in danger. She was certain her name was on a list in the town hall.'

Arnis chewed his lip. That was exactly what his mother had said.

'When she told me, I told her to leave Latvia,' Kurmis continued. 'But she wouldn't.' He closed his eyes for a moment, as if in prayer. 'Thank God she did leave eventually.' Again he stopped to think. 'At least she saved herself from ... God knows what.'

Arnis looked at him wondering if he knew exactly

what she escaped to. 'It wasn't all milk and honey,' he said. 'She had a hard life in Scotland. She worked her fingers to the bone to give me a start in life.'

Kurmis's eyes confirmed his understanding though it was obviously something he could only envisage in his mind; a life that could be the best or worst of two evils.

'So why was she so desperate to make me think that Vilks was my father? Especially after we got to England. I don't understand...' said Arnis, voicing his thoughts out loud.

Anna answered his question. 'I can tell you why,' she said in a deep guttural tone that sounded exactly like his mother's. 'It was money.'

'Money?'

'Yes,' said Anna. 'Vilks's mother was very wealthy. She was Russian. The daughter of a prestigious jeweller on Nevsky Prospekt in St Petersburg. It was her money that helped to build the Vilks mill in Kuldīga.'

'What happened to her?' He knew so little about the Vilks family for reasons that were becoming all too clear.

Anna continued. 'She fled in 1945 like your mother. We assumed she'd gone to Paris. Her sister was there and people said she had got the family fortune out of Russia before 1917. Think about it, Arnis. Your mother probably thought Vilks might come back one day. If so, she would have wanted to be sure he thought you were his son. You would have stood to inherit a fortune. That's my opinion anyway.'

They all fell silent. A few drops of rain spattered against the window and Arnis became conscious of his heart beating in time to the dull thump of some distant music. For a few moments no-one said a word then Kurmis broke the silence. 'I can understand her reasons but I wish she'd told you, all the same.'

Arnis felt more confused than ever. It all sounded believable but somehow it didn't feel right and he suddenly felt he needed more space. Time to think; time to make sure he wasn't being duped.

He glanced at his watch. It was getting very late and Siliņš had already yawned a few times.

Again Kurmis seemed to read his thoughts. He stood up and offered his hand to his sister. 'I'm sorry,' he said. 'We've already taken up too much of your time. You have a lot to think about and we respect that. Take as long as you need. If you want to contact us, you know where we are.'

He pulled his sister to her feet and helped her on with her coat. As they reached the door, he said, 'If we don't hear from you, we will understand.'

When he turned to say goodbye it was as if he thought it might be for the last time. Then he saw something behind Arnis and his tired eyes seemed to be suddenly hypnotised. He swayed a little and Arnis stepped forward to support him. Kurmis raised his hand to signal he was all right but his eyes never moved from whatever had caught his attention. Arnis was quite worried and watched him carefully.

Then Kurmis spoke. 'I see you still have Sprīdītis,' he said, his gaze unwavering.

Arnis spun his head to look at the puppet, still suspended from the place he had put it after his mother washed its clothes. 'You know Sprīdītis?' he asked.

'I should,' Kurmis said. 'It was the first puppet I made. I gave it to your mother and she made its clothes.'

Arnis fetched a chair and lifted Sprīdītis off his hook. Gently, he lowered the puppet to the floor and then held it in an upright position in front of the old man.

Kurmis stared at Sprīdītis and a few tears trickled down his cheeks. Slowly, he reached out to the puppet. 'May I?' he asked Arnis.

'Of course you may,' Arnis replied, and handed Edgars the strings.

With shaking hands, Kurmis made Sprīdītis take a couple of faltering steps across the parquet floor. As his hands began to steady, he made him jump on to the coffee table where with great deftness he began to work the puppet into a fast dance. Then, he picked the puppet up and hugged it close to his chest, his eyes tightly closed; as if memories of happier days were flooding through him like a surging tide.

He lifted the puppet's tails deftly and slid its coat up to expose its back. 'See. My initial is carved on its back.'

As he pointed, Arnis noticed for the first time that his little finger was very crooked and his mind immediately carried him back to the day his eldest son was born. It was the first thing his mother noticed.

'Look, Arnis. His little finger is crooked,' she said, holding his tiny right hand and gazing at the bent finger which curved gently inwards.

'Just like his grandfather's,' she said. 'Just like his grandfather's.'

ACKNOWLEDGEMENTS

This book could not have been written without an enormous amount of help from other people. Thanks are due to Sandra Bērziņa, Vice-President of the Latvian Pharmacy Association and to Dr Ilze Aisilniece, without whose kindness I could not have visited doctors' surgeries in Rīga. Indra Vilmane at the tourist office in Kuldīga and Matthew Kott at the Occupation Museum in Rīga were very vital sources of information.

As my hosts on visits to Latvia, Charlotte and Emil Sveilis deserve special mention. Were it not for their help in checking facts about day to day life in, my research would have been so much more difficult. Thanks are also due to the late Melanie Sveilis for being willing to share her experiences of being forced to leave Latvia in 1944.

In London, I am particularly grateful to Douglas Simpson, previous editor of *The Pharmaceutical Journal*, without whose constant encouragement to write about pharmacy in different countries, I would never have had the courage to approach doctors and pharmacists in Rīga.

Zigrida Daskevica shared her experiences of pre-war Latvia and her life as a Latvian ex-patriot in Britain. She also invited me to several events at the Latvian embassy in London and the Latvian Independence Day celebration on November 18 in 2000.

I would also like to thank Sheila Weston who arranged for me to meet her cousin in Rīga, Jānis, whose memories of farming life in Kurzeme in the 1930s were so helpful. Vieda Skultans provided me with invaluable background information and her mother told me the story of Sprīdītis. Latvians Online gave me useful insight into the wider Latvian émigré community.

Sunyana Shah is everything anyone could ever wish for in a friend. Countless are the times she heard this story in all its detail and never once glazed over, even at the end of a busy day. Ailsa Benson could not have been more generous with her support, not to mention her willingness to read and comment on the manuscript at a very early stage. Thanks are due to my late father-in-law, Hugh Mason, who also read the manuscript and provided invaluable comments. Jo Barnes, Mike Carver, Brenda Ecclestone, Erik Kristensen, Jo Lumb, Joan Mason, Anna Morgan, Denis and Maria Moss and Doug Watts provided valuable support at various times.

I would especially like to thank my mother and father. Unlike Arnis's mother, Mrs Rozenvalda, my own mother moved just ten miles – from one side of Manchester to the other – in the eighty-six years of her life. Yet it was her stories of pre-war and wartime England, particularly the industrial North and the Lancashire countryside where her father worked on a farm, which in a strange, unfathomable way inspired my writing. I began work on this book six months after she died.

Finally, Ambrose, who had to put up with my constant struggle to write this story, but was always there with cups of tea when it looked as if I was going to stay up late into the night to finish one more chapter. In 1998, had it not been for his job as Director of Ministry for the Diocese in Europe, I would never have made my first of many visits to Latvia, where, despite having no family links whatsoever, I have always been made so welcome.

Pamela Mason, October 2005
Email: pamelamason@apotek.org.uk

BIBLIOGRAPHY

I could not have written this book without reading many others and this bibliography represents some of the more valuable ones.

1. Brigadere A. *Spreedeets.* A Latvian children's play in seven acts. Sprīdītis, Rīga, 1993.
2. Eksteins M. *Walking Since Daybreak.* Houghton Mifflin, New York, 1999.
3. Kahn F. *Rīga and its Beaches.* Landmark Publishing, Ashbourne, Derbyshire, 2000.
4. Lieven A. *The Baltic Revolution.* Yale University Press, New Haven and London, 1993.
5. Lingard J. *Tug of War.* Puffin Books, London, 1995.
6. Lingard J. *Between Two Worlds.* Puffin Books, London, 1995.
7. Nesaule A. *A Woman in Amber.* Penguin, New York, 1997.
8. Skultans V. *The Testimony of Lives.* Routledge, London and New York, 1998.
9. Volanska A. *Kuldīga.* SIA "Apgāds Jāṇa sēta", Rīga, 1998.
10. Williams E. *Gulag to Independence. Personal Accounts of Gulag Survivors,* 1992.
11. Williams MO. *Latvia, Home of the Letts.* National Geographic Magazine, Washington DC 1924: 401-443.
12. *The Anti-Soviet Resistance in the Baltic States.* Du Ka, Vilnius, 1999.
13. *The Wreck of the Latvian Cargo Ship Helena Faulbaums.* The Scottish Slate Islands Heritage Trust. The Heritage Centre, Ellenabeich, By Oban.
14. *We Sang Through Tears.* Jānis Roze, Rīga, 1999.

ABOUT THE AUTHOR

Pamela Mason began her happily varied career as a pharmacist working for Boots in the North of England after which she owned her own community pharmacy in North Wales for five years. A move to London in 1983 enabled her to study for an MSc and PhD in nutrition. She then worked at the Royal Pharmaceutical Society of Great Britain as an editorial assistant on the British National Formulary and at the National Pharmacy Association as a writer of training and education materials.

Since 1994, she has been self-employed as a pharmaceutical writer and consultant and has written four non-fiction books. An interest in pharmacy and medical practice overseas together with her fascination for Eastern Europe has resulted in her visiting most of the former countries of the Soviet bloc, including Latvia, about which she has written numerous articles in the pharmaceutical press. Since 1999, she has been an honorary member of the Latvian Pharmacy Association.

She is married to Ambrose, a Rector of four rural churches in Monmouthshire, South Wales. *Puppet Maker* is her first novel.